# the

# wild

# man

ALEX
USA TODAY BESTSELLING AUTHOR
GRAYSON

To those with a wild animal in them.

## one

EVERLEE

"**A**re you sure this is smart, Ever? I mean, you aren't exactly the outdoorsy type."

I peek my head around my closet door frame and look at Lyrika, my best friend since middle school. With bright-red, waist length hair, exotic aqua-colored eyes surrounded by thick eyelashes, and a killer body with curves in all the right places, I've always felt lacking when standing next to her. Not that I think I'm not pretty, but my shit-brown hair, with my shittier brown eyes, and the extra twenty pounds I can't seem to diet or exercise off can't compare to her perfectly gorgeous model features. But hey, bright side, at least the extra weight is proportionate and not all in one place.

She's sitting with her legs crossed in the middle of my bed, eyeing the small pile of clothes I've tossed on the end like they've personally offended her.

"I don't know what you're talking about. I love nature and being outdoors." Grabbing a flannel shirt that I haven't worn in years, I throw it at her. "You remember all those camping trips my dad and brothers took me on in middle and high school. You even went once."

She pinches the shoulders of the shirt, her eyes meeting mine over the printed material as she expertly folds it. "I remember you hating it."

I scoff and roll my eyes, even though I've already moved back into the closet and she can't see it. She knows me well enough to hear the action in my voice. "I did not. You were the one who hated it." Bending, I pick up a pair of old hiking boots and toss them between my legs through the doorway and into the room. They clunk against the footboard. "Which is why Dad made Ethan take you home early and wouldn't let me invite you again."

"Girls were not designed to squat in the woods, Ever."

"They are if you do it right."

"And do you have any idea how itchy poison ivy is when it gets in your butt crack?" she continues, ignoring my statement. I can practically see the shuddered look on her face in my mind.

It wasn't funny at the time—or rather, it kind of was, but to keep my friend from slaughtering me, I kept my mirth to myself— but thinking back, I can't help the laugh that slips out.

"That shit was *not* funny," Rika grumbles, her bitterness from that experience still alive and kicking. "I must have looked like a whore with herpes with all my squirming and scratching at my crotch." Another spurt of laughter comes out before I can stop it. "I blame that one experience on why Mad and I never married and had two-point-five kids."

Rika has had a lady boner for my oldest brother for years. Despite the eight year age difference, she used to swear she was going to marry Maddox one day and they'd live happily ever after with the perfect life. Much to her displeasure, he's never shown any interest in my friend, and over the years, that crush has faded.

"Does David and the guys know what you're doing?" she asks, folding another shirt I tossed on the bed.

"Not yet," I admit reluctantly. "I'm calling Dad on the way out. He'll pass along the information to my brothers."

I avoid Rika's eyes when I leave the closet and move to my dresser. I know what she's thinking. And she knows that I know.

"You've had this planned for weeks, so there's only one reason why you're waiting until now to tell them." She pauses, and I can feel her eyes on the back of my head as I dig through my panties drawer, searching for the most utilitarian undies I have. Silk, lace, and satin would be wasted on where I'm going. "You know they would stop you from going if they knew ahead of time."

I snort, even though she's right. Dad is going to go ballistic when he finds out what I plan to do. And my brothers, they'd tie me to the metal pipes in the basement to keep me from going. I love my dad and brothers, but they can be hella overprotective.

"You're delusional. I didn't tell them because I've been busy and it slipped my mind," I reply, playing dumb.

"Oh, come on, Ever. We both know that's bull. What you're doing is dangerous, and quite frankly, stupid. There's no way the Horde would let you step a foot out of the house if they had any clue what you were up to."

The Horde.

That's what Rika calls my dad and brothers.

I lift a shoulder nonchalantly. "Maybe, maybe not. Either way, they won't have the chance."

I carry a stack of plain cotton panties and a couple of sports bras to the duffle bag on the bed, carelessly stuffing them inside. I go back to the dresser for some socks, feeling Rika's concerned gaze on the side of my face the whole time.

"You have no idea how dangerous this man could be, if he even exists," she continues in her pursuit to try to talk me out of going. Nothing short of an apocalypse could stop me. "He could be a psycho killer who waits for hikers to wander his way. You remember that guy who disappeared last year, right?"

"Yes. He was found weeks later." I stop and face Rika. "He died from a broken neck after he fell from that cliff."

"That's what the papers say," she says, one of her brows lifting in question. "They claim he *fell*, but he could have been pushed."

I let out an exaggerated puff of air. "You watch too many true crime shows." I leave her and go to the bathroom for some toiletries.

"That may be so, but it's still very plausible that man could have been pushed. There's no way to know for sure."

I raise my voice so she can hear me. "I like to believe people are innocent until proven guilty. There's no evidence that comes even close to linking that hiker's death with Wild Man."

"Okay, so let's forget about that for a moment," she hollers back. "What about other dangers? Wild animals, for instance."

I toss in some shampoo and conditioner into a small travel bag, along with body wash, a toothbrush, toothpaste, and a few other things. No make-up is needed where I'm headed. "I'll have my taser and gun."

"You've thought of everything, haven't you?" she asks, her tone full of sarcasm.

"Yep," I chirp, leaving the bathroom.

After dropping the bag on the bed, I sit on the side and face my friend. I reach out and grab her hand.

"You need to stop worrying. I'll be fine. I'll only be gone for a couple of weeks at the most. And I'll have my sat phone with me. If it makes you feel better, I'll call you every day."

Her eyes narrow and she gives me a look I imagine moms giving their children. I can only imagine it because I've never had one. Or rather, I did, but she died when I was two from breast cancer.

"You better. If I don't get a call at least once every twenty-four hours, or I'll send the Horde after you."

I laugh, dropping her hand and getting up from the bed. "You won't have to." I pick up the thick notebook that's full of notes from my nightstand. "They'll already be pissed that I only told Dad, and didn't give them a chance to stop me. I'll be lucky to spend two days out there."

"I still don't like this." She slides her ass across the bed to get up from the mattress. "I have a very bad feeling. Are you sure there's nothing I can say to get you to nix this crazy idea?"

"No." I shove the rest of the clothes on my bed inside the duffle bag, putting the notepad on top before zipping it. "You know how much this means to me. I've been researching Wild Man for years. I've finally found what I believe is his location. I can't pass up this opportunity."

She sighs, her shoulders drooping in acceptance. "Yeah, I know. Can't blame me for trying."

I walk around the bed and pull my friend into a hug. Her embrace is tight.

"Just promise you'll be careful and smart," she says, her voice muffled by my hair. "You don't know what this guy is capable of."

"I'll be fine. Everything will be okay. I'll be back before you know it." I give her cheek a loud smacking kiss. "Now walk me to the door."

I grab my duffle by the handles and she picks up my bathroom bag. We leave the room and go out to the living room. At the front door, I drop the bag and scoop up Mr. Bones. I snuggle the thick-haired ginger cat against my chest. His soothing purr vibrates in my ear.

"You be good for Auntie Rika." I kiss the top of his head. "I'll be back soon."

I set him back on the floor and he scurries off, having had enough cuddles for the moment.

"Thank you for staying here and watching Mr. Bones for me," I tell Rika.

"You're doing me a favor by letting me stay. The damn neighbors were at it again last night. It'll be nice to sleep in peace for a change."

After getting one more hug from my best friend and reiterating my promise to call her every day, I finally make it out of my house and shove my stuff in the trunk of my car.

One obstacle down, one to go.

---

"THE FUCK YOU'RE GOING, EVERLEE!" my dad's harsh voice booms in my ear. "Have you lost your goddamn mind?"

I wince and pull the phone away from my ear. It's not often Dad loses his temper and yells, which says a lot about his patience after raising four sons and a rambunctious daughter on his own. When he does, though, anyone who knows him knows to stay the hell back.

I wait until I'm not in danger of having my eardrums blown before I bring the phone back to my ear.

"Are you done?" I ask, keeping my tone calm, even though I want to yell right back at him. I learned early as a child, you have to give as good as you get with the Adair men.

"Ever, so help me God—"

I cut him off before he can start again. "I'm going, Dad, and you're just going to have to find a way to deal with it. And to keep the guys away. I won't have them or you mess this up. Dillon and Linzi are depending on me. And besides, you know how important this is to me."

His deep rumbly growl comes across the line. Dad's a control freak. He hates not getting his way, especially with me. There are some things I'll relent and give up on because it's not worth the trouble of fighting him or my brothers, but there are some times, now for instance, I put my foot down. No one is taking this opportunity away from me.

"At least let me send one of your brothers with you," he suggests, his tone has calmed but I still hear the anger and worry behind his words.

"No," I reply stubbornly. "I want to do this on my own."

"Jesus Christ, Ever," he mutters in exasperation. "You'll put me in an early grave one of these days."

"Oh stop being dramatic, Daddy. You'll be fine."

"The hell I will. You'll be out in the middle of fucking nowhere. There's a number of different predators in that area of the wilderness. Not just the four-legged kind. I'm more worried about this man you're so dead-set on finding. Do you have any fucking clue how dangerous this can be?"

"Yes, I understand. I'm not an idiot. You raised me to be a smart, independent, and strong woman. I'm taking precautions. I'll have my sat phone, taser, and my gun." I give the same reassurances I gave Rika not even an hour ago.

"None of that will do you any good if this guy sneaks up on you."

"That may be so, but I've also got all the physical training you and the guys taught me."

I'm not complaining about the number of countless hours Dad and my brothers forced me down in the basement to the training room to learn self-defense maneuvers. It may have been annoying back then, but I appreciate it now. Especially considering the incident that happened in high school.

Rika and I had just finished watching a movie at the theater. Her mom picked her up, but I stayed behind because I wanted to hang out with my boyfriend Lucas, who worked at the ticket sales booth. Instead of calling Dad or one of my brothers to pick me up afterward, I decided to walk home. We lived a few blocks away, so it was only a fifteen minute walk.

I had just passed the drug store, which was closing up for the night, when I was grabbed from behind and dragged down an alley. At first, I was stunned frozen. It wasn't until he was rucking up my skirt that I was knocked out of my rigid state. The man, whom I didn't know until later was Jerry Bishop because of the ski mask he wore, was not prepared when I kneed him in the balls.

Then when he was bent over double, I grabbed his head and rammed his face against the same knee. He fell on his ass, and I took off running.

I went straight home and told Dad what happened. My brothers wanted to find the guy and take care of the problem themselves, but Dad put his foot down. He said he didn't want any of his son's going to prison for murder. And I have no doubt the man wouldn't have lived through what my brother's would have done to him. I know it took a lot for Dad to back down from hunting the guy himself, but luckily, he had a clearer head.

It was because of their training I was able to get myself out of a situation that could have ended a lot worse. It was later discovered that I wasn't the first person Jerry, one of the janitors at my high school, had attacked. Once word got out, two girls came forward, claiming he had attacked and raped them. The news rocked the town. Shit like that just didn't happen here.

"I still don't like this," Dad grumbles, pulling me out of the past and back to the present. "Why does this mean so much to you?"

I don't have an answer for him. I'm just as stumped as he is. I've been obsessed with the story of Wild Man for the last five years. Ever since I overheard Mrs. Crocker talking about him in the grocery store.

"It doesn't matter why. It just is."

His breath crackles across the line. "I expect daily reports. If I don't hear from you—"

I finish the sentence for him. "You and the boys will storm the area until you find me. Got it."

"I'm serious, Ever," he warns unrepentantly.

"I know." My lips tip up into a smile, relieved he's finally relenting. Surprisingly, talking him into backing off was easier than I thought it would be.

"Keep the sat on you at all times. And keep the gun loaded."

"Already planned on it."

8

"Daily reports, Everlee," he repeats like I didn't hear him the first time.

"Yes, Dad."

"Love you."

"Love you too. And send my love to the guys."

I press the End Call button on the screen just as I reach the Black Ridge National Forest sign. Adrenaline and excitement course through my veins.

After years of curiosity and tons of research, I'll finally be able to uncover the story of the mysterious Wild Man.

## two

EVERLEE

I swipe my fingers over my chin and the corners of my mouth, checking to make sure no drool has pooled out between my lips.

Never in all my twenty-seven years, out of all the guys I've dated or the ones I've met, or even the men in the few pornos I've watched, have I ever seen a more gorgeous man.

Handsome is too tame a word. Attractive pales in comparison. Sexy comes close, but it's still not strong enough. Outrageously, devastatingly gorgeous is the only way to describe the man fifty feet away from me.

Wild Man.

It took me years, but I finally found him.

And holy mother of everything, it was well worth the wait.

He's currently bathing in one of the springs the area is rumored to have. One end has a pool of crystal clear water with thick green foliage surrounding the sides. There's a small path between a section of the foliage that invites a person to dip into the cool water. The other end has a small waterfall that has just enough of a trickle that it perfectly mimics a shower.

Wild Man runs a thick green leaf up and down his muscular arm, using it like a washcloth. He does the same to the other. When he switches to running it over his deeply chiseled chest, my eyes are helpless but to follow the movement.

He's not built like a linebacker. More like a surfer. He's stacked with muscles, but they aren't bulky and excessive. Instead of a six pack, there are eight sharply-cut ridges running down his stomach until they meet a V that I've always found ridiculously sexy on men. His pecs flex with each movement of his arms. Other than a small scattering of dark hair on his pecs that travels down his abs, his chest appears smooth and flawless. His skin is deeply tanned, which is expected since he lives outdoors.

My eyes slowly move down the line of muscles and stop where the water gently laps at his waist. Just a small portion of his cock sticks out of the surface. Disappointment is the first thing I feel at not being able to see the full package. If I were a little closer, I'd be able to see through the crystal clear water. Then I feel like a pervert for spying on an unsuspecting man and shame coats my cheeks. Even so, no matter how much guilt I feel, I can't tear my eyes away from him.

He's just too damn beautiful to not look at.

His dark hair, which goes halfway down his back, is wet and glistens in the sun peeking through the heavy canopy of trees. His cheeks and chin are covered in a thick layer of hair. It's shorter than what I would have expected, considering the man has lived in the wilderness for most of his life. How does he keep it trimmed? I can't imagine him having a razer or even know how to use one.

He starts moving toward the edge of the water, and my breath catches. I no longer have to worry about drooling because my mouth dries of moisture. I'm pretty sure every bit of it went between my legs.

I have the perfect profile view of him. And sweet Lord have

mercy, if I thought from the waist up he looked good, the view below is damn near perfection.

A tapered waist and a round ass with luscious muscular globes are just as tanned as the rest of his body. But it's not that part that has my stomach clenching and my legs scissoring back and forth to relieve a needy ache.

With the leaf still in his hand, he wraps his fingers around a dick so thick and long that I can tell all the way from here it would be difficult for any woman to accommodate. I thought I had seen big dicks before, but good God, this one is mammoth. It has to be as thick as my wrist and nearly the length of my forearm.

A shutter ripples down my spine, and I send out imaginary sympathy to any woman who encounters that thing.

As intimidating as it is though, I can't stop staring at it. Or the way he carelessly strokes his hand up and down. From root to the tip, he twists his wrists. He drops the leaf and fists it bare-handed. He jerks his hand back and forth, the muscles in his arm bulging, moving slowly at first but picking up speed. He looks like he's squeezing that thing to death.

I move my gaze to his face. His head is tipped back, a sliver of sun shining down on him. It's hard for me to see from where I am and the beard covering his cheeks, but I can imagine his jaw is clenched.

My eyes travel down his back just in time to see his asscheeks clench. I know that reflex. He's getting ready to come. Not wanting to miss it, I ignore my mind's demand that I look away and jerk my eyes back to his cock. Seconds later, a rope of cum spurts from the tip, splashing into the water. Three more arcs of clearish liquid squirts out as Wild Man's hand slows on his cock.

My cheeks must be the color of cherries and sweat dots my forehead. I suck in a sharp breath, trying to regulate my breathing and heart rate. I can't believe I just watched this man ejaculate. Watched him like a pervert while he was none the wiser.

*You are a fucking creepy freak, Everlee.* I admonish myself.

Even with that thought in my head, the camera hanging around my neck taunts me. A little teasing voice in the back of my mind whispers for me to take a picture of Wild Man and all his gorgeous glory. I bring the camera to my face, focus the lens, and press the shutter button. I take a couple more for good measure, because you know, just in case the first was blurry.

I disregard my conscience telling me this is for my own pleasure and not for the public's eyes. Obviously, I can't put these images in the article I'm writing. I tell myself it's normal for journalists to document things that never actually make it to the public. It's strictly for research purposes.

I almost snort out loud at the thought.

Wild Man releases his dick and it flops forward. It bounced to and fro as he exits the water. His legs are toned, tanned, and covered in a dark layer of hair. Water drips down his body, and for a miniscule of a moment, I'm jealous of the drops.

*What in the hell is wrong with you, Ever?* I reprimand myself. *Your job is to witness and document, not ogle the subject.*

Wild Man shakes his head like wild creatures do and water flies everywhere. The movement also has his dick flapping about so hard it looks painful. Picking up a cloth, he roughly drags it up and down his arms and across his chest.

The shutter on my camera is silent as I take picture after picture.

The cloth gets dropped on a nearby bush. I hold my breath, wondering what he'll do next. He does nothing. He just stands there, so still he looks like a statue. I hold just as still.

After several moments, he walks out of view, leaving the drying cloth behind. I wait and wait and wait for him to reappear. I found Wild Man and where he bathes, but that's it. I don't know where he went or where he came from. This part of the forest is thick and spans hundreds of acres on all sides. I've been wandering around this part since the sun came up this morning. Who knows how long it'll take me to find him again.

My next move is to get closer to the pool of water and try to track his movements from there, hoping he's left a trail behind to follow.

A loud buzzing sound fills my ear seconds before there's a sharp sting on my arm. I slap my bicep, feeling the squish of the bug beneath my palm. So much for the bug spray I used earlier. I scrub my hand on my shorts, wiping away the bug guts.

Rika wasn't lying when she said I don't like the outdoors. Well, I *do* like it. I just hate the inconveniences that come with it. Like the bugs. I *hate* bugs.

Making sure the straps of my backpack are secure on my shoulders, I turn to make my way to Wild Man's bathing pool. I don't even get fully turned around before I'm smacking into a solid wall.

A solid wall that has firm muscles and smells like pure male. A delicious scent that has moisture pooling back into my mouth.

What does one do when they bump into something? They throw their hands up to catch themselves. And of course, that's exactly what I do.

My nails dig into the tanned and firm muscles that my hands rest against. The muscles twitch, and I swear my heart lurches at the same time.

My eyes are pinpointed on the center of Wild Man's bare chest, right between the delicious dip of his very defined pecs.

I should probably look up, but I'm finding it difficult to do so. I'm still very much enjoying where my eyes are currently pointed.

I'm in big fucking trouble here. If his chest is this mesmerizing and looking at him from fifty feet away had me drooling like an idiot, there's no telling what condition I'll be in when I look him directly in the eyes.

I give myself a firm mental talking to and an imaginary slap on the side of my head

*Act professional, Ever. This is no more and no less than a job. You've got this. Be cool.*

I search for and locate my proverbial big girl panties and pull them up. Taking a deep fortifying breath, I tilt my head back. Way back, because the man towers over me by at least a foot. My eyes clash with a pair so black, it's like looking into an empty void. Thick lashes frame the black orbs. I can't tell if he feels nothing, or if he's just damn good at hiding it.

He just stares at me with no indication of what he's thinking. No curiosity. No animosity. No intrigue. Absolutely nothing.

I clear my throat, briefly wondering if I should have taken better heed of Dad's and Rika's warnings.

Did I make a mistake coming out here? Did my foolish curiosity of learning more about Wild Man earn me a way one ticket to my deathbed?

My brothers always said my innate need to know things was going to get me in big trouble one day. It's going to suck if I have to hear *I told you so* for the rest of my life.

That is, if I'm around for them to taunt me with it.

Something tells me the gun and taser on my hip may not do me any good with Wild Man so close.

"Hi." I mentally wince when the word comes out a squeak.

Wild Man says nothing. He doesn't even so much as twitch a single muscle.

He's so close that I feel the hot air of his breath fanning across my face. Surprisingly, his breath doesn't stink. Considering he's lived on his own in the wild since he was a young child, I assumed dental hygiene isn't something he remembers or even has the means to keep up with. If I'm not mistaken, I believe I smell a hint of mint.

With his head tilted down, his eerie dark eyes bore into me. They leave chills popping up on my arms and cause my heart to race an uneven beat. His lips, behind the scruff of his beard, are full and a deep shape of red. I didn't notice before because he was so far away, but his hair isn't just black, it almost has a hint of blue in it.

I blink away my mesmerized state and bring my attention back to the reason I'm here. To get information. To learn this man's story. To uncover the secrets surrounding Wild Man.

I open my mouth to introduce myself, but the words get stuck in my throat. They literally get stuck, because Wild Man wraps one of his big hands around my neck and tightens his fingers so much that I barely manage to draw in air to breathe, let alone speak.

I'm pushed backward until I'm forced against a tree, my backpack digging into my skin. I arch my spine when Wild Man dips his face closer to mine. My hand twitches to reach for my gun, but I hold off for the moment. He's not fully cutting off my air supply, just merely holding me in place.

He may have not shown his interest, but he's got to be just as curious about me as I am about him.

Even so, I slowly bring my hand up and wrap my fingers around his wrist. His eyes slightly narrow and he tightens his hold even more. I barely refrain from pulling at his hand. I get the feeling if I struggle, it'll agitate him, and that's the last thing I want to do.

I slowly drop my hand, keeping my eyes on him for his reaction. He gives none, except to loosen his hold a fraction.

Then, all of a sudden, he drops his head and his face goes to my neck. I don't know why, but I tilt my head to the side, which stupidly gives him easier access to whatever he's doing.

What in the hell *is* he doing?

It only takes me a moment to figure it out. The touch of his nose slides along the column of my neck and he breathes in deeply. He does it a couple more times.

He's... sniffing me?

For some reason, that has the hairs on my arms rising and the back of my neck prickles.

He keeps his face buried in my neck and steps closer. Something hard pokes into my stomach. My eyes widen, and my body stiffens at the realization of what it is. He's still fucking naked and he's pushing his humongous dick against me.

My instincts kick in, and I reach for his wrist with one hand while going for my taser with the other. I don't get to either before my neck is released and both of my hands are captured in his. He transfers them to one of his and lifts them above my head.

His lips are a flat line as he stares down at me with his unfeeling black eyes. His hair, still damp from his bath, partially hides his face as it falls forward. The hand not holding mine goes back around my throat. The heat of his fingers is scalding.

I straighten my spine as much as I can and stare back at him.

"No," I say, adding strength into my voice that I don't actually feel.

The only response I get in return is a deep grunt.

His face goes back into my neck and he continues sniffing me. With my arms raised, it limits his access, so using his grip around my neck, he tilts my head to the side.

Another grunt comes at the same time he pushes his hips forward, digging his abnormally large dick into my stomach.

"Stop!" I say louder.

When he doesn't even acknowledge my demand and continues his ministrations, I try to raise my knee, but it's no use. Wild Man has effectively trapped me. The only thing I can do is wait for him to finish and hope like hell this is as far as he'll take it.

I don't believe his intent is to get off while dry humping me. I think he's simply using the movement to keep me in place while he takes his fill of my scent.

Something wet touches my neck, and it only takes a second to comprehend that it's his tongue. He's fucking licking me, and from the deep rumble that vibrates in his chest, he's not displeased with the way I taste.

As he continues to rub his nose and tongue up and down my neck, the prickles of his beard abrading my skin, I open my eyes and stare up at the blue slivers of sky through the thick canopy of trees. Birds chirp in the distance, along with the buzz of insects. Off to the right, in the direction of the spring, the whoosh of the waterfall fills the air. Sweat trickles down my temples, between my breasts, and down my back. It's hot as blazes out here. Why does mother nature have to pick now to be unseasonably hot for the beginning of fall? I bet that spring would feel heavenly right about now.

My eyes widen and my breath hitches when Wild Man leaves my neck and pushes his face against my chest. His nose pokes into the space between my breasts just above the line of my t-shirt and he inhales deep. I ball my hands into fists, the bark cutting into my flesh. I pull against his hold to test his grip, but it's locked tight.

A gruff groan reverberates from his chest and he digs his face deeper, stretching my shirt down until my breasts almost fall out. I wiggle against his hold, but he just keeps me in place with his hands and groin tucked against me.

Then, before panic can set in, I'm released. It happens so fast, I stagger forward and nearly fall. My gaze shoots to Wild Man standing a few feet away, his body rigid with his nostrils flaring. Before I can stop myself, my eyes lower. Down and down they go until they fall on the rock hard appendage hanging between his legs. I thought it was big from fifty feet away. This close... I had no idea they were made that fat and long. Dark hair surrounds the root. The twin balls just below hang low.

I don't get a chance to look at it for long before Wild Man turns around and walks away, giving me a close up view of the backside of him. I'm not ashamed to admit, the back is just as appealing as the front.

I stand there for several seconds, watching him get further away from me as I contemplate on following him or getting the hell out of there. The smart thing to do would be to leave and maybe bring one of my brothers back with me. Just one look at Wild Man, and I know he's more than I can handle, should things get out of hand, even with my gun and taser.

But I'm impatient. I've been curious about this man for years. And the magazine I work for is depending on this article. I promised Dillon I would have something for him no later than a couple of weeks. I won't let him and Linzi down. It's just not an option.

Call me naïve, and maybe I'm making the biggest mistake of my life, but I really don't think this man will hurt me. Not truly.

So, with a deep breath of courage and a prayer to the big man upstairs asking Him to watch over me, and ignoring all the blaringly obvious warning signs, I take the first step toward uncertainty.

*three*

EVERLEE

I follow behind Wild Man, but I keep my distance. It's better to not be close if he makes any sudden movements toward me. I rest my hand on the butt of my gun I have holstered to my hip.

I watch my surroundings as we trek through the forest, memorizing landmarks so I won't be lost when I leave. Having been forced to live half of my life outdoors with my dad and brothers has its perks. They taught me all about nature. How to navigate it. How to recognize certain things. How to track through it. How to identify poisonous plants and critters.

While I'm aware of what's going on around me, my eyes keep straying ahead. Wild Man is about twenty feet in front of me, still wearing his birthday suit. With each step he takes, the muscles in his ass and legs flex, and I can't help but watch. That butt looks good enough to bite, or maybe sink my nails into. What can I say, I've always been a butt gal.

He suddenly stops and turns his head, his eyes meeting mine. My cheeks grow hot at being caught looking at his backside. His blank expression doesn't change. He just turns back around and keeps walking.

His feet are bare, and I wonder how in the hell he's able to walk on such rough terrain and not hurt himself. Living in the wild has toughened up his feet, I'm sure, but there are things that would scratch and cut through the toughest of skin.

His steps are light. So quiet that if I didn't see him, I wouldn't even know he was in front of me. No wonder he was able to sneak up on me unawares. My father and brothers are masters at being outdoorsmen, but they have nothing on Wild Man.

After about twenty minutes, we come up to a thick brush of green bushes. Wild Man doesn't hesitate as he walks through the mass of green and goes out of view.

I *do* hesitate. I have no clue what's beyond that wall of vegetation. I don't know what's going to happen on the other side. Of what I'll find. It's a worrisome notion, and I recognize I'd be stupid to chance it. But dammit, I've waited years for this opportunity.

My head jerks to the side when a branch snaps. It sounds like it's a good distance away, but there's no telling what or how close it is. It didn't sound small though. A noise comes from the bushes in front of me, and my head swivels in that direction. I look up at the sky, or what I can see of it through the trees, and notice how far down the sun has gone. It's on its descent into the west. Which means I only have a couple hours of daylight left.

I estimate I have about an hour of steady walking before I make it back to my campsite, so I have a little time to spare. Why not use that hour to try and learn more about Wild Man. To see where he lives. Or attempt to get him to speak with me.

Can he even speak? I mean, I'm sure he can make noises, but does he remember how to form words? He was five years old when he was left alone in the wild. From the little research I've been able to find on him, it's rumored that he's never left. He raised himself in this forest. Other than the two people who have claimed to have glimpsed a man in the forest, there are no accounts of anyone approaching him. There's been no one for him to talk to, so maybe he's forgotten how.

That thought pulls on my heartstrings. I can't imagine growing up utterly alone, especially at such a young age. I was two when Mom died, but I had Dad and my brothers, and later in life, my friends. I don't remember Mom, but my family wasn't the type to shy away from talking about her. I know her through pictures, their memories, and the many stories they've shared about her.

Wild Man had no one. He lost his parents so young and had no one to take care of him, comfort him, shield him from danger. How in the hell did he survive out here on his own? How did he manage to find food? How did he escape the many deadly creatures that roam the area? How did he survive the harsh weather elements?

I'm determined to get the answers to my questions. And to do that, I need to grow a pair of steel balls and move forward.

So that's what I do.

My first step is hesitant, but the ones that follow are stronger and more steadfast. I step up to the thick overgrowth of brush and reach out. When I push it aside and walk through the small opening, I stop just on the other side.

My mouth drops open in awe at what I find.

It's like a mini-oasis. The focal point of the hidden spot is a big white oak tree with thick branches that hang surprisingly low. Surrounding the tree are make-shift walls made out of tree branches and foliage. There's a big open space where one can walk inside the structure. Between the large tree above and the branches and foliage, the area is protected from the rain. More walls are along the outside of the living space, giving a sense of privacy. The ground has a thick layer of old leaves and underbrush, which I'm sure makes the ground softer to walk on. Along one wall is a pile of random stuff that looks like it's been there for years. I wonder how and when he started collecting it. Up against another wall, there are several long sticks with pointy ends. Weapons? Hunting tools?

From where I'm standing, I can't get a good look inside the covered portion, but it fills me with curiosity. Is that where he sleeps?

The smell of burning wood has my gaze jerking around, looking for the source. To my left, Wild Man is squatting in front of a small fire. Before I can stop them, my eyes drop to the thick appendage hanging between his legs. It damn near brushes the ground. Does he always go around naked? Does he not own any clothes? It's a silly question, since this forest is his home. He would have no way of getting clothes.

I move my gaze before he catches me staring at his junk and take a tentative step forward. His long hair falls forward, some draping over his wide shoulders while the rest falls down his back. One of his big tanned hands rests on his knee, while the other arm is stretched out. He's holding a long stick with what looks like a piece of meat stuck on the end. I don't even want to think about what animal it is.

He doesn't look at me or acknowledge my presence as I slowly move closer.

"Hello." I keep my voice low and even. "My name is Everlee. Or you can call me Ever."

Nothing. He just flips the meat on the stick to the other side..

I stop on the opposite side of the fire from him, keeping the flames between us. "Do you have a name?"

Again, he doesn't say anything. He ignores me and keeps his black gaze on the meat.

Spotting a log a few feet away, I roll it toward the fire and take a seat. I set my backpack beside me. I'm quiet for a few minutes, just watching the silent man in front of me, giving him time to get used to my presence. Every minute or so, he flips the meat over.

"The people in town call you Wild Man," I say casually. "So I'll just keep calling you that until you feel comfortable telling me your name. Is that okay?"

I'm not surprised when he doesn't respond. It's a good thing I have plenty of patience and a ton of tenacity. I knew this endeavor wouldn't be easy. It would be shocking if Wild Man took to me immediately and told me his life's story from the get go. Having not been around people for so long, I knew he would be wary and probably wouldn't know how to socialize. I have to build his trust and show him I mean him no harm.

When I told Dillon I wanted to write an article about Wild Man, one of the stipulations I made with him and Linzi was that the location of Wild Man would stay out of the magazine. He's lived in this forest peacefully for more than twenty years, and I didn't want that to change for him. I didn't want people to swarm the area on a hunt to locate the man who raised himself in the wilderness since he was a child. He has the right to continue living in peace, and I won't be responsible for disrupting that. I merely want to observe him and document his journey, if he allows it.

"I work for a magazine," I say conversationally. "I heard about you years ago and have been fascinated by what happened." I internally cringe at how the words come out. It makes me sound like I get enjoyment from his suffering. "What I mean is, I'm interested to learn your story. How you came to live in the wild. How you survived. And if you're okay with it, I'd like to document it."

Not a peep or twitch.

I sigh. Rome wasn't built in a day. Thankfully, I'm a freelance writer, so I can spend as much time as needed to get the information I want.

I watch Wild Man as he watches the meat he's cooking. The light beneath the canopy of trees is growing dimmer by the minute, which means I need to leave soon. I'd rather not be traipsing through the forest at night. I have a cabin I go to every couple of days to shower and charge my sat phone, but mostly I stay in my tent. It's weird camping on my own, but it's also peaceful, relaxing.

I'm just getting ready to stand and inform him that I'm leaving and to ask if he minds if I return tomorrow, but he gets to his feet first, startling me. I tense, unsure what he's about to do.

What he *does* do is more than unexpected. As he rounds the fire to my side, he yanks the piece of meat from the stick and tears off a portion of it. It has to be hot, but he shows no sign of it burning his hand.

I hold still, preparing to pull the gun from my hip should I need it. He stops a foot away from me and holds out the small piece of meat. My gaze switches from the meat in his hand to his face and back again several times before I realize what he's doing.

He... wants me to eat.

This wild and untamed man is trying to feed me.

I look back at the meat, inspecting it with a critical eye. There's no telling what animal it is. There are a number of creatures known to inhabit this part of the forest. Bears, coyotes, bobcats, wolves, and foxes are just to name a few of them of the deadlier kind. None of them sound appealing to eat. But it would be rude and offensive to refuse his offering.

I reach out and take the piece of meat from him, ignoring the way my stomach flips on its side at not knowing exactly what I'll be putting in my mouth. Surprisingly, it looks good and the smell isn't bad either.

Wild Man waits a moment before he turns and goes back to his side of the fire. He resumes his squatted position, but he doesn't eat. His dark, brooding eyes stay latched onto me, as if he's waiting on something.

*Here goes nothing, Ever.*

I bring the meat to my lips and take a small bite. Wild Man watches me, and if I'm not mistaken, there's a hint of expectancy in his blank expression. The look makes me think he's waiting for my reaction to the food, and maybe even hopes I like it.

It doesn't taste bad. It actually reminds me of one of the grilled steaks Dad is known for during cookouts. It's charred perfectly, is tender, and has just the right amount of juices.

"This is good." I don't even know if he can understand me, but I still feel the need to voice my praise. "What animal is it?"

No response.

I take another bite, this time bigger. Wild Man seems satisfied with my reaction and starts eating his own piece. Unlike me, he tears into it with zero amount of grace. He just digs his teeth into it and yanks a piece off. He finishes before me, despite his piece being twice as big as mine. The simple meal settles in my stomach, leaving me satisfied.

He stands again, and I watch as he walks inside the covered area and comes back out a moment later. He carries a small plastic jug. Stopping beside me in the same spot as before, he holds the jug out. I slowly take it from him. It looks filthy on the outside, but when I look inside the little opening, the clear liquid looks fresh and clean.

I don't know why I feel compelled to eat this man's food and drink his water—assuming it *is* water. It wouldn't be a stretch for him to poison me somehow. Afterall, I'm a complete stranger that wandered into his camp. He has every reason to get rid of me.

Even so, I lift the jug to my mouth and take a small sip. The water is cool and refreshing against my parched tongue. I swallow two more mouthfuls before I hand it back to Wild Man with a smile. He looks down at the jug, flips it around, and drinks from the exact spot that I drank from. For some reason, that move heats my cheeks and makes my stomach swirl.

Droplets of water cling to his lips and beard when he pulls the jug away. Lifting his arm, he used the back of his hand to smear away the lingering moisture. Unconsciously, and of their own accord, my eyes fall back down. Right to his groin, which is only a couple of feet in front of me, right at eye level.

This whole time, I've done an excellent job at avoiding it, no matter how often my eyes want to stray. It's just so damn big, it's hard to miss. It's like a huge fucking log, swaying in the wind each time he moves.

When I realize I've been staring at it for too long, and I've even gone so far as to licked my lips, I jerk my eyes back up to where they should be. This view isn't much better. The man is a work of God-like art. I'm pretty sure the man upstairs spent way too much time perfecting the body in front of me.

His eyes, which are as black as obsidian, are focused on me. Something lurks behind the darkness, barely noticeable, and the look sends a ripple down my spine. Not the pleasant kind of ripple, but the kind someone gets when they instinctively know something bad is about to happen. The kind that kicks in right before the fight or flight response activates.

And that's my cue to leave.

That's when I make my first mistake.

My attention is on my backpack as I get up from the log. "Thank you for the food," I say, grabbing the pack with the intention of throwing it over my shoulder. "I'm going to lea—"

My words fall short when I look up. Wild Man has moved closer. So close that he's in my personal bubble, and I can see a few faint freckles dotting his forehead and feel the heat coming off his naked body. He looms over me, his expression an unreadable mask. I'm forced to tilt my head way back to keep him in view.

When I try to take a step away, he darts his hand out, wrapping his long fingers around my much smaller bicep. His grip isn't tight enough to bruise, but it's also unyielding.

"Let go," I demand in a no-nonsense tone.

That's where I make my second mistake. Thinking I can force him to release me.

In response, Wild Man tightens his grip. Fear shoots through me at the defiant look that darkens his already unfathomable eyes. Just that look alone tells me he has no intentions of following my order.

I drop my pack and reach for my gun. My fingertips barely graze the butt of it when my hand is snatched away. Before I have a chance to reach for my taser, my arms are pulled behind me and my wrists are captured into one of his big hands. He yanks me forward and my breasts are smashed against his firm chest. I can feel the thick length of his cock trapped between our bodies. This close, I can smell him. The scent of primal male radiates off him. A slight musk, pine, and a hint of earth.

I tip my head back, the fear of before growing tenfold.

His face is only inches away from mine. The warmth of his steady breath fans across my cheeks, heating them further. The long strands of his ebony hair surround us as he glares down at me.

He drops his face closer and bares his teeth, growling out a single word.

"Mine."

*four*

EVERLEE

"**M**ine."

That's the only word Wild Man says.

That one word, along with the intent written all over his face, has true terror filling my veins, freezing the life-giving blood flowing through them.

Up until this point, I didn't truly fear the situation or Wild Man. One look at him, and I knew he was capable of harming me, but I didn't get the sense that he would. I felt more like an unusual nuisance to him. An inconvenient tolerance he would deal with until I was gone.

Boy was I ever wrong.

With the straight line of his lips, the puffing of his nostrils, narrowed eyes as dark as night on a starless sky, and the hard bulges of his muscles as he stands over me, I realize I was stupid. So fucking stupid. I made a colossal mistake coming here, and an even bigger one finding this untamed man. Thinking back, how in the hell could I have ever thought this was a good idea.

This man is uncivilized. He's never been in society or around people. Aside from when he was still a young child, memories that have probably faded over time, he's never been taught right from wrong. He doesn't know what a person should or shouldn't do. He has no laws to follow and no morals he was taught. He's going on pure animal instinct.

"*Mine.*"

His growled voice saying that word echoes in my head over and over again.

What does he mean? Surely he's not saying *I'm* his. That would be ridiculous, and if I'm honest, frightening as hell.

Knowing it'll be a fruitless effort, I still test out his strength and willingness to let me go. His grip doesn't lessen even a fraction.

What in the hell do I do now? The gun and taser are my only chance, but he has to let me go long enough for me to get to one of them.

As if sensing my thoughts, Wild Man pulls the gun from the holster, looks at it for a moment with his jaw clenched, before he tosses it somewhere behind me.

"Wait!" I yell, pulling hard against his unforgiving hold.

He does the same to the black taser.

His free hand latches around my throat at the same time his eyes jerk to mine. I tremble at the deadly look he gives me.

He tilts my head back by his grip. "Mine," he growls again.

I suck in a deep breath, barely able to get air in my lungs, trying to not let the panic that's quickly filling me show on my face.

"No, I'm not yours," I reply firmly.

His expression darkens and the bite of his fingers around my wrists dig against the bones.

"Mine," he grits out, baring his gleaming white teeth.

Is that the only word he knows? Something tells me he knows and understands more, but he probably so rarely talks—if ever—that he doesn't like to.

I open my mouth to protest again, but my breath is cut short when his fingers tighten around my neck. Terror stops me cold when I can't even pull in a breath.

Wild Man puts his face so close to mine that our noses touch.

"Mine."

One moment I'm standing on my feet ready to start fighting the brute tooth and nail, and the next, I'm up in the air hanging upside down. The move is so sudden and shocking that I'm stunned immobile. It only takes seconds to realize the asshole has tossed me over his shoulder.

"Put me down!" I yell, balling my hands into fists and whacking them against his back. His bare ass is right in my face, and I'm tempted to bite the fuck out of it. It's almost funny that I thought about biting his ass earlier in a more carnal way. "Let me go!"

I get a stinging slap on my butt for my efforts. The action was meant to get me to stop beating against his back, but it only fuels the angry fire building inside me.

I buck my body in an attempt to throw myself from his shoulder, but it doesn't work. One of his thick arms wraps around the back of my thighs, and I get another smack on my butt. This one much harder. I cry out at the sharp sting.

I dig my nails into the globes of his asscheeks so hard I'm surprised blood doesn't start flowing. Two can play this game. He hurts me, I hurt him in return.

I get my wish to be let go a moment later. Only it's not in the way I wanted. I'm tossed down on a surprisingly soft pile of blankets, which thrusts me into a new nightmare. This one more potent and chillingly disturbing.

Before I have a chance to scramble from the bed, Wild Man is on top of me, wedging his hips between my legs and settling himself down until his chest is pressed against mine.

"What in the hell are you doing?" I ask, trying to keep myself calm. I push against his chest, my nails biting into the hard muscles.

My wrists are captured again with one of his hands and brought above my head, where he slams them against the blankets. I buck my hips, but I stop immediately when I feel the hard ridge of his erection.

*Holy hell. He's fucking hard.* That does not bode well for me.

I have got to find a way out of this situation before it gets out of hand. Before Wild Man does something that can't be undone. Fighting and yelling isn't working, so I try something else.

Relaxing my muscles, I hold still, going lax beneath him. From the way his eyes narrow, Wild Man seems suspicious of my capitulation.

"Hey." I keep my voice soft.

Wild Man stays quiet, but his head tilts to the side. I try to pull one of my hands free, but he doesn't let go.

"Let me go," I say quietly.

The muscles in his jaw bunch and his left eye twitches. "Mine," he repeats what seems like the only word in his literary library.

I shake my head slowly. "No."

"Mine," he growls.

If I never hear that word again, it would still be too many times.

Frustration tries to outweigh my limited patience, and it takes effort to push it away.

It all goes to hell, and I know I've lost when Wild Man's eyes drop to my chest and something else altogether fills the blackness.

Pure, raw lust. And it scares the shit out of me.

Looking down, I mentally groan when I notice my shirt has been pulled down in my struggles and is showing off the top part of my purple sports bra. I've always thought my breasts were my best asset. Big, but not overly so. Perky, but not to the point where they sit right below my chin.

Right now, with my cleavage playing peek-a-boo, I wish I was one of those girls who complains about being flat chested. My firm C's are not working in my favor at the moment.

"Hey!" I say loudly, digging my booted heels into the back of his legs, hoping to get his attention away from my boobs. "Eyes up here, buddy!"

He scowls when he focuses back on my face. With his eyes still locked with mine, as if daring me to try and stop him, the hand not holding my wrists lifts and his fingers curl into the top of my shirt. I know what he's going to do before I hear the rip of material. He yanks and the shirt rips as easily as if it were paper.

"Stop that!" I yell, and once again, it falls on deaf ears. Or rather, he hears me, he's just choosing to ignore my demands.

I start bucking in earnest, adding my feet to the mix. I'm wearing heavy hiking boots, so I know the jabs can't feel good against his legs, but it's like I'm not even doing anything to him. My wrists are starting to turn raw from pulling on them so much, and I know I'll have bruises later.

My ruined shirt gets tossed to the side and Wild Man immediately reaches for the front of my sports bra.

Oh sweet Jesus, this can't be happening. This seriously can *not* be happening.

"Please stop." My voice cracks.

He ignores my struggles and pleas and easily rips my sports bra off like it was made of the flimsiest of material. How in the fuck did he rip is so easily? The fresh air slides across my sweat-dampened skin. I'm dimly aware of my nipples tightening. Not from desire, but from the air hitting my sweaty flesh.

Lifting my hips, I try to knock him free, uncaring that I'm probably making it worse by rubbing against his shaft. I just need him off me. I need to leave this place. To get away from this savage man. Because I know what's coming next, and I want no part of it.

I squeeze my eyes closed when Wild Man drops his head and I feel the warmth of something wet against my nipple. His teeth scrape against the tender flesh, and if this situation weren't what it was—if his machinations weren't being forced on me—it might have felt good. Right now, it feels anything but.

A hiss slips past my lips and tears sting the back of my eyes when he palms my other breast and squeezes. His fingers pinch the nipple at the same time he sucks the other one deep into his mouth. He bites down and the pain is nearly too much.

His rusty groan rumbles in his chest, and I feel the vibration of it against mine. A tear slips out the corner of my eye and rolls down my cheek and onto my ear.

Feelings of helplessness and hopelessness weigh heavy in my stomach, mixing with the nausea that's been slowly building since I realized what a monstrous mistake I made coming out here. This man is too big to fight off and all of my weapons are useless. There is no telling him no. There is no begging him to stop. He's taking what he wants and for some reason he wants me.

I am utterly and truly fucked, in the literal sense.

"Mine."

My eyes snap open at the snarled word and the painful grip on my breast. Wild Man looks up at me, his hair covering one of his black eyes. Even in the waning light, I see the glistening of his lips.

Fear pitches my stomach upside down.

When I don't respond, his lips peel back from his teeth and he growls the word again. "*Mine!*"

I shake my head. I'll be damned if I'll willingly give him what he wants. He's a fucking lunatic if he thinks otherwise.

He lets my breast go and his weight leaves me. I don't get the chance to suck in a full breath of air before I'm suddenly flipped over onto my stomach.

Renewed determination whips through me, and I scramble to my knees with the intent to roll off the other side of the pile of blankets. My ankle is grabbed in a firm grip, and I fall back to my stomach when I'm pulled backward.

"Get your fucking hands off me!" I screech, slamming my foot backward, hoping to connect with something. All I meet is air.

Then there's a weight on the back of my thighs and hands are reaching between me and the blankets. I fight and buck and scream so loud the sound pierces my ears. But no matter how much I struggle, my shorts and underwear are pulled roughly down my legs. They get caught on my boots only long enough for them to be taken off as well.

Then I'm naked. And Wild man is naked. There's not a stitch of clothing separating our bodies. Nothing to prevent him forcing himself on me. Taking from me something I don't want to give.

Long fingers wrap around my hips and my ass is pulled up. I curl my hands into the blanket and try to crawl away. My breath leaves me on a whoosh when my arms are yanked behind me and trapped, once again, in one of his hands. He presses them to my lower back.

"Wild Man!" I scream the name, wishing I knew what his *real* name was. Maybe if I made him feel more human, reminded him that he *is* human, he'll stop acting like a fucking animal.

A grunt is my only response.

I feel something hard poking at my entrance.

"Stop!" I cry hoarsely.

With no support of my arms, my cheek is smashed against the blankets. I try to drop my weight to the bed, anything to get his dick away from me, but with my arms pulled back, I can't go anywhere without popping them from their sockets.

Wild Man pays me no attention, his crazed lust-filled mind set on only one thing. Satisfying one of man's most basic needs, uncaring of the destruction it'll cause.

I go limp below him and brace myself, knowing there's not a damn thing I can do. Tears fill my eyes, dropping to the soft dark-green blanket below me.

"Please," I whisper. I don't know if I'm asking God for help or begging Wild Man to stop.

Regardless, my request goes unheeded.

With the fingers of one hand wrapped around my hip and his other hand still holding my wrists, Wild Man, with no compunction at all and a low grunt, slams his hips forward, seating himself completely in one go.

I cry out at the sudden sharp pain, my body tensing, trying to expel him. He's too fucking big. Even if I were fully prepared and willing, there *is* no preparing for a man of his size. It feels like he's in my stomach, rearranging my organs to accommodate him.

Knowing it's useless, I try again to get away. I'm held back by my wrists and my hip.

Thankfully, Wild Man doesn't move. He holds still, grinding his hips into my ass. My nails dig into my hands, no doubt leaving crescent marks in my palms, and I turn my head to the side. Out the corner of my eye, I see him with his head tipped down, looking at the place he's violating me, his hair falling forward. His gaze appears crazed, more hungry than he was before.

He lets my waist go and moves his hand to the back of my neck. All too soon, he pulls his hips back slowly, only to thrust back in just as hard as the first time. The growl he lets out sounds animalistic. Another low cry leaves me and more tears stream down my face. The pain isn't as bad, but it's still there, stealing my breath and searing into my soul.

Resolve firms my spine. I can get through this. I can endure this savage brutality, and once it's over, leave this place and forget my stupid fascination with Wild Man.

He picks up speed, his deep grunts and groans filling the small space around us. Each slap of his hips against my ass has me rocking forward, and with each one, he pulls me back by my wrists and neck, holding me in place.

The only thing I can do is lay there and take it. Let this man use my body for his sick pleasure.

And that's what I do. With my head laying sideways, I stare across the small room, ignoring the way my body jerks and wincing every few thrusts when Wild Man hits a spot too deep. My stomach cramps at the invasion of my body and low sobs escape my lips. The slide of his too-large shaft scrapes against dry walls, sending shards of pain through me.

After what feels like hours later, but could only be minutes, he buries himself deep inside me, smashing our bodies together. "Mine," he snarls and lets out a guttural growl. Warmth coats my insides.

I'm both grateful it seems to be over, but disgusted to have this man's cum inside me.

He holds me still for several seconds before he lets me go. I fall to my stomach and then roll to my side, tucking my knees up to my chest. My eyes immediately go to him.

He's still on his knees in the same place. His eyes are pointed down at his glistening cock before lifting to mine. Heat fills them and my stomach clenches painfully when I realize he may not be done with me.

Then another thought occurs. Was that the first time he's had sex? It has to be, right?

I crab crawl backward, the rough bark of the tree meeting my back, when he gets to his feet. A couple of long steps and he's standing over me, leering down. His half hard cock sways right in front of my face, but I ignore it. His expression is blank, and I'm not sure if that's a good thing or bad.

He just stands there a moment before he turns on his heel and leaves the structure. I feel disgusted and my body hurts everywhere. Bile rises in my throat when I feel his cum leak out of me and slides down my thighs. I want a blistering hot shower and a scoring pad to scrub away every drop of him.

Wild Man returns. In his hand and trailing behind him is a rope about a quarter inch thick. My gaze snaps up, meeting his. Before I have a chance to even think about getting away from him, he's down on his knees before me.

"Stop!" I screech, clawing at his hands when he reaches forward and winds the rope around my waist.

It's like a fucking baby is attacking him with all my attempt it's doing to him.

Once he has the rope secured around my waist, he ties it, using a knot I've never seen before. My breath stutters out and dread coats my insides when he takes the other end of the rope and ties it around his wrist.

Are you fucking kidding me? He's attaching me to him? There goes my chance of escaping while he's asleep. Unless I can untie the knot or figure out a way to cut the rope. I look at it and the knot looks complicated as hell. Hopefully he's a heavy sleeper.

Once he's satisfied, he sits back on his heels, looking pleased with himself.

Grabbing the length of the rope, I tug on it so hard it lifts his arm. "Release me," I demand. "Now."

I know he understands me—I can see it in his eyes—but he only does his stupid grunt thing.

Quick as lightning, he darts his arm out, and before I realize what's happening, we're both down on the blankets on our sides. I grit my teeth and bite back my own growl when I feel the whole front of his body plastered to the back of mine. His semi-hard dick included. He shifts his hips until the length of his shaft is wedged between my buttcheeks. I'd much rather take this spooning shit than have him fuck me again.

Reaching down, he pulls one of the thinner blankets over the top of us to our hips. The arm I'm lying on curls around my torso so his fingers wrap around my shoulder, effectively holding me in place. His other arm is around my waist with hand going down my body. He cups his entire hand over my sore pussy possessively.

After he's done with all of that, his face goes into my air and he inhales deeply.

Seriously, what is up with him sniffing me?

His voice, when he speaks, is deep and dark and it sends creepy vibes sliding down my spine.

*"Mine."*

My eyes spring open when a gut-wrenching pain explodes in my lower stomach. Disorientation has me in its grip for all of two seconds before I realize what the pain is from.

I'm on my stomach with Wild Man's heaving body on top of me.

He gives a brutal thrust, and I scream because it feels like he's ripping me apart from the inside.

I grab the blanket underneath my hands and start bucking and twisting my hips, anything to get him off me. All it does is make him go deeper, which adds to my suffering. I scream and yell and cry until my voice goes hoarse and the cloth beneath my face is soaked with my tears.

I can do nothing. I'm stuck beneath this merciless and unhinged man as he continues to violate me over and over again.

Wild Man grabs my hair and yanks my head back. His other arm slides between me and the bed and up until his fingers wrap around my throat. Between the hair pulling and his harsh grip barely allowing me to breathe, black dots dance on the outside of my vision.

Wild Man buries his face in my neck and his hot breath scorches my skin. His grunts of pleasure mix with my cries of pain. He continues to rut, pounding his hard flesh into my abused body. His pelvis rams against my butt, retreats, and slams back forward. Revulsion and pain mix together, pulling me down into a terrifying void.

The black dots grow bigger, filling my vision. I welcome the thought of going unconscious. Anything to block out what's being done to me.

Seconds or maybe minutes later, my body goes completely lax as my reprieve finally takes me under.

*five*

EVERLEE

Memories of what happened yesterday and during the night and the situation I put myself in flash behind my closed eyelids before I come fully awake. I don't want to open my eyes. Ignorance is bliss and all that shit. If I stay asleep, or at least pretend to be, maybe I can forget where I am and hold onto the hope that it was all a nightmare. Opening my eyes will make the situation real again.

Unfortunately, it's not something I can avoid. Not if I want to find a way out of this mess. Also unfortunately, I can feel the rope around my waist. Unfortunately again, the soreness between my legs and the stickiness on my thighs is a harsh reminder, so my wishful ignorance would be unattainable regardless.

I don't get the sense that Wild Man is in bed, so maybe I'll be lucky and he'll be gone somewhere so I can escape.

I crack my eyes open just a sliver, enough to see that it's daylight. When I open them more, I damn near have a heart attack. Right in front of me, only a foot away from my face, is a pair of hollow eye sockets staring back at me. Fucking eye sockets! Inside of—what I assume—a human skull.

My stomach churns violently and bile threatens to make an appearance. I barely manage to swallow down the need to vomit.

I inch back from the nasty looking thing, keeping a watchful eye on it like it'll suddenly come alive and attack me. I hold the cover to my chest, because surprise, I'm still naked. Warily, I take my eyes off the skull and look around the space for my clothes. I slap my hand over my mouth as a small screech leaves my lips when I find another skull on the other side of the pallet of blankets. This one is pointed at me as well, its hollow eyes staring at me as if in judgment.

*What in the actual hell?*

Are these people he's killed and he's keeping their skulls as trophies?

Jesus fuck, Ever, you've really done it this time.

I back off the end of the pallet, away from both skulls, dragging the cover and rope with me. Once I'm on my feet with the cover wrapped around me and tucked beneath my arms, I look toward the opening of the space where the other end of the rope leads out of. I tip my ear that way, listening for any indication that Wild Man is out there. When I hear nothing, I let out a breath of relief.

After a quick look around, I don't find my clothes or anything I can use as clothes. Looks like I'll be running through the forest in nothing but a bed cloth. At this point, I couldn't give two craps, so long as I make it back to my car and away from the crazy man in the forest.

I keep my eyes locked to where the rope leads out and pick up the slack to give it a small tug. The rope pulls taunt, but doesn't otherwise move. Which means the chances are high that the other end is tied to some*thing* and not some*one*.

Last night, after waiting what felt like hours for Wild Man to drift off to sleep, I meant to try to work the knot loose. But when he finally did fall asleep, the bastard's arms and legs were wrapped around me too tightly. The last thing I wanted to happen was for him to wake up. So I waited some more, hoping he would roll away or at least relax his hold enough for me to slip away. Of course, I stupidly fell asleep before that could happen. Only to be woken up sometime later to him fucking me again. Thankfully, my mind checked out.

Now I have to hope he's gone long enough. Or maybe I can find something sharp to cut away the rope.

A quick look around shows nothing I can use at the moment. Nor nothing I can use as a weapon. I eye the skulls. I could use those. Maybe try to break one of them and use a pointed end. But just the thought of touching either one has my stomach churning furiously.

Hearing no noises coming from the opening, maybe I'll get lucky and find the gun or taser he threw away. Or maybe my pack is still out by the fire so I can get to my satellite phone inside to at least turn the GPS tracking on. Dad and my brothers are probably already out looking for me since I didn't report in last night. Of course, my stupid self purposely kept the GPS tracking turned off because I didn't want any of them to hunt me down and drag me back home. And they would have.

Sucking in a fortifying breath and making sure the cloth is securely tucked around me, I slowly approach the entrance and peek my head around the doorway. Relief relaxes my tense muscles when I don't see Wild Man. I step outside, my bare feet crunching against the leafy ground, and dart my gaze around, looking for the forest green backpack I came with. Not finding it, I start looking for the glint of my gun.

Just as I see the shine of metal and hope blossoms in my chest, movement out the corner of my eye has me jerking to the side. Dread and trepidation curdles in my gut when the tall form of Wild Man steps into view from the small opening of the bushes.

There's a piece of cloth tied around his waist. It covers his dick, and from the looks of it, his backside. At least there's that. I don't have to stare at the mammoth-sized piece of meat between his legs.

I take a step back, my heart jumping to my throat, when he approaches. But I need not have worried. He doesn't even acknowledge my presence as he walks past. He stops where several dishes sit on a flat rock and picks up a bowl. After, he turns, and I brace again as he walks toward me. This time, I do have to worry, as his thick fingers wrap around my upper arm and he pulls me behind him.

"Hey!" I yell, yanking on my arm. It's apparent that when he grabs me, there is no getting loose from him. "Let me go!"

He does so, but only when we reach a log by the fire pit and he takes a seat. The bark has been ripped away and the wood beneath is smooth. Which is good for him, because his cloth isn't long enough to cover his ass when he sits.

My arm is pulled, and I'm forced to sit between Wild Man's splayed legs. I bite back a few dirty words and opt to choose my battles wisely. Sitting between his spread legs, although degrading, isn't as bad as say, being forced to take his cock.

Thankfully, the cock in question is hidden behind the cloth, because my face is way too close to it in this position.

I sit stiffly, my legs tucked beneath me. One of my hands is holding the edge of the blanket under my arm. I'm sideways with one of his long legs at my back and the other bent in front of me. The hair on his legs is as dark as the hair on his head and the scruff on his face. The events of the last twelve hours must be turning my head to mush because for some idiotic reason, I wonder how coarse the hair is.

My eyes move down to his feet. Big feet with long slender toes and a small scattering of lighter-colored hair on the top. I'm mildly surprised that his toenails look clean and are clipped. I would have thought they would be long with dirt underneath.

I pull my eyes away and look up at his face. I've never particularly cared for men with beards. I prefer them with clean-shaven faces. But on Wild Man, I can't imagine him without the hair covering his cheeks and chin. With his long, thick dark hair falling down his tanned, bare shoulders, it gives him a caveman-type look and suits him perfectly. And although I loathe to admit it because of what he's done to me, he really is the most beautiful man I've ever seen. Too bad looks can be deceiving.

"You have to let me go," I tell him quietly, hoping to touch the part of him that has to still be human. "You can't keep me."

Instead of acknowledging my words, he pinches something from the bowl between his fingers and holds it up to me. My eyes briefly bounce off it, noticing an orangy-yellow piece of fruit, before I lift them back to him. He looks at me, his expression only holding expectancy as he waits for me to take it.

I shake my head. "No."

His eyes turn to narrow slits and a grunt leaves his throat when he shoves the fruit closer.

I've got two options here. I can continue to refuse the fruit, not giving him what he wants—this is the option I prefer, because I want to deny him anything he wants. I've no doubt he can force me to eat if he so chooses, but I damn sure don't want to make it easy for him.

Or I can give in and hope my acquiesce earns me brownie points with him. Maybe enough to where he'll untie the rope around my waist.

With no small amount of reserve, I lift my hand, intending to take the fruit from his fingers. I don't get the opportunity to. He pulls his hand back, his face forming a scowl when he shakes his head. His other hand comes up and pushes my hand away. The fruit is again lifted, this time closer to my mouth.

My own eyes narrow when I realize he wants me to take it from his fingers with my mouth. He wants to *hand feed* me.

Seriously?

We hold each other's eyes for several moments. His black bottomless ones to my determined brown ones.

In the end, it's me who gives in. Picking my battles, I feel I'll quickly learn, will be more difficult than I imagined.

I lean forward, never moving my gaze away from his face and slowly open my mouth. As soon as my lips part, his eyes move there. I manage to take the fruit without my tongue touching his fingers, but my lips still graze the tips. His eyes darken at the touch, and it sends a fissure of fear racing over my scalp.

I quickly jerk my head away and chew the sweet fruit, swallowing it past the dryness forming in my throat.

He holds up another piece, and it's on the tip of my tongue to say no. But I once again lean forward, this time managing to avoid touching his fingers with any part of my mouth. Apparently, Wild Man notices and finds my actions irritating, for he pinches his lips into a firm line when I lean back, slowly chewing.

The next piece he picks up, he does so where I'll have no choice but to touch my lips to his fingers. The moment my lips come in contact with the tip of his thumb, the muscle beside his eyes twitch and a low, rough sound emits from his throat.

I yank my head back and swallow the fruit before it's all the way chewed. A movement to my left catches my attention and my eyes move there. Then they widen as the cloth covering his shaft jerks and begins to point outward.

My attempt to scramble backward, away from that thing and the man it's attached to is thwarted by a hand gripping my hair. My head is jerked back, and I'm forced to look up into a pair of black eyes. The hand not holding the sheet latches onto the thigh in front of me. I dig my nails deep into the flesh, not enough to break skin, but enough he should feel a pinch of pain.

His jaw is clenched, the muscles on either side of his cheeks flexing, and his eyes blaze a message that says there will be dire consequences if I don't do what he wants.

45

"Mine," he growls, lowering his face so close to mine I can feel his breath. His hair hangs forward and a piece falls on my cheek.

"Fuck you," I seethe right back at him. I am sick and fucking tired of hearing that word.

With my head still tilted back by the hand in my hair, another piece of fruit is brought up to my lips, but I keep them sealed shut this time, glaring at him. Surprise filters through me when, instead of trying to force the fruit into my mouth, he gently runs it across the seam of my lips. His eyes track the movement, and I really don't like the attention he's giving my mouth.

Just as I decide to take the fucking fruit, he lifts it away and brings it to his own mouth. He chews slowly, the lump in his throat from his Adam's apple bobbing up and down.

Another piece is brought to my lips, and this time, I open them. But instead of him pulling his fingers away, he keeps them in my mouth. Just inside, the tips grazing my tongue. Another rumbly growl leaves his throat.

I relax my jaw and let my teeth lightly close against his fingers. I apply light pressure. Not enough to hurt, but the threat is no doubt felt. I should bite his fucking fingers off, but something tells me the consequences would be dire.

Wild Man lifts his onyx gaze to mine and a look of challenge flashes in the dark orbs. The grip he has on my hair flexes tighter, and I feel some of the strands pop. My head is jerked back further, the angle nearly too far.

For a split second, I let my teeth sink deeper into his skin, silently letting him know, he may hurt me, but I can cause pain too.

When I release my teeth from their grip, he doesn't yank his fingers from my mouth like I expected him to. Rather, he slides them along my tongue to the back of my throat, nearly activating my gag reflex. He slowly pulls them free and releases his grip on my hair. Reaching to his right, he picks up another piece of fruit and brings it to his mouth. He closes his lips around his fingers before he slowly pulls the digit out, tasting not only the fruit, but also *me*.

He again reaches to his left, but instead of fruit, he holds up the same jug I drank from last night. Knowing it would be foolish to refuse him, I grab the small jug with my free hand and bring it to my lips, once again surprised at the cool freshness of the water.

Wild Man takes the jug from me when I'm finished and does the same thing he did last night. He moves it around so his lips touch the same spot where mine were. He does this while keeping his eyes on me. The hand holding the sheet under my arm tightens.

Once he's finished drinking, he drops the jug to the ground and it tips sideways, the last of the water leaking out to soak the ground.

The next moment, I'm pulled to my feet and turned to face him. The cloth is ripped from my arms, and I'm left standing in front of him bare-ass naked. All of this is done within seconds, before I'm able to even comprehend what's happening.

Natural instinct has my hand darting out, balling into a fist to slam against his face. Inches before I'm able to connect with his cheek, my wrist is caught. I try with my other fist, but that wrist is caught too.

I release an unladylike growl and try jerking up my knee. He's still sitting and I'm standing between his spread legs, so it's the perfect height to nail him in his nose. But once again, I'm stopped prematurely, this time by his legs closing around my thighs and his hands, which have moved mine behind me to my lower back, yanking me forward. I'm immobilized, and the worse part is, my bare breasts are right in his face. I shoot daggers down at him from my eyes as he looks past my breasts and up at me. His nostrils flare and he looks angry.

Well, boo-fucking-hoo. I'm goddamn livid.

I wiggle and jerk against his hold, which is a mistake because it causes my boobs to bounce in front of him. His eyes drop and zero in on them.

"Shit," I mutter under my breath.

It might be my imagination, but it looks like he might drool.

His eyes flash to me at my expletive, and I hold completely still, afraid to move.

My spine goes straight when I feel the hand not holding mine touch the outside of one of my legs. It starts below my knee. Slowly, as if gauging my reaction, he moves it upward.

I'm pretty sure my expression must show my distaste but he doesn't seem to care, because he continues his movement.

When he reaches my upper thigh, his hand veers and his palm comes in contact with my ass. His fingers flex there when I clench my butt cheeks together. A distressed sound leaves my throat, and I shake my head rapidly from side to side, telling him, begging him, without words, that I don't want this.

His brows drop low, as if my negative reaction confuses him. It doesn't stop him though. His hand moves from my butt and around to my front. It travels up and up until it stops just below my breasts. He pauses and his eyes jump to mine.

I shake my head again and his look becomes a scowl. The hand holding mine tightens their grip at the same time he pulls me forward.

"No!" I yell, knowing it's a vain attempt, but refusing to give in without a fight. "Stop!" He easily holds me in place with his arm around my waist as he uses his other hand to settle his long fingers around one of my breasts. He palms it gently at first, the look in his eyes almost reverent. As if he's fascinated just by the weight of it in his hand.

I refuse to allow that curious look to get to me. I give not one shit that this man may not know any better. That the female body is an anomaly he's never seen before and the differences between my body and his are fascinating. That, at this moment, he's

48

exploring something new to him and he enjoys the way it looks and feels.

He may not remember what the word no means, but he has to know just from my struggles right now and my fighting him last night that I did not, and still do not, like what he's doing. Therefore, he should stop.

I wince and break eye contact with him when his gentle grip around my breast flexes and tightens. I look over his head and my eyes immediately fall on the shiny piece of metal I saw earlier. What I thought could possibly be my gun. My shoulders sag with disappointment when I realize it's not my gun but a stupid utensil. It's not even a knife or fork—either of which I could have used as a weapon—but a spoon. I could still use it against Wild Man, but it wouldn't be near as effective.

Something rough and prickly grazes the skin of my breast, and I jerk my chin down. A noise, a cross between a strangled cry of surprise and a grunt, leaves my lips. I stare down at Wild Man as he plumps up one breast with his palm and rubs his cheek against the soft skin. He does it again on his other cheek. His nose is next. He runs it over my flesh like he's smelling me.

Against my legs, I ignore the hardness of his cock as it begins growing behind the cloth covering him.

Because of the stimulation, my nipple has become a hard little point, and of course, this interests Wild Man. Nipples aren't new to him—he has his own—but a woman's are different. More sensitive and bigger.

He shows his interest by forcing my body forward at the waist so I'm slightly bent backward. When my nipple brushes against his mouth, his lips fall open and his tongue peeks out. He runs the tip over the tight bud, just barely touching it. I bite my bottom lip until I taste blood.

I watch with mutinous eyes as Wild Man draws more of my nipple into his mouth. He sucks the bud, flicking it this way and that with his hot tongue. I feel the rumble against my skin as he releases a low growl from his throat.

My breath stutters and a small sound escapes me when the sharp edge of his teeth bite down. With my flesh still in his mouth, his eyes raise to mine. I twist my features into a scowl, letting him know just how much I hate what he's doing.

I'm unsure if it's my unwillingness to show something he wishes to see on my face or if it's something more untamed within him, but he releases my nipple and lifts his head. For a brief moment, my mind celebrates, believing he's done with his exploration. But it falls flat not even a second later.

Using my hands and his free one at my hip, he turns me around until I'm facing away from him. My legs are kicked apart by one of his and then he pulls me backward. With a renewed burst of energy, I try to yank my hands from his. All I managed to do is strain the joints in my shoulders enough to send pain blazing through me. He pulls me backward again. The new position has my legs straddling his. I'm forced down until I'm sitting on his lap with my legs spread. He opens his knees, which causes my legs to open more.

And then I feel it.

My eyes grow wide and my hands behind me ball into fists. My head falls forward, and I look down between my legs. The cloth that was covering Wild Man has been pushed to the side and his big cock is sticking out, the length of it pressing against the lips of my pussy.

My back snaps straight and the joints in my shoulders feel like they'll pop out of their sockets when I start struggling in earnest.

"Goddamn it!" I screech. "No! Not again!"

How many times do I have to say the word before I realize that Wild Man just doesn't care if I want this or not?

My wrists are let go, only for Wild Man to wrap his arm around me tightly, trapping them at my sides. I'm lifted high off his lap and he reaches between my ass and his groin. He lowers me a second later and the tip of his cock touches my entrance. I don't get the chance to prepare before he jerks me all the way down on his shaft.

I scream at the sudden painful fullness of him. Tears prick my eyes and my stomach spasms, the fruit threatening to make a reappearance. I dig my nails into my thighs, hard enough that I feel the skin break. I slam my head backward, hoping to smash it into his face, but it's no good.

I squeeze my eyes shut and try to hold back any sounds, but a whimper manages to slip free when Wild Man holds me against him, pushing his hips up at the same time he grinds me downward. He touches a part of my insides that sends a sharp pain through my stomach.

He grunts behind me.

The arm not surrounding my waist, holding my arms captive at my sides, comes in front of me. His hand goes up my stomach, between my breasts, then he wraps his long fingers around my throat. He doesn't choke me, but it helps hold me in place as he uses his other arm to lift me up, only to bring me back down so hard my boobs bounce.

Another pain-filled whimper rips from my lips.

Three more times he forces me to slip to the tip of his cock and slams me back down. More deep grunts leave him.

His chest presses against my back. I let out a squeak when I'm pushed forward until I feel like I'm going to fall over. I lock my ankles around his calves. With his hand around my throat, barely loose enough to let me breathe, and his hands holding my wrists captive again, he keeps me from tipping over.

I'm basically hanging there, staring at the ground.

He uses both of his holds on me to use me for his pleasure.

When I hear the sound of his low growls as he slides me up and down his shaft, I block it out. When the feeling of him scraping against the walls of my dry pussy becomes too unbearable, I force the feeling away. When the smell of our joining invades my senses, I ignore it.

All of my efforts go to waste when I open my eyes and they land between my legs. The evidence of what's happening is right there. My gaze locks on his long shaft as it keeps appearing and disappearing inside my body.

Wild Man picks up speed, which adds to my discomfort and brings forth a dose of mortification. The harder he fucks me, the looser I get. While I'm glad the pain isn't so intense, I don't like that my body is getting accustomed to the abuse.

I'm roughly pulled tightly against him and a warm feeling fills me where we're connected. A low guttural growl emits from his throat.

I keep my eyes closed and feel the hot streak of tears blazing a path down my cheeks as he releases inside me.

After his cock stops jerking, I'm pulled by my waist until I'm once again sitting properly on his lap with me still impaled on him. His sweat slicked chest meets my back, and I can feel the rapid beat of his heart against me.

His breath fans against my ear when he mutters the same single word in a low voice. "Mine."

His arm moves from my waist which leaves mine finally free. But I'm completely drained emotionally to even attempt to get away. He lifts me from his lap and sets me to my feet. My hips are grabbed, and I'm spun around to face him.

Because he's still sitting on the log, I'm forced to drop my head down, meeting his dark eyes with a deadly glare. I want to smack the satiated look off his face. Claw his eyes out and jam my fingers in their fleshy sockets. He sits there like he doesn't have a care in the world, while I silently fume inside as I feel the scalding hot evidence of his brutal rape sliding down my legs.

We stay like that for several moments. Me mentally coming up with all the ways I'd like to kill the bastard. There's no telling what's going through his mind.

His head drops, his eyes tracing my torso, down over the small line of hair on my pubic area, to the slick liquid coating my thighs.

My jaw clenches and the muscle in my thighs tense when his hand comes up between my legs. He slides the tip of his fingers through his release. Revulsion fills me.

He continues the trek with his fingers until they graze my opening. He lifts his head to watch my face when he slips a finger inside. I hold a blank expression, giving him absolutely nothing, while on the inside I want to take that finger and shove it up his ass.

His finger goes in to the knuckle, comes back out, then goes back in. After several more slow thrusts of his finger, he pulls it out and holds it up between us. His gaze drops to his finger, a curious look entering his eyes as he looks at the glistening digit.

When he brings his finger to his mouth, I can't hide the twitch in my brows when he slides it between his lips. He sucks his release from his fingers, his eyes having moved back to me. Something dark and desirous mixes with the blackness in them.

He pulls his finger free and moves it back between my legs, this time adding a second one. He does the same as he did before; sliding a finger inside a few times before pulling it free. Only this time, he doesn't bring it to his mouth, but to mine.

I press my lips together determinedly. His brows drop into a scowl, irritation tightening the lines on his face. He reaches up, grabs a handful of hair, and forces me back to my knees. My head is pulled back so fair, I have no option but to open my mouth.

And of course, he takes advantage by slipping his fingers past my lips.

The taste of him is not what I expected. I've had men come in my mouth before, and while I'm not a fan of the taste, it's always been just on this side of tolerable.

Wild Man's though, it's not the salty bitterness that I'm accustomed to. It's both, but not as strong and there's something else. Almost something that has a hint of sweetness.

If I were to be honest, I'd admit that it doesn't taste bad. That thought has me wanting to spit every drop back into his face.

Wild Man's eyes heat and flare as he slides his finger over my tongue. I debate biting his finger or at least threatening him with it again, but it got me nowhere last time, so it would be a waste to do it again.

So I give him what he wants and suck his finger until he's satisfied.

*six*

EVERLEE

I sit with my knees drawn to my chest and both arms wrapped around my legs. I'm not sure how much time has passed, but it's been at least a couple hours since Wild Man got done with me. I can still taste him, despite having rinsed my mouth with water.

I eye the opening of the bed area, where Wild Man threw the cloth I was using earlier.

Once I had sucked his finger to his satisfaction, he pulled it from my mouth and slipped it into his. The whole time he watched me, and I know he was analyzing my reaction, which I find strange. Why would he care how I felt about what he was doing when he didn't care he was hurting me while he was raping me?

I made sure to keep my expression vacant. Afterward, I was forced back several feet when he got up from the log. I was grateful our time was over and reached for the cloth that had been yanked from me.

However, before I could even put it around my shoulders it was again pulled from my hands. He stalked to the bed area and threw it inside. I shot him a glare and got a glower in return. Since then,

I've been sitting on a piece of burlap trying to come up with an escape plan. So far, I've come up with a whole damn lot of nothing. At the moment, the only chance I have is my family. As I promised Dad I would, each night before I went to bed I called him.

Until last night.

I have no doubt Dad and my brothers are already out looking for me. The only problem is, they're looking in the wrong place.

The last time I spoke with him, I told him I was in the northern part of the Black Ridge National Forest. And at the time, I was, and had been since I started this venture. But yesterday morning, I decided to go in a different direction since the area I was in hadn't shown any signs of Wild Man. I'm in the most southern part. I was going to call Dad last night and tell him of the new location, but never got the chance. So, even though my family is looking for me, they're nearly seventy miles away searching in an area I'm nowhere near.

Black Ridge is seventy square miles, expanding between two states. It could take them months of searching before they found me.

I could kick myself for making the sudden change to my plans without telling someone. If I make it out of here, Dad and my brothers will never let me live it down. I'll be lucky if they even let me leave the house again.

And poor Rika. I know she must be worried just as much.

I tighten my arms around my legs, feeling the friction of the rope rub against my ribs. The other end is tied to a tree. Like I'm a fucking dog.

Wild Man sits on the same log he was before. He's sharpening the end of a stick with a wicked looking knife, bringing the end to a point. Probably to stab unsuspecting animals for dinner.

My mind whirls with ways to get my hands on the knife. Even the stick will do. I just need something I can use against him.

I let my gaze drift over the man. His blue-black hair is long and thick enough to make most women envious. It hangs halfway down his back in soft waves with a few strands falling over his shoulders. His beard is thick and full, but not long. His face is narrow with a straight nose, high cheekbones, and full lips so red it almost looks like he's wearing lipstick. His tanned shoulders are broad, his biceps thick with defined muscles, and his torso is stacked with dips and valleys before it leads down to a tapered waist. The V just above the cloth is deeply pronounced.

From the outside, the man appears to be in excellent condition.

It's his mental state that's questionable.

His head lifts, and for the first time since I sat my ass on this burlap sack, he looks at me.

I really wish he wouldn't. The man has creepy, but fascinating eyes that easily captures and can hold a person's attention. Like right now. I'm an unwilling captive caught in his ominous dark stare, helpless to look away.

"You can't keep me here forever."

He says nothing, not that I expected him to. He pulls his eyes away from mine to look back down at his stick and knife.

"My father and brothers are looking for me."

Nothing. Not even an eye twitch.

"This is wrong, Wild Man," I continue, trying to get through to him. "What you're doing is illegal. It's called kidnapping and you could get in a lot of trouble."

I closely watch his face for any signs that he understands what I'm saying. I get nothing. Frustration wells and has my hands curling around my legs, my nails digging into my skin.

"They've probably already called the police, which means they'll be looking for me too."

He continues chiseling away at the stick.

"You've got to let me go," I say, desperation raising my voice. "They'll hurt you if my family finds me here."

Strangely, the thought of Wild Man being hurt isn't as appealing as it should be. As painful as what he's done to me is, the man is following his baser instincts. But it's going to happen if he doesn't let me go. It'll be a race to who gets to him first. My family or the police. For a person like Wild Man, being put in a prison cell would be torture, but it would be the lesser of two evils. At least if he's incarcerated, he'd be alive. If my father and brothers find him first, I can't guarantee that outcome. My family is capable of anything when it comes to protecting their own.

I continue to try to get him to understand the severity of the situation he's put himself in.

"When my family finds me, they're going to be angry." I blow out an aggravated puff of air. "They'll hurt you and take me far away from you."

That last part gets a reaction. One that has fear slithering through my bloodstream and wishing I could take the words back.

In the blink of an eye, Wild Man is up from the log and is looming over me, his feet planted apart and a vicious look on his face. He reaches down, wraps his long fingers around my throat and hauls me up from my seated position. He brings my face so close to his there's only an inch of space separating us, and the tips of my toes barely touch the ground. His grip is tighter than all the other times he's held me like this. Panic sets in, and I start clawing at his hand, desperate to draw in air.

My feeble attempts at fighting don't phase him in the slightest as he continues to glare down at me.

Just as my vision starts to blur, he loosens his hold just enough for me to suck in a lungful of air.

"Mine!" he snarls in my face. He lifts his other hand, his fingers balled into a fist. I flinch and try to move away, worried that fist is meant for me. But then he surprises me when he slams it against his chest hard and repeats in a harsh tone, "Mine. You stay. I kill family."

My eyes widen. I'm not sure what I'm more shocked about. The fact that he spoke more than one word, or that he wants to kill my family. All because they may find me and take me away from him.

"No!" I croak, barely able to draw enough air to say the word.

Using his grip around my neck, Wild Man brings me closer. Our noses brush against each other.

"Kill family. My Ever."

Holy motherfucking hell.

*My* Ever.

I have got to get away from this crazy-ass man. Before my family finds me. Because as deranged as it is, I still don't want my father or brothers to hurt him. Or the police to find him. If Wild Man isn't insane yet, he certainly will be if he's locked up in prison.

And what's worse, I know deep down to the very depth of my soul, this man won't ever willingly let me go.

I try once again to knee him between his legs. I need him incapacitated long enough to get free of the rope and to run away. If I get a head start, maybe I can hide. I know I can't outrun him. His feet may be used to the forest floor, but mine aren't. I'll need to hide somewhere long enough for him to get tired of searching for me.

As if he can read my mind, his hips jerk to the side just as I swiftly lift my knee. He catches the underside of my leg and hooks it over his hip. I freeze, my breath stuttering, when I feel the ridge of his shaft against my bare pussy. The thin cloth he has covering himself is the only thing separating his bareness from mine.

Planting my hands on his hard chest, I try to shove myself away and pull my leg from his hip. His reaction is to tighten his hand around my throat and to pull my bottom half firmer against him. He's hard. Like brick fucking hard.

I tense, preparing to fight him more if he tries to put that huge thing inside me again.

A girl can only take so much. Being taken by him three times already was three times too many.

I'm roughly pulled closer, which makes my hands useless between us. There's no way I can overpower him, no matter how much I tell myself that I'll fight him tooth and nail and this time I'll manage to stop him from raping me.

A moment later, he lets me go. My jaw slackens, my mouth dropping open, as I'm suddenly back on my ass on the burlap sack and Wild Man is stalking away from me. After stopping and grabbing the knife and spear he was working on, he leaves through the leafy opening, disappearing out of sight.

*What the hell?* I silently ask myself. He was hard. Not that I'm complaining, but I thought for sure he would have another go at me.

I don't waste time thinking on the reason why he abruptly left and instead focus on getting the fuck out of this place. The first thing I need to do is get this godforsaken rope off me. Then find something I can use as a weapon.

I pluck up the rope and stare down at the knot. I've learned from my dad and brothers several different knot styles. But this one is unfamiliar and looks complicated as hell. It only takes me a couple of moments of struggling with the intricate tightly woven knot to realize I don't have enough time to figure it out. I walk to where the other end is tied, only to find the same style knot.

Okay, time to move on and look for something to cut the rope with. Ten minutes later, I let out a growl of hopeless frustration. There's not one damn thing I can use that's sharp enough. Even the spears I spotted earlier are gone. Either Wild Man has nothing of use or he's anticipated me looking and has hidden everything. There's no sign of my backpack, gun, or taser either.

My stomach cramps, and I wrap my arm around my lower torso. So far, I've managed to ignore my full bladder, but it's getting increasingly hard to continue to do so. Growing up with men who love the outdoors and camping, peeing outside is nothing new to me. What I have an issue with is doing it not knowing where Wild Man is or when he'll return.

And anyway, I don't have time to search for a spot to relieve myself. I need to spend this time looking for a way to escape before he comes back.

I drag the rope behind me as I make my way back to the small opening where the bed is. I've already searched the area, but it wouldn't hurt to take a closer look. Maybe I missed something.

My eyes immediately go to the two skulls sitting on either side of the bed, and a shiver of revulsion skates through me. I walk to the pile of blankets and pick them up, giving them a firm shake before tossing them to the side. It jostles one of the skulls and it rolls to the side. I ignore it and grab the sheet I used earlier to cover myself. I wrap the material around my torso twice and tuck the extra in itself to secure it as best as I can.

I start walking along the edges of the makeshift walls, kicking shit out of my way as I search the ground. I wince when the tip of my big toe encounters something hard. Squatting, I brush away leaves and twigs and find a metal rod about two feet long. It's hollow, is only about a quarter inch in diameter, and looks like it might be part of a frame from a tent.

Picking it up, I stand and continue looking in case I find something better. A few minutes later, when I don't find anything else, I come to the conclusion that the rod will have to be my weapon. It's not the best choice, but it'll have to do.

With determined steps, I leave the sleeping area, ignoring the painful spasm in my bladder. I go back to my burlap sack and get to my knees, resting my butt on my heels. I set the rod beside me, making sure to keep it hidden under some brush, and point my eyes in the direction of where Wild Man left.

I don't have to wait long before he's stomping back through the opening. I hold my breath, forcing myself to wait instead of immediately attacking him. I need to time this perfectly.

He stops just inside the entrance and looks at me. His eyes slide to the sheet I have wrapped around my chest, and his lip curls up like the material is the most disgusting thing he's ever seen. I brace, curling my fingers around the rod, when he starts in my direction. I wait until he's only a foot away and is reaching down to grab my arm. I spring up to my feet, taking the piece of metal with me. I lift my arm, ready to take a swing at him. I aim it for the side of his head. I don't want to do permanent damage. Just enough to knock him out for a while to give myself a head start.

I scream out in rage when the stupid fucking man catches the rod before I can connect it with his head. He yanks it from my hand and throws it to the side, where it lands somewhere with a soft thump.

Beyond furious, I screech and start lashing out with my hands, raking my nails down his chest. The sheet falls from around me, but I can't give any shits at the moment. All I care about right now is getting away from this madman.

Finally, I manage to land a fist in his stomach and he lets out a grunt. My victory only lasts for a couple of seconds before I'm spun around and Wild Man has his arms wrapped around me, pinning my arms to my side. He squeezes my torso, and the air in my lungs whoosh out. My bladder protests violently and a new worry develops. It would serve the asshole right if I peed on him.

His hard dick, still separated by the cloth, wedges itself between my asscheeks. My hair is grabbed and my head is yanked back so far it's a wonder he hasn't snapped my neck. Out the corner of my eye, I see his harsh stare boring into the side of my face. I shoot my gaze sideways, glaring back at him with all the hatred I feel toward him right now. If looks could kill, he'd be dead on the ground, sightlessly staring up at the dense canopy of trees above us.

"Stop!" he growls the word, once again reminding me he *can* speak. He just chooses not to.

"Then let me go," I spew back at him.

"Never. Mine."

I dig my nails into the flesh of the arm he has wrapped tightly around me. "I'm only yours until I find a way to escape. Or until my family finds me. And when they do, you're dead."

My father has always told me that my mouth was going to get me in trouble one day. That I needed to learn to think before I spoke. I've never taken his warning seriously. I should have.

My head is pulled to the side, and I let out a shriek of pain when Wild Man sinks his teeth into the side of my neck. I don't know if he broke the skin, but it damn sure feels like it. My nails dig deeper until I break the skin, the warm trickle of blood meeting my fingertips.

Wild Man grunts against my neck as he continues to bite and suck on my skin, making the pain sharper.

I wiggle, trying to break his hold on me, but it only manages to wedge his dick deeper into the crack of my ass. My body stiffens when I feel the head grazing my puckered hole. I suck in a breath and hold it, hoping by some miracle he doesn't get any ideas. There's no way in hell I can fit that thing in my ass. It would tear me beyond repair.

I somewhat relax when my feet hit the ground and Wild Man lets me go. I stumble forward a step and whip around. Wild Man stands there, his chest rising and falling with his harsh breaths and his hands balled into fists at his sides. Satisfaction soothes some of my anger when I see the scratches on his chest. His eyes bore into me, and I'm not sure if the dark look he's giving me is filled with desire or anger. Maybe a bit of both.

Before I can stop them, my eyes dart down. From the way his dick is poking at the cloth, I would say desire is probably the dominant feeling, which does not bode well for me.

"I have to pee." I blurt the first thing that comes to mind, hoping to use it as a distraction.

His brows scrunch together, and at first he looks like he might be confused. The look quickly fades and his expression turns blank. His hand whips out and he grabs my wrist. He turns on his heel, and I'm practically dragged behind him as he takes me to the tree the rope is tied to. He unties the knot too fast for me to try to watch and learn. Once he's done, he grabs the rope and pulls me from his little hut. I'm so stunned that I don't even try to yank away from him. But I do have trouble keeping up with his long strides.

I'm just about to open my mouth to tell him to slow the hell down, when we come to a sudden stop. We're about a hundred feet away from the tree hut in a semi-clearing. We stop near a bush that has big leafy leaves.

He lets my hand go and points to the bush. I look from him to the bush before glancing back at him.

"What?"

"Pee."

I kinda figured that's what he was getting at.

I cross my arms over my chest. "Turn around."

He doesn't say anything. Just glares at me as he mirrors my stance by crossing his arms over his own chest.

My lips tighten. This is fucking ridiculous. Has the man ever heard of privacy?

I mentally snort at that thought. Of course he hasn't. He wouldn't know what the word meant if it slapped him in the face. He's had plenty of privacy himself, living out in the wilderness all alone, but only because no one comes out here.

If I didn't have to relieve my bladder so badly, I'd fight him on the issue, but I'm barely holding it in just standing here.

Shooting him a heated glare, I stomp over to where Wild Man indicated. I turn so he only has a side view of me. I damn sure don't plan to give him more of a view than he already has.

At least I don't have to worry about my stream getting on my clothes. I like to consider myself a half-glass full kind of girl.

My eyes fall closed at the instant relief.

They jerk open a fraction of a second later when I hear the trickle of more liquid hit the ground.

I damn near fall on my ass when Wild Man stands in front of me, his dick in his hand, letting his own urine flow. What has my mouth dropping open in shock—which is stupid given the circumstances—is that he's aiming his stream so it hits mine.

What in the hell kind of sick shit is he doing?

But then it dawns on me.

64

He's a fucking animal marking his territory.

I try to stop my flow so I can get the hell away from him, but I can't. My bladder is too full to stop now. So I stay squatted. My eyes drop and they get caught by the combined stream splashing on the ground below me. His pee comes so close to hitting me, but Wild Man has good aim, apparently.

We finish at the same time, and I hurriedly wiggle my ass to get rid of any drips before I stand. Wild Man lets his dick go and it just flops there. Before the cloth falls in place, I notice a drop of clear liquid still clinging to the tip. I'm careful where I put my feet so I don't step in our urine.

## seven

EVERLEE

Hours of doing nothing as I sit on my burlap sack and watch Wild Man piddle around is driving me fucking crazy. I've tried talking to him a few times, but all I get in response is nothing or a stupid grunt.

Earlier, he brought me the water jug and a few dried pieces of meat. When I asked him if I could have my cloth back, he ignored the request and continued skinning a squirrel. A fucking squirrel. It made the meat I ate earlier sour in my stomach.

I'm currently sitting with my legs out in front of me, my ankles crossed together. I've lost all modesty. Being forcefully taken by a man then sitting naked in front of him all day does that to a woman.

I haven't been sitting idle though. I've been slowly, and discreetly, trying to work at the knots on the rope. So far, the dumb thing hasn't budged. I'll eventually get it though. It's only a matter of time. Then a new worry will follow. How in the hell I'm going to get away.

Sweat trickles between my breasts and the grit of dirt abrades my skin anytime I move. I hate being dirty. Especially my hands and feet. It's a pet peeve I have. Even the slightest bit of dirt on my hands or feet has me rushing to the bathroom to clean them. I've been this way since I became an adult. You'd think it strange since I spent a good portion of my childhood outside.

I abandon the rope when I notice dirt beneath my nails. I use my thumb nail to try to scrape it out, but I can't get all the flecks. My eyes slide past my hands and land on my feet. My toenails are worse. I even have dirt between my toes.

I'm pulled from my thoughts when a shadow looms over me. I didn't even notice Wild Man get up from his spot. That goes to show how much I detest dirty hands and feet.

I say nothing as he stares down at me. If he wants to play the silent game, so can I.

The staring contest only lasts for a few seconds before he's reaching down and grabbing my wrist. He pulls me up from the ground so fast that I slam against his chest. My hands land on the hard plains of his abs. If this were any other guy and any other situation, I may have curled my fingertips against those firm muscles, because let's face it, he has a killer body. You'd have to be blind to not appreciate the dips and valleys.

But this is Wild Man and he's holding me against my will, so I push against those delicious muscles and take a step away from him. I tilt my head, way back because he's so tall, waiting to see what his next move is. His long, thick hair falls over his shoulders, a few strands getting stuck in his beard. The black in his eyes as he looks at me seems bottomless and it makes me wonder what he's thinking. What he's been thinking since he brought me here. What made him decide he wanted to keep me? What is it about me that makes him think I'm his? Is it really me, or would he have felt this way about any female?

I tense, preparing to attack when he lifts a hand toward me. But instead of grabbing me and doing whatever the hell he wants, he takes hold of the rope. At first I think he's going to use it to drag me somewhere, so I'm surprised when he actually starts working on the knot.

Is he letting me go? Hope flutters in my stomach at the thought.

Once the rope is untied, he drops it to the ground. His brows fall into a frown when he notices the red marks around my waist from where the rope rubbed against me. His fingers are surprisingly gentle when he slides them over the spot. I would have never thought the man was capable of being any type of soft.

Then suddenly, he grabs my upper arm and bends at the waist. The breath whooshes out of me, and I let out a squeak when he rams his shoulder into my stomach. In the next second, I'm up in the air, dangling upside down. The move leaves me speechless. For all of two seconds.

"Put me down, you brute!" I pound my fists anywhere they can reach. His back, the too firm globes of his ass, his thighs. My hits are like feather-light taps, for all the good they do me. "Hey, asshole!"

A loud smack fills the air, followed quickly by the sharp sting on my butt. The mother fucker spanked me again.

I turn stiff as a board, clenching my butt cheeks, in case he delivers another one. I wait a few seconds, and when he doesn't slap me again, I slowly relax and just hang there. Over the last twenty-hours, I've learned the sooner I stop fighting him, the sooner he quits whatever he's doing. No matter what I do, he wants me over his shoulder—presumably to cart me somewhere —so I may as well just suck it up and let him take me wherever he wants.

My arms hang down, and I remain pliant. I expect Wild Man to stomp through the dense forest, jostling me to and fro, but surprisingly, his steps are fluid and graceful. I barely feel them.

I turn my head left and right, taking mental notes of anything I can use as markers when I finally manage to escape. And I will escape. I refuse to believe anything otherwise. Wild Man will make a mistake sometime or another, and I'll be ready to take advantage.

I don't know how long Wild Man carries me. A slow pounding starts in my head where all the blood has rushed to it. I can imagine how red my face must be.

After a few minutes, I hear the splash of water. Wild Man flips me over to my feet, and I look around. We're in the same spot as when I first found him. The little waterfall oasis. It really is pretty out here. Even prettier being this close.

The crystal clear water looks refreshing, and my dirty hands and feet beg me to dive in.

I turn and look at Wild Man and find him naked with his loin-cloth tossed on the ground behind him.

I take a step back. He takes one forward, a look forming in his eyes that I don't like. I take two more steps, wincing when something sharp presses against the sole of my foot. I ignore the pain. I don't have time to think about it because Wild Man keeps stalking toward me.

A few more steps, and I feel the cool water on my feet. It feels so damn good that I almost forget the precarious situation I'm in.

Keeping my eyes on Wild Man, I continue moving backward. He matches each step I take, but his are longer, so he's easily closing the distance between us. Why he's not rushing me, I'm not sure, but I'm prepared for it. I don't look down, but I can see in my peripheral vision that he's hard.

The water laps at my knees. It's cool and feels wonderful against my heated flesh. It irritates me because I can't enjoy it more with the crazed man in front of me.

When the water reaches my hips, Wild Man makes his move. Before I can register what he's doing, he eats up the space between us until he's practically in my face. I try to move backward, but he stops me with his fingers wrapped around my throat. This time, I don't fight him. It's useless anyway.

He lifts his other hand and puts it on my shoulder. It's then I

69

realize he's holding something. It's the same kind of leave he used when I watched him bathe.

"Wash," he grunts in his deep voice. Slowly, he slides the leaf from my shoulder down my arm.

He wants to... bathe me?

For some reason, the notion of him cleaning me isn't as abhorrent as it should be. I tell myself it's only because I'm desperate to feel clean again, but a little niggle in the back of my head—something that I refuse to acknowledge—says it's more than that.

I stand still and watch him curiously as he runs the leaf down to my fingertips. I flip my hand over and he washes my palm. I don't know what kind of leaf he's using, but it leaves a sudsy film behind. I rub my fingers together and they feel slick.

He moves the leaf up my forearm and all the way back to my shoulder. Then he rubs it over my collarbone. The leaf is gently abrasive. It kind of feels like those bath gloves people use for exfoliating.

His fingers release my neck and he works the leaf over my other collarbone to my other shoulder. Down my arm he goes, and I again flip up my palm.

We keep our eyes on each other while he does this. I don't know what his thoughts are, but mine are all over the place. Thinking about things I don't want to think about. Stuff that should never even cross my mind, given what Wild Man has done to me.

With his free hand, he cups some water and dribbles it on my shoulder then runs his bare hand down my arm. He does the same to the other side.

He washes my neck and starts moving the leaf down my chest between my breasts. My muscles stiffen and my knees lock into place when he moves it to the top of my right boob. A curious note enters his eyes and he tilts his head to the side as he moves down the slope and over my nipple.

I press my lips into a firm line, fighting back the need to tell him to stop. I tell myself that I *do* want him to stop, and the reason I keep quiet is only because it would be useless. It's not like he would listen anyway. It's certainly *not* because what he's doing actually feels good.

*Liar, liar, Ever.*

I shake my head and ignore the taunting voice.

Using the leaf, Wild Man slides it down my breast until he reaches the underside. He cups my flesh and uses his thumb and forefinger to pinch my nipple.

I bite the inside of my cheek, willing away the unwanted feelings he's slowly invoking in me.

This has turned into more than bathing. I still don't try to stop him though. Again, there's no sense in even trying. Wild Man will do whatever he wants.

I drop my eyes from his, unable to hold his gaze any longer. Not with the way he's watching me, like he's waiting to see what I'll do, how I'll react to his ministrations.

He moves to my other breast and gives it the same treatment. My toes curl into the soft sandy ground, and I ball my hands into fists.

Disgust sours my stomach at my body's betrayal. How can I find anything this man does to me even remotely pleasurable? He's done nothing so far to constitute such a reaction from me.

My eyes focus on the tanned skin of his chest. He has coarse hair over his pecs, but not much. It thickens slightly further down his stomach, leading to his happy trail. I've never understood the term 'happy trail' more than I do right now. From the thing that's bobbing out of the water, a part of Wild Man is very happy. Not to mention that ordinarily, that thing could make a woman very happy.

It's only brought me pain so far.

My eyes jerk up when Wild Man moves the leaf slowly down my stomach, on a path to parts of me that I don't want him to touch. I clench my stomach muscles and my hand darts out to grab his wrist. The muscles in his jaw bunches as he grinds his teeth. I can see the determination in his eyes to continue, but he surprises me by dropping his hand.

He latches them around my waist and spins me around so my back is facing him. Part of me likes this position better because it means I can't get lost in his black eyes. But it also spikes up my anxiety because I won't know what's coming.

I suck is a startled breath when Wild Man sets his hand on the center of my back right below my neck. The slightly rough texture tells me he's still using the leaf. With leisurely movements, he washes my back, going from one shoulder blade to the other and sliding the leaf down my spine. I close my eyes, and let myself, just for a moment, imagine that I'm somewhere else and enjoy the feeling of being taken care of.

His ministrations are unhurried, as if he's getting just as much enjoyment as I am.

My eyes flutter open when he reaches my lower back. He stops just above my butt, then cups more water and lets it rain down my back. I feel the trickles of water run down the crease of my ass.

I'm turned around and my eyes drop when Wild Man holds out the leaf.

He thumps his closed fist against his chest and grunts. "Me."

Seeing no way around it, I tentatively take the leaf, understanding what he wants. It's my turn to bath him now. I don't know why, but the idea of me washing him is more daunting than him washing me.

I swallow the saliva that's gathered in my mouth and drag my eyes up to his to find him watching me with a look of eagerness.

Licking my lips then rubbing them together, I place the leaf on his shoulder. It takes me a moment to gather my thoughts enough to glide my hand down his arm. It's no surprise the man is so darkly tanned and has the muscles he's built over the years, but it's a whole new experience feeling those muscles beneath my hands. Even through the leaf, I feel every single hard ridge.

It makes me wonder how they would feel if there was no leaf in the way.

Again, I shove those thoughts out of my head.

I move the leaf to his other arm. I feel his eyes on me, but I don't look up. I'm not sure what I'll do if I see the look in his eyes. I know he's enjoying my hands on him, but I don't want to see the proof. It's already hard enough ignoring the huge dick that's bobbing in the water.

When I finish with his arm, I follow the same path he took with me. I start at his collarbones and slowly move the leaf across the hollow of his throat then down the firm plains of his stomach. My gaze gets caught on two marks beside his belly button. They're scars, about an inch apart and each about three inches in length. They look like slash marks. Like maybe an animal attack. They're old and faded, which makes me believe whatever happened was years ago.

I want to ask him about them, but hold back the words. I came here to learn about the mysterious Wild Man, but this trip has turned into so much more. I worry that if I hear any of the horrors this man must have endured, it may lessen the hatred I've formed for him. I need to hold on to that hatred, keep it strong, because he doesn't deserve anything softer than that.

I steer clear of the appendage popping out of the water as I finish washing his stomach. No prompt is needed once I'm done. He turns around and gives me his back. Doing this side of him is a little easier. I don't have to worry about his eyes on me, and while the backside of him is no less appealing, it's not quite as distracting.

His hair, thicker and softer than I realized now that I've touched it, goes almost to the middle of his back. I brush the strands out of my way. Starting at his shoulders, I work my way across both. With his eyes not on me, I selfishly enjoy looking at him. His shoulders are wide and his trap muscles are deliciously defined. I run the leaf over them, and a stupid part of me wishes I could feel them beneath my bare hands.

I move to the center of his back between his shoulder blades. When I reach his lats, they feel tense, as if he's holding his body stiff. The urge to massage those muscles to loosen them hits me all of a sudden, but I ignore it.

I reach his waist, and I quickly move the leaf across his skin. I don't want to linger too long in this area because it's way too close to his tanned ass.

Thankfully, as soon as I'm done and I take the leaf away, Wild Man spins back around. My eyes spring up to his before they can latch onto his cock. I hold the leaf out to him and he takes it.

My hair isn't wet, so I take a step back to dunk myself, but before I get the chance to, Wild Man grabs me by the waist and pulls me toward him until our chests are pressed together. I tell myself the feeling of our skin touching, of my breasts smashed against his firm chest, my nipples scraping against the coarse hairs on his pecs, isn't arousing. I tell myself that, knowing deep down inside this isn't the first lie I've told myself in the last ten minutes.

My hands latch onto his shoulders, whether to push him away or to simply hold onto him, I'm not sure.

"Legs."

I know what he wants and before my brain can compute my actions, I wrap my legs around his waist. It's a mistake that I should have foreseen. I'm an idiot for not thinking before acting.

The length of his cock wedges itself perfectly between the lips of my pussy. Sensations that could lead to stupid things if I let them smack me right between my legs.

I wiggle my hips, unhooking my legs, and push against his shoulders. "Put me down," I say with no small amount of panic filling my voice. I can't afford to let anything he does to me feel the smallest bit of good.

My movements become frantic, and I don't even care that I'm wasting my time. I shove and dig my nails into his shoulders, trying my best to jerk my hips away from him. To get his dick away from me.

He puts both hands on my butt, pulls me snug against him, and the next thing I know, Wild Man submerges us both in the water, holding us beneath the surface for several seconds. The water is so clear that I can clearly see his face. Little bubbles form and pop out of his nostrils and his long hair floats around him. I'm still wrapped around him, but I've stopped my struggles.

When he brings us to the surface, I suck in several deep breaths. I open my mouth to tell him exactly how I feel about his stupid maneuver, but I snap it shut when he starts swimming further out into the water. He's heading toward the waterfall and a giddy sort of excitement makes my belly squirm. I've always wanted to play in a waterfall.

Before we reach it though, Wild Man veers to the right and stops us at a couple of rocks jutting out of the water. One rock sits lower than the other. There must be more rocks underneath the surface or it's not as deep, because he lifts us both and sets me down on the lower rock. He moves back, and my shoulders relax when our bodies separate, giving me the relief of no longer having his dick pressed against me.

I try to close my legs, but Wild Man stops me by putting his hands on my knees. "Stay," he says. His voice is low and rough as his eyes stay locked between my legs.

A warm blush coats my cheeks. I want to argue, but I press my lips together to hold the words in.

He holds the leaf out to me. "Bathe."

I don't take it at first. I sit stubbornly on the rock, my back ramrod straight and my hands balled into fists on my thighs. It takes him a moment to realize this and when he does, his eyes slowly lift to mine. I swear every inch his eyes touch, it's like a caress to my skin. I don't like the feeling.

When his gaze finally meets mine and he sees the determination in my expression, the pulse in his temple begins to pound. I can literally see the vibration of that pulse.

He takes my hand in one of his big ones and uses the other to uncurl my fingers. He slaps the leaf in my palm, leans over me, and issues with a low growl, "Bathe me."

I'm tempted to rip up the stupid leaf and throw it in his face for good measure. But I haven't reached that level of tantrum yet. Besides, he'll just get another one.

I let out a huff of hot air through my nose and grit out, "Fine."

Seeming satisfied with my capitulation, he leans back. I drop my gaze and come face to face with his groin. Our positions puts my head even with his waist, and of course, he's still hard, so his dick juts out at me.

I've already washed him from the waist up, so what's left is right in front of me. There are his legs too, but something tells me it's not those body parts he wants me to concentrate on.

The hand holding the leaf shakes. I'm nervous for some reason. I've seen plenty of dicks in my lifetime, but the one in front of me has been used against me. Half of my brain urges me to grab it and yank the fuck out of it until it detaches from the owner's body. That's one way to incapacitate Wild Man so I can get away.

The other half—the dirty devil on my shoulder—is curious and wonders if Wild Man's cock is as smooth as it looks. Each time I see it, it astounds me that it actually fits inside my body. It's not only long, but thick. It's a wonder he didn't do permanent damage to my insides. Bluish, prominent veins run the length of it and the head is an angry deep shade of red. A patch of dark hair surrounds the root and the two balls below it hang low. My eyes zero in on the clear drop of liquid that clings to the slit.

A guttural groan has my eyes jerking up. A lump lodges itself in my throat when I see the desirous look in Wild Man's eyes.

Clearing my throat and getting back to the task at hand, I don't touch the dangerous thing nearly slapping me in my face like I know he wants me to. I lean to the side away from it and press the leaf to the top of his thigh, methodically rubbing it down his leg. The hair on his legs is thick and dark, matching the hair on the rest of his body.

On the outside of his thigh, I come across another scar. This one is two small round holes about an inch apart.

I force my eyes to not focus on the two puncture wounds, even though my curiosity has more than piqued. What kind of snake bit him? How old was he when it happened?

I shove those questions out of my head. They won't help me escape. If anything, they'll hinder me.

I make sure to wash the rest of him slowly, because I know once I'm done with his legs, Wild Man will give me no choice but to move on to his dick. I wash his feet too, even between his toes, just to give myself more time.

All too soon, I'm finished. I lean up and tilt my head back. Wild Man looks at me expectantly, and I grit my teeth.

My eyes drop to his cock just as it bounces in the air between us. Like it has a mind of its own and it's waving to get my attention. I know if I don't do this on my own, he'll just force me to do it anyway.

So I wrap the leaf and my fingers around it, intending to get this over with as soon as possible. At least I'll have the leaf as a barrier.

But the moment I touch him, Wild Man darts his hand out and grabs my wrist. I release him and he takes the leaf from my hand, dropping it on the rock beside me. Then he puts my hand back on him.

A swarm of butterflies form in my belly at my first real touch of him. He's much smoother than I thought he would be. And dear God, he's so damn hard it's like touching titanium.

A hissed breath blows out between his stiff lips.

Without being ordered to, I slowly glide my hand down his shaft all the way to the root. He's so big, I can't wrap my fingers all the way around him.

I slide my hand back and by the time I reach the tip, a small bead of precum has formed on the slit.

Unconsciously, I imagine myself leaning forward with my tongue sticking out to catch the drop before it falls away.

Sometimes, my mind is stupid and likes to think about things that it shouldn't be thinking about. Like willingly taking this man's cock in my mouth. I must be certifiably insane for the thought to even cross my mind.

I don't know exactly what Wild Man expects of me, so I twist my wrist and do my best to make him feel good, even though good is the last thing I want him to feel. He doesn't deserve to feel good. But the sooner I make him come, the sooner this will be over.

More precum leaks from the tip and it drips down my hand. To hopefully speed things up, I reach up with my free hand and grab his balls, gently rolling them around.

I don't look at his face as I work his cock and balls, but I don't look at said body parts either. I can't. I'm afraid if I do, they'll catch too much of my attention. It's already hard enough trying to ignore the small grunts of pleasure I hear coming from him. Instead, I stare at his belly button. It's an innie and it's surrounded by dark, coarse hair.

I'm so focused on that part of his body, that I startle when my head is suddenly jerked back. The hair on the back of my head nearly snaps at the harsh way he's fisting the strands. His eyes bore down on me and his nostrils flare with his heavy breathing.

With his head tipped down, his wet hair falls forward, framing his face. I want to reach up, grab a handful, and yank with all my might to see how much he likes having his hair pulled.

I let his dick go when my head was pulled back. Now he has it in his hand and is pointing the tip at my mouth. I press my lips together and shoot him 'fuck you' vibes with my eyes. One corner of his mouth tips up and it pisses me off even more that he seems to be amused at my refusal. So much so, I barely manage to quell the urge to bite the tip of his dick off. I bet he'd lose that dumb smirk then.

He presses the wet tip to my mouth and coats my lips with his precum. "Open," he orders in a gruff tone.

I smash my lips together harder. Lifting my hands, I set them on his thighs and use my nails as words to tell him he can take his demand and shove it up his ass.

It's like he doesn't even feel them digging into his flesh because he shows no reaction.

After swiping his dick across my lips a few more times, he lets my hair go. I'm so stunned by the move, I just manage to catch myself from tumbling backward off the rock.

This man confuses the fuck out of me. One minute he harshly forces himself on me, demanding I give him exactly what he wants. But in other instances, he stops himself before he goes all the way. Why? Why give in to his urges one moment, then stop himself in the next?

I'm pulled from my thoughts when Wild Man grabs my ankle and lifts my leg. I'm forced to set my hands behind me before I fall over. He sets my foot on his thigh, which puts me in a very uncomfortable position. Uncomfortable because my legs are spread and my pussy is more exposed than before.

I try to pull my foot away, but he just latches onto my ankle with a firmer grip. The muscles in my calf tenses, preparing to shove him backward with all my might, but the look in his eyes gives me pause. It's a look of daring, one that says the retribution of such an act would be swift and very unpleasant. Releasing a sigh of resignation, I relax my muscles and let him do whatever he wants.

He grabs the leaf he set away a few minutes ago and places it on my shin, then slowly begins rubbing it in circles. I have to admit, rather reluctantly, it does feel good to have someone bathe me.

He works on my lower leg, including my foot, before he moves to my knee and then my thigh. The closer he gets to the junction of my thighs, the tenser I become. But he stops before he gets there. Setting my foot down, he grabs my other leg and does the same to that one. Again, he stops before he reaches the center between my legs.

He puts that foot on the ground, and I wonder, with no small amount of trepidation, what's going to happen next. I don't have to worry for long. Grabbing my upper arms, he brings me to my feet, which puts me on even ground with him. He spins me around so my back is facing him. Pressing a hand between my shoulder blades, he tries to shove my top half over.

I resist. "What are—?"

My words are cut off when he applies more pressure to my back and my hands automatically reach out for the rock so I don't land face first against it. I feel the slap of the leaf against my lower back. I'm tempted to try and wiggle away from him, but I know he'll only grab me to keep me in place.

So I drop my head and silently count to ten over and over in my mind.

I'm halfway through my third round when I'm pulled from my numerical thoughts. Wild Man, still using the leaf as his wash-cloth, moves it down over my right butt cheek. I turn my head to the side and watch him through my peripheral vision. His eyes are laser focused on his task, which happens to be my ass, like it's the most fascinating thing he's ever seen.

He disappears from sight when he squats and moves the leaf down my legs. So far, he's left my private parts alone. I wonder how long my luck will last, or if he has no plans to touch me there.

It's like God has something against me, because as soon as the thought crosses my mind, I feel the slightest of touches on the outside of my pussy. The touch becomes firmer, and it's not coming from a leaf. It's Wild Man's fingers.

He flicks my lower lips before pinching them between his fingers and tugging on them gently. I bite my tongue almost to the point of drawing blood. The muscles in my back go stiff, and I'm just about to stand up to try to get away from him, but he anticipates my move and stops me with a hand on my back.

"Stay."

The way that one word leaves his lips, the deepness in his voice, has me freezing. It sounds sinister, like he's on the verge of something. And it's something I instinctively know I want no part of.

So I stay still. I close my eyes and pray that what comes next will happen fast and it won't cost me more than I've already given.

## eight

EVERLEE

I try to keep my breathing even and hold onto the disgust I'm supposed to feel, but my wayward body isn't on board. It likes the way Wild Man's rough fingers slide between my folds and nudges the bundle of nerves housed at the top of my slit. No matter how much I want to abhor his touch, my stupid fucking body won't stay on track with my mind.

I feel myself get wet and it turns my stomach. I want to purge all the moisture from my system so there's none left to form between my legs.

My nails dig into the rock beneath my hand so hard, I worry I'll break them off.

When I get home, my family won't have to worry about locking me in the house. I have every intention of committing myself to a mental facility. That's apparently where I belong, because somewhere along the way I must have lost my mind. That's the only explanation there could be for actually reacting in a positive way to Wild Man's touch.

One of his hands rests on my ass while he uses the fingers of his other hand against me. He rubs one between my lower lips, gathering the moisture there, and leads it to my clit. A warm blast of copper explodes in my mouth when I bite my tongue too hard. It's either that or moan in pleasure from the way he presses against that little button. He manipulates it with an expertise that shouldn't come from someone who's never had sex until yesterday.

Or rather, I don't think he's had sex. As far as I know, he's never had the opportunity. But who knows, maybe I'm wrong. Maybe I'm not the first female he's held captive and used for depraved things. I try to think back if there have been any cases of missing females over the years, but my brain won't function properly. It's being overrun by the explicit pleasure I'm too weak to ignore and too ashamed to acknowledge.

The disgust I feel for him has flipped around and points its accusing finger at me.

Wild Man pushes a finger inside me, and I rise to my toes, trying and failing to get away from the sensation. He pulls it out, but only so he can insert a second finger. He fucks me with those two fingers a couple of times before he adds a third. It stretches the ring of my pussy to almost uncomfortable levels. Especially when he thrusts them in deep, only his knuckles preventing him from going in further.

A bead of sweat rolls down my cheek and drips onto the back of my hand.

Then suddenly I'm empty, and because my body hates me, a feeling of loss hollows my stomach.

I not only hate Wild Man for the sexual abuse he's forced on me, but for also manipulating my body to fit his needs.

I sense him moving behind me and a moment later I feel something else at my entrance. Something broader and less abrasive than his fingers.

He tunnels his fingers in my hair, grabbing a fistful. Then with his grip in my hair and his fingers curled around my waist, he ruth-lessly plunges forward with no warning at all.

My screams at the intrusive invasion of my body drowns out any noises he makes. The intense feeling of being too full is almost too much for me and those familiar black spots appear in my vision. I sway forward, half expecting to slam face first into the rock I'm leaning over, but Wild Man holds me up by my hair.

My stomach revolts and saliva gathers in my mouth. I feel like I might throw up from the pain.

I get a short break as Wild Man holds still inside me. I feel the bristly hair on his groin press against my butt. He lets out a noise, sort of like a muted rumbly growl and his fingers dig deeper into my waist.

The pain slowly begins to ease, and I'm both grateful and resentful. Grateful because that shit was not pleasant. Resentful because the feeling that replaces the pain is not one I want to feel.

Wild Man slides out slowly, and once just the tip is left inside me, he rams back forward, filling me to overflowing once again. I clench my jaw and curl my fingers against the rock at the way his hardness glides against the walls of my pussy. It should be crim-inal for something so bad to feel so good.

Each slow slide backward and harsh thrust forward has stars sparking behind my closed eyes. The good kind of stars. The kind that has me catching my breath and wishing that things were different.

Wild Man lets my hair go and my head falls forward. There's an ache in my chest from holding back the whimpers I refuse to release. My body may be betraying me, but I'll be damned if I let Wild Man know by voicing any sort of sounds of desire.

I stiffen and jerk my head to the side when he stops moving, and I feel something slide against my back entrance. I can barely make out Wild Man's face from this angle. His hair hangs forward with his head tipped down, his concentration on parts of me that has my worry growing anew.

My jaw locks, along with my knees, when I feel pressure against my asshole. I prepare to fight when that pressure increases. I've never been taken there before, have never even been interested in the carnal act.

When the tip of his finger slides past the tight muscles, I expect to feel pain, but the opposite happens. Something deep in my core spasms and before I can stop myself, a low moan works its way past my lips.

Wild Man pauses and raises his head. His black as sin eyes meet mine. I want to look away, but something in his gaze holds me captive.

I've seen desire from men when they look at me. I've felt desire for those men. But the look in Wild Man's eyes goes much deeper. He looks wild and untamed, possessed, and on the verge of something that the tiniest of nudges would push him over.

And for some reason, the crazed look does unwanted things to me. Things that I'll never admit to and will keep hidden from the world until the day I die.

His eyes stay on me as he slowly pushes his finger in. Without permission, the walls of my pussy clench around his cock that's still lodged deep inside me. His eyes flare and the maniacal look in them intensifies. It scares the shit out of me, but it also has more wetness pooling between my legs.

Every woman wants to be desired, but I've always had a secret craving to be wanted to the point of obsession. It's a hidden part of me that I've kept under lock and key because just the idea of it is irrational and can't be healthy.

Wild Man obviously wanted me like that from the beginning because he took me without any compunction or compassion. And while the rational part of my brain, hates him for taking away my choice and freedom, I can't deny the way he's looking at me right now, like I'm the sole reason for existing, doesn't secretly please me.

My bottom lip gets caught between my teeth as he works his

finger in deeper. My walls flex around his cock and he hisses out a breath of air. When he pushes all the way inside me, I don't even attempt to stop the whimper of pleasure that falls from my lips.

With his finger lodged all the way inside my asshole, he pulls his hips back and slowly slides back inside this time. We don't look away from each other. It's like we're both caught by the other's gaze, and no matter what happens, nothing could break that connection.

He picks up speed, fucking me with his cock in one hole and using his finger in the other.

I let out an embarrassing cry of disappointment when his finger leaves me. But it's soon cut off when Wild Man grabs my hair in his fist and pulls me up from the rock. He wraps his other arm around my stomach and pulls me until my back is flush against his chest. The hand in my hair releases and moves to my throat, where he wraps his long fingers around the delicate column.

He's way taller than me, so his hips aren't exactly aligned with mine, so the new position practically has me hooked on his cock with only my toes barely touching the ground. I feel even more full of him.

I feel like if I don't hold onto something, I'll fall forward, so I grab onto his arm that's around me.

Before my body has time to adjust to the new sensations, he uses his arm around my waist to lift me up. He releases his hold slightly, and I fall back down, impaling me on his shaft.

Over and over again, he uses my body as his personal fuck toy. My breasts bounce with the forceful up and down motion. Ashamedly, I don't feel quite as disgusted as I did the first three times he took me.

Later, I'll dredge up the appropriate emotions I should be feeling and worry about getting away. Right now, I close my eyes and let the shameful feelings take over me.

Wild Man buries his face in the crook of my neck, and I drop my head to the side. He growls against my sensitive skin and then the blunt edge of his teeth scrape against it. He bites down, in the same spot as before. The area is still tender, but it surprisingly doesn't hurt when he refreshes the mark.

The animalistic sounds coming from him adds fuel to the inferno that's already raging inside me. It's not fair, and quite frankly wrong on so many levels, for me to be enjoying this. But I'm too weak to deny it.

Wild Man bounces me up and down his cock as if I weigh the equivalent of a bag of cotton candy. I drop my head back on his shoulder when it becomes too heavy to hold up. The hand he has wrapped around my throat tightens and white spots dance on the outside edges of my vision. I can't even muster up the worry of potentially blacking out, because what he's doing to my body takes my full attention.

When my orgasm hits, it does so hard and out of the blue. I dig my nails into the flesh of his arm and my mouth drops open on a long, loud cry.

Just when the tremors start to fade from my release, I'm put back on my feet. Wild Man pushes me over at the waist, but not far enough for me to rest my hands on the rock. He keeps me in my suspended position by grabbing a handful of my hair and laying his forearm on my back. I'm kept bent over by the pressure of his arm, but he keeps me from falling forward by the grip in my hair. His other hand latches around my waist.

And then he fucks me. I mean, he really fucks me. Like a savage animal who's been taken over by pure lust and if he doesn't take his female in that very second, he'd die a gruesome and painful death.

He rumbles out a grunt with each harsh thrust and with each thrust he hits something inside me that has explicit pleasure building.

I let out a cry as another release slams through me and the sound echoes against the rock walls of our oasis. Wild Man growls and rams his hips forward, then grinds himself against me. His cock thickens and a warm blast coats my insides.

His fingers in my hair and around my waist loosen, and I start to fall forward, but he catches me around my stomach before I can tip over.

He pulls his still mostly hard cock out of me. A trail of cum leaks out and begins spilling down my thighs. It's feeling his release slide out of me that has reality crashing back into place.

What in the hell have I done? How could I allow myself to enjoy what just happened? Is there something mentally wrong with me? I've heard of Stockholm's Syndrome before but I haven't been held long enough for that to develop, right? Maybe it's because I already had a preconceived notion of sympathy for the man before I even met him.

I'm pulled from my thoughts with a brutal reminder that my feelings are irrational when Wild Man slips his fingers between my legs and smears his cum over my pussy lips. He slides his fingers past my folds, as if he's trying to push the cum that's leaked out of me back inside.

A shudder runs through me, and it's not only from the lingering pleasure he forced on me, one I desperately wish to get rid of.

But from the very real possibility that, even if I do get out of this situation and never see Wild Man again, we could be creating something that will forever be a reminder of my time spent with him.

*nine*

EVERLEE

I'm bound again by the stupid fucking rope. I thought I got a reprieve and was able to walk around free when we came back to the tree hut yesterday after our bath and he didn't immediately attach the rope around my waist. My freedom lasted until it was time to go to bed.

I fought and kicked and screamed and even tried to run when he picked up the rope and looked at me with expectation. Like I would willingly go to him and let him tight me up again. He's delusional if he thinks that'll ever happen.

After he secured the rope around my waist, he tossed me over his shoulder like a sack of potatoes and carted me to his bed. He pushed me to my hands and knees and fucked me again. I tried to force myself to not react, but my treacherous body is working against me. My only consolation was I was able to hide my reaction from him. As far as he knows, I hated every minute of his rough fucking.

And I could tell he didn't like that, me not reacting the same way I did at the pool of water. The displeasure on his face was palpable. I wanted to give him the middle finger, but I figured that would come across as childish.

Now I'm lying on the pile of blankets and the warmth at my back indicates that Wild Man is still in bed with me. It's still mostly dark outside. Only a sliver of light peaks through the leafy roof, but it's enough to break up the pitch blackness.

Slowly, so as to hopefully not wake him, I roll to my back and turn my head in his direction. He's on his back with one arm lying above his head. And although the other end of the rope is tied around his wrist, he still grips it tightly in his fist.

His face is turned toward me. There's just enough light that I can make out his features. Long, dark lashes rest against his high cheeks. His thick beard almost looks like it would be soft to the touch. I have to curl my fingers into a fist to keep from reaching out and testing that theory.

Full lips, redder than you'd expect on a man, peeks out from the beard. They're parted, and I hear the soft sound of his breathing. The thought of what kind of kisser he would be filters through my mind. I push it away, but it's replaced by something more dangerous. Like how it would feel to have his lips on other parts of my body.

I close my eyes and shove the dirty devil who conjured those thoughts off my shoulder. She has no place here.

I open them again and take in the rest of his body. His slender neck, wide shoulders, and the dark hair under his arm that looks oddly appealing. Who knew armpit hair could be attractive. The thin blanket is pushed down and barely covers his hips. I narrow my eyes and dip my head for a closer look, then jerk it back when I see the head of his cock poking out of the blanket.

And then it moves and peeks out even further.

I snap my head up to his face, only to find his onyx eyes watching me. Sitting up, I suck in a sharp breath and the air gets lodged into my throat. I brace my arms behind me, ready to scramble backward, but at the last second, I stop. I don't know why. I should be doing everything I can think of to get away from this man. Even just lying there, relaxed and barely awake, he exudes power. A power that scares me shitless and can force me to do whatever he pleases.

We both stay still for several minutes, each watching the other. I'm wearily waiting for his next move, and what pisses me off and confuses me is that I don't know if I'm waiting with anticipation or dread.

His hand comes up and his fingers catch around a lock of my hair. He rubs the strands between the pad of his thumb and forefinger. The act seems so inconsequential, something a normal man would do. Certainly not this primitive male.

I don't know how long we stare at each other, but something catches my attention over his shoulder. It's one of the skulls I saw yesterday. A shiver races down my spine at the way its hollow eyes seem to be watching me, as if judging me for something. I felt the same thing yesterday.

Who are they and why does he have them by his bed?

I open my mouth to ask, but snap it shut when Wild Man moves. He lowers the arm that the rope is attached to. Grabbing the loose portion, he begins sliding it through his fingers, gathering the extra. He does this slowly, never removing his eyes from me.

What does he want once he reaches the end of the rope where I'm attached to it?

All too soon, I feel a tug around my waist. I strengthen my stomach muscles, not giving in to the pull he has on me.

He tugs harder, and unless I want the rope to leave hellacious bruises around my waist, I've got no choice but to give in. I brace my hands on his firm chest and the hard muscles under my palms flex. He keeps pulling until I'm hovering over him, our mouths only inches away from each other.

His eyes move to my lips and his tongue darts out and runs along his, leaving a glistening sheen behind. He moves his other hand to the back of my head and slides his fingers through the strands. I want to fight and pull away from him, but I'm oddly caught up in the look in his obsidian gaze as he looks at my mouth.

His grip on my hair tightens and then I'm being tugged down more. I press my lips together when his surprisingly soft ones touch mine. The rough hairs above and below his lips tickles my flesh.

My head is pulled back by my hair an inch. Just enough for him to rumble out, "Open."

I smash my lips together tighter and shake my head.

His eyes narrow. "Open," he growls.

I dig my nails into his pecs, reminding him that there are some things he may be able to force me to do, but kissing isn't one of them. He won't ever get that from me.

The muscle in his jaw tics and his eyes flare with ire, but he doesn't repeat his demand, even though I can tell he wants to.

*Yeah, buddy. How does it feel to want something and not get it?*

He pulls my head back down, but instead of pressing our lips together again, his tongue darts out and runs along my bottom one. I'm so startled by the move that I almost open my lips to suck in a breath.

I keep my mouth closed as he continues to explore my lips with his tongue in soft licks. He groans a few times and the sound vibrates against me, sending unwanted shockwaves into my stomach. A couple of times I nearly give in, but at the last second I remember why I'm here.

He leaves my mouth and moves his lips down my chin to my neck, nipping and sucking the flesh into his mouth. When he hits the spot that he's bitten and sucked a couple times before, I squeeze my eyes shut. The area is tender to the touch, but he doesn't seem to care, because he latches his lips around it and sucks hard.

A whimper tries to escape my mouth, but I forcefully hold it back.

He lets my flesh go, but then lightly runs his tongue over it, like he's lapping at it to take away the sting of pain. He licks the spot for several moments before he pulls my head back by my hair.

I'm let go, and I scramble back on my ass to the edge of the bed. He doesn't look at me as he slowly gets to his feet. I watch him wearily with my arms wrapped around my raised knees. Once he's on his feet, he pulls on the rope, indicating he wants me to come with him. Because I have no choice and I'm still picking my battles, not to mention, my bladder is screaming at me, I get up and walk after him.

He leads me out of the tree hut. I recognize the way he's going and a breath of relief loosens the muscles in my back. A few minutes later, we stop in the same spot we did yesterday. I move before he tells me too, my stomach cramping with the need to pee. It hurts so much that I can't even feel embarrassed that I'm doing it in front of him again. I turn so he has my profile and squat.

Once again, the moment my stream hits the ground, he's in front of me, aiming his to mix with mine.

I've owned dogs before. They do the same shit Wild Man is doing. Marking his territory. I assume other alpha animals do as well. It's fucking weird, but a part of me realizes, for Wild Man at least, it makes sense. He was raised in the wild, so it's logical for him to pick up some animal characteristics.

After we're both done, he turns on his heel and starts walking. I wait until the rope is almost pulled tight before I start following. When we're back in the leafy walls of his home, I come to a stop. I don't know what to do with myself.

My decision is made for me a few minutes later when he yanks on the rope. He's gathered some food and is sitting on the same log as yesterday. When he pulls on the rope again, I reluctantly make my way over to him. His legs are spread wide, his dick swaying, and he indicates for me to sit between them.

As soon as I'm down on my knees with my ass on my heels, he

offers me a piece of meat. I try to take it from him, but he shakes his head and grunts, "Open."

With an eye roll, I part my lips and he slips the meat inside, his finger lingering on my bottom lip too long. I chomp on the meat, more hungry than I realized. He gives me two more pieces before he pops one into his mouth.

I lick my lips, the savory flavor of the meat tasting better with each bite.

I keep my hands limp in my lap as I peek up at him through my lashes. "Who do the skulls belong to?" I ask, my voice low.

I don't really expect him to answer, so I'm surprised when he does.

"Noeny and Peepa."

My brows drop at the unusual names.

He holds up a dried piece of fruit, and I automatically open my mouth. It's the same fruit as yesterday.

"Who are they? What happened to them?" I ask after I've swallowed the bite.

"Dead," he answers, his eyes on the bowl as he brushes his fingers over the fruit, flicking several pieces out of the way.

"I know they're dead. How did they die?"

Seeming to find the piece he wants, he holds it up to my lips. It's bigger than all of the other pieces. He takes one of the smaller pieces and pops it in his mouth. He plucks up a piece of meat and offers it to me.

"Bear."

My eyes snap to him. "A bear killed them?"

A grunt is my only reply. He digs through the bowl of meat until he finds the one he wants. My lips are already open waiting for his offer.

I quickly chew and swallow. "Who were they?"

He waits until he drops another piece of meat into my mouth.

"Noeny and Peepa."

"Did you know them?"

He just repeats the names again.

We sit in silence for several moments as he continues to feed me, alternating from the meat to fruit. I eat a few of each before he indulges himself. I've noticed that he always gives me the bigger pieces, leaving the smaller ones for himself. When he holds the water jug to my lips, I greedily take several swallows. Again, he takes his own sip from the same spot my lips touch.

I think of the names he said. I've never heard of such strange names before and they sound made up. I say them over and over in my head.

*Noeny and Peepa.*

Then something clicks.

Could it be?

"Mommy and Papa." I say out loud, looking up at Wild Man.

A line forms between his eyes. "Mommy and Papa." He says the two names slowly.

I look to the opening where the skulls are then back to him. "Are they your parents? Your Mommy and Papa?"

It takes a minute for him to answer. "Yes."

Having already suspected it doesn't make his confirmation any less heartbreaking. Now I understand why he has them. It's the only way for him to keep his parents with him so he wasn't alone. How utterly fucking devastating.

A part of me wants to wrap my arms around him. To comfort the little boy who lost his parents at such a young age and was forced to care for himself in the wild. I can't imagine how scared he must have been back then. How much he cried for them. It's a miracle he survived. I knew he had lost his parents—or rather, that's what the rumors say—but to lose them in such a horrific way was probably terrorizing. Was he there when the bear attacked his parents? Did he witness it? He was a child when they died—again, according to rumors—so how did he get away? How did he not become a victim himself?

Despite the direness of my situation, I still want to know the mysteries of his life.

"Did you... see it happen? Were you there when your parents died?"

"Yes."

The corners of my mouth tip down. "How did you manage to get away?"

"Run," he grunts. "Peepa said run. Hide."

My heart breaks for the little boy he was and for the man he is now, because he must still feel the grief over the death of his parents.

"I'm sorry that happened to you," I say quietly.

He doesn't acknowledge my sympathy, not that I really expected him to. He may still grieve his parents, but he's understandably built a protective wall around himself. It's what helped him survive so long out here.

## ten

## WILD MAN

I focused on the two pieces of wood I'm rubbing together to start a fire, but most of my attention is on the female sitting on the ground not far from me.

*My* female.

The one I've claimed as my mate and will never let go.

Even if she says her people will come for her.

I'll rip apart and shred anything and everything that dares come between us.

I knew long before I showed myself to her after bathing she was watching me. I knew the moment she first spotted me. Even before that. I awoke that morning with an odd feeling in my stomach. I've learned to trust my instinct, so every move I made, every step I took, I was aware of my surroundings. I'm always aware—not being so could cost me my life in a place like this—but I was even more so because of that weird feeling.

Hours before I went to the bathing pool, I sensed another presence in the forest. I hunted for that presence until I came across the female sitting on a log with a big piece of paper spread out on the ground in front of her. She was beautiful. Long brown hair, soft looking skin, and eyes the color of tree bark.

Her body intrigued me. She was fully clothed, and I wanted to rip it all off so I could see what was underneath. The mounds on her chest and the fullness of her backside. Both tempted me. I wanted to feel them in my palms, to run my hands over every part of her.

I watched her and took in everything I could, fighting the basic animal instinct inside me demanding I take and keep her. She was there, right in front of me.

Instead, I followed her for a while, making sure none of the deadly creatures that roamed the forest came near her. Then I set my trap. A trap I knew she would fall into, because she was there for a reason, and I was guessing *I* was the reason. She's not the first to wander into my territory, but she is the first that I didn't want to steer clear of. All the others, I purposely left signs of life leading away from my home.

With this female, I led her to the pool of water, knowing her curiosity would have her following. The whole time she watched me bathing and I acted oblivious, I again fought my instinct to grab her, throw her on the ground, and rut between her legs like I've seen the wild animals do.

Having her eyes on me had the thing between my legs getting hard. It happens often, especially in the mornings. But this was different. Knowing that she watched had it growing harder than it ever had before. It felt like more than just her eyes were touching me. It was as though *she* was touching me.

I grabbed the thing and stroked, knowing she would continue to watch. I wanted her to. It was a part of me that I planned to push inside her like I've seen wild animals do.

That instinct to take her grew to nearly uncontrollable levels when I finally approached her. I did lose it for a moment when I had her against the tree. Up close, enough for me to smell her scent, a scent that drove me insane.

I've never wanted anything more than I wanted her. Not even for Noeny and Peepa to be alive.

It only made the feeling worse when I had my lips on her and *tasted* her flesh. I wanted to mark her right then and there, so if any creatures came across her, they would know she's mine. I only barely stopped myself.

But all of my control vanished when she thought she could leave. I let her believe she was there by choice, but she wasn't. She was where I led her. She was in my home because that's where she belonged and where she would stay. Forever. I never let go of the things I claim. And this female was my most prized possession.

I took her. I marked her flesh for all to see. I left my scent on her as a warning to all other predators. I planted my seed inside her, the first of many times to create an offspring.

This female was mine. I would protect her and our babies with my life. I would destroy anything that threatens her.

She's mine, and nothing, not even her, would change that.

Everlee, or Ever, is what she called herself.

She twirls a small twig in her fingers, having bent and twisted it until it makes a loop. She slides it over her wrist and looks down at it, her lips curving slightly, as if she likes the thing she made.

She hasn't spoken in a while. Not since she asked me about the skulls I have where we sleep.

Mommy and Papa. That's what she called Noeny and Peepa. My parents.

A very vague memory of me using those terms slides through my mind. I barely remember what they looked like. Or what life was like before the big brown bear ate them.

Words are foreign to me because I rarely have the need to use them. I remember some, but they feel strange coming from my lips and my voice sounds weird to my ears.

My female's voice though... I like the sound of it. I want to hear it again.

Smoke billows up from the sticks, and I lean over to blow on them. A small fire sparks to life, so I drop some dried leaves on top to make it bigger. Once it's big enough, I add some sticks, then some logs.

It doesn't take long before the fire is big enough to cook the small fox I killed earlier. Grabbing one of the sticks that has a point on it, I poke it onto one of the bloody pieces of meat I have beside me before placing it over the flames.

Feeling eyes on me, I lift my head and catch the female looking at the meat. Her face looks whiter than normal. The muscle in her throat moves, like she's swallowing over and over again. If I'm right, it looks like she's trying to not expel the food in her stomach.

I grab another piece of meat, watching her reaction as I stab it on another stick. She's definitely fighting the urge to puke.

I don't understand why she's reacting this way. It's like the sight of the meat is making her sick. How do her people hunt and eat? Maybe she's not the one who handles the meat. Maybe it's the males in her group.

My female does a lot of things that I don't understand.

Like the thing she did with the twig. Why did she look pleased when she put it around her wrist?

Or the way her cheeks turn pink when she urinates? Every living creature does it, so why does she appear uncomfortable? Is it because I'm with her? And why does it look like she's on the verge of running when I mark her urine with mine? Do her people not do that to mask their female's scent to keep predators away?

And why is she still fighting me when I want to breed with her? I expected a fight the first time. It's up to the male to master his female to show her he's strong enough to provide and protect her. Does she not believe I'm a worthy mate?

Just the thought of her believing that has my hackles rising and the thing between my legs getting hard. I will show her that I'm the only male for her. That I can be strong enough to protect her from all dangers. That I can provide her with food and water and shelter. That any offsprings we create will be shielded from harm until I teach them to defend themselves.

There are other things about the female that confuses me. Like how she makes me feel.

Her mouth for one thing. I've never seen any of the wild animals push their mouths together. But for some reason, I want to do that with her. I have a faded memory of Noeny and Peepa doing the same thing. I remember thinking it was gross because they used their tongues, licking inside each other's mouths.

I want to do that with my female. I want to know what her mouth tastes like. I want to slide my tongue against hers and breathe in the air that comes from her lungs.

If my memory is right, Noeny and Peepa did it all the time, so I would think it was normal, so why does my female keep her mouth from me?

The sizzle from the juices from the meat pulls my attention back to it. I flip the sticks over to cook the other side.

My eyes move back to her. She has her legs pulled up to her chest with her arms wrapped around them. Her feet hide her female parts, and I don't like it. I like looking at her. I like the pink and the softness of the lips between her legs. And I like the way it smells. That's another part of her I want to taste with my tongue. To lick her from the tight little hole in her backside, up to the hole I push my thing inside of to the little button at the top.

The first few times I pushed inside her, she was dry between her legs, but yesterday, when I had her in the water, she had liquid seeping out of her. At first I thought it was urine or maybe just the water, but it felt different. It was slippery, and it made pushing my thing inside her much easier.

She acted differently too. She didn't fight me as hard, and even made noises that I knew meant she liked what I was doing. And then she tightened around my shaft until it almost hurt and let out a cry that sounded like she was in pain, but I knew she wasn't.

But then last night when I had her, she was wet and her walls gripped me, but she didn't give me any cries. I wanted her cries. I really liked the way they sounded.

The first time I pushed my thing inside her body was unlike anything I had ever felt before. I've used my hand many times to rub myself until it felt good and I expelled my seed. But being inside my female, having the warmth of her body wrapped around me, I couldn't imagine anything feeling better. But I was wrong. Sliding inside her when she was wet and feeling her spasm around my thing, hearing her cry out and knowing she felt good too.... I will make sure every time I take her, it will be like that.

After checking the meat, I get to my feet and rinse my hands in a small bowl of water before I walk to my female. She digs her nails into her legs as she watches me approach. I want to burrow myself in her mind so I know what she's thinking.

Once I'm standing over her, she tips her head back to keep her eyes on me. My thing bobs out from my body, and I feel a drop of liquid hanging from the tip.

An image pops in my head of her licking away the clear drop with her wet tongue. It manifests into her lips wrapping around my thing as she takes me into her mouth. I've seen wild animals lick themselves and even each other.

I can help her by grabbing her hair and using it to thrust into her mouth like I do when I take her between her legs.

My shaft moves and more liquid seeps from the head at the thought.

When I pressed the tip against her lips in the water, she refused to take me in her mouth. It angered me, and I almost forced her. I didn't only because I knew I wouldn't last long. I was already close to releasing my seed, and I wanted to do it inside her. I want to plant my baby in her belly.

There would be time for that later. I'll teach her how to take my thing in her mouth and suck it like I do the hard little tips on the mounds on her chest. I wonder how much I can get in there. If I could reach all the way to the back of her mouth and if I could even fit down her throat. How tight that passage would be.

As much as I want to show her now, it'll have to wait until the sun goes down. I've taken my female hard since I first claimed her. I don't want her sore in too many places, and I know taking her mouth won't be easy.

I look down at her legs that are still drawn to her chest, hiding the spot I want to see. Her nails dig so hard into her flesh that her skin is white around her fingers. Her eyes track me with an expression that makes me believe I scare her. The look angers me. Doesn't this female not know that I would never intentionally hurt her? That I'd rather naw off my own limbs than ever see her in pain.

I look at the marks on her neck, shoulders, and arms made by my teeth and hands. More are on her thighs, but I can't see those with her legs pulled up. I press my back teeth together until my jaw hurts.

Those marks may indicate I've hurt her, but they're a show of power and a warning to any creature who dares to come near her. They're my mark of ownership. They show any and all things, including my female, that she's mine.

I unlock my jaw and jut my chin to her arms. "Stop," I grunt, still unused to hearing my voice.

Lines appear on her forehead. "What?"

I point to her arms and repeat, "Stop."

Her head drops and she looks at her arms. Her nails release their grip in her flesh and she lifts her hands, flexing her fingers. She tilts her head back to look at me again. "I don't understand. What do—?"

I don't let her finish. Reaching down, I slide my fingers in her hair, grip the thick strands and tug her up to her feet. A strangled noise leaves her throat and she pulls against my hold. I tighten my grip so she doesn't get away. Her eyes blaze a deep color when she glares up at me.

"Stop," I hiss, pulling her face closer to me.

"Stop, what?" she asks, only her lips moving since her teeth are clamped together.

Instead of answering, I pull her to the log I was sitting on and force her down until her butt is on the ground. She was too far away where she was sitting. I want her closer to me.

The ground is covered in crushed leaves, so it won't scrape her skin. She huffs out a breath, and her eyes say that if she had a weapon right now, she'd use it against me. Part of me wants her to try, to feel her fight me, just so I can overpower her and prove to her again that I'm the stronger one. That I'm the alpha.

Once she settles down, her body going lax, I sit on the log. I'm reaching for the stick over the fire with the meat on it when she starts pulling her legs up again. Like she intends to sit the way she was a moment ago. I grab her arms before she can wrap them around her legs and push them back down to her sides.

"No."

She presses her lips together at my demand. I wait a moment before I let her arms go, but I'm still not satisfied with her position. I push her knees until her legs are straight in front of her. I have a clear view of her breasts, but I want to see more of her. Taking one of her feet, I move it away from the other so her legs are spread open.

She tries to close her legs. "What the hell are you doing?"

I slap the inside of her thigh and she freezes, a small sound leaving her throat. She looks at me with surprise, her eyes big circles and her lips open. I see her pink tongue pressed against the inside of her bottom teeth. I really want to slide my own tongue against hers. To press it inside her mouth. To suck it and take a couple of small bites.

I don't know if she stays still with her legs open because of shock or because she finally understands what I want and knows I won't allow anything else. I release her leg and she still doesn't move. Not even her eyes. They stare up at me with a look I don't understand.

Without taking my eyes away from her, I remove the meat from the fire and set it to the side. My eyes slowly move from her face and go down. Her chest moves faster than normal and it makes the mounds quiver. The tips are hard little points. Her stomach is flat and the small hole on the lower part—I think it's called a belly button—looks deep.

My gaze tracks further down, to the part I'm most interested in. The hair that covers her female parts is thinner and shorter than the hair that surrounds my thing. It looks like it was cut and is starting to grow back. Just below that, my gaze focuses on soft, pink lips. They look dry from the outside, but between them, I see a drop of clear liquid forming. I want to lick that drop away. I know what she tastes like from the time I licked her from my fingers, but I want to eat her directly between the legs. To taste only her, not mixed with my seed.

My thing moves between my legs, growing in length and width, readying itself to take my female again, to plant my seed inside her womb.

"Touch," I grunt.

She doesn't move, so I lift my head to look at her. Her bottom lip is trapped between her teeth and there's a line between her eyes.

"I don't understand," she says.

I look back between her legs and grunt again, "Touch."

"Y-you want me to touch myself... down there?" Her question sounds like she doesn't believe what she's saying.

"Yes."

I expect her to say no or start fighting me, even if it would be pointless. But she doesn't. She doesn't do anything at first. It's like she's frozen.

I grow impatient and I'm just about to force her hand between her legs, but then she moves. It's slow at first, but her hand moves down her stomach passed the hair between her legs. She presses two fingers on either side of her lips. My thing gives another jerk. Her lips down there open more, and I see more liquid seeping from her. It slides down and disappears under her bottom to the ground.

I can't look away as she takes two fingers and glides them between the lips to her hole. My eyes jerk up when a small sound comes from her. Her eyes look halfway closed and redness covers her cheeks. She's breathing heavier now. Living in the wilderness has left me ignorant to a lot of the ways of the world, but I'd have to be dead to not recognize the look on my female's face. What she's doing with her fingers feels good.

I move my eyes back down. Her legs are wider and she slips one of her fingers inside her hole. When she pulls it out, it's covered in her clear liquid. She drags that same finger between the lips and stops when she reaches the little bump at the top, where she swirls it around. This must feel really good because the noises coming from her become louder.

Feeling my thing jump, I wrap my fingers around it. I've stroked myself plenty of times, but doing it in front of her feels different. Better, more sensitive.

Noticing where my hand is, her eyes move there and her tongue darts out to lick her lips.

Is she thinking the same thing as me? About my thing sliding inside her mouth. It wouldn't be as tight as the hole between her legs, but I'd bet it would still feel good.

I slide my hand up and down. When a drop of liquid appears at the slit, I swipe it with my finger. I get to my knees in front of her, moving forward until my thighs are between hers. It would be so easy to fall forward and thrust inside her. She's spread out in front of me, open and appearing like she may want it to.

But I stop myself.

I lift my finger that has the liquid on it to her lips. Her mouth is already open, so I slip it inside and touch her wet tongue. Surprising us both, her lips close around my finger and she starts sucking on it. I push more of my finger inside and touch the back of her throat. Her eyes widen a little, but she doesn't pull away. I go further and the muscles in her throat tighten. She gags like she's trying to not throw up.

I bet that would feel good against my thing. I want to jam it inside her mouth to find out how tight and warm it is.

Her hand has stopped moving, so I pull my finger from her mouth and move it back to my thing. When I pointedly look between her legs, her hand moves again. I settle back on my heels, slowly moving my hand up and down. The more I watch the female in front of me, the harder I get, and the harder it becomes to not fall on top of her and rut between her legs.

She pushes two of her fingers deep inside her. So far that the rest of her hand is the only thing stopping more from going in. When she pulls them free, the need to taste her is too much to ignore. So, I grab her wrist and bring her fingers to my mouth. The taste of her is like eating my favorite meal. I swipe my tongue between her fingers, making sure to get it all.

My eyes dart to hers when she sucks in a sharp breath. Seeing the look in her eyes that says she likes what I'm doing has the two balls below my thing getting tight.

I pull her fingers from my mouth and place my hand on her chest, pushing her back until she's lying down. I grab her waist and lift her butt until only the top of her back is still on the ground. I attack her like a starved man. Like if I don't have her in my mouth at that moment, I'll die. Because that's the way I feel. I need her taste. I swipe my tongue between her lips and eat away every single drop that's leaking from her. I devour her, pushing my tongue in as far as it'll go until I've lapped it all away. It's not enough. I need more of her.

"Mine," I snarl against her.

I drag my tongue up and press it against the spot she kept playing with. I suck it between my lips and scrape my teeth against it. I growl when her fingers slide through my hair, thinking she means to push my head away. Nothing could move me from where my mouth is right now.

But she doesn't try to get away. Instead, she pulls me closer. Her nails dig into my scalp so hard that marks will be left behind. I want her to leave marks on me just as much as my need to leave mine on her. It's a show of ownership. I'm her mate, just as she's mine.

Low cries fill the air around us and her thighs squeeze tight against my head. More liquid seeps out of her, and I lick it away before it can slide to the ground below her, not wanting to waste even a drop.

When I slip my tongue back inside her, her walls clamp around it, attempting to suck me in.

"Oh God!" she cries while gouging my scalp with her nails.

I grab the back of her thighs and push her legs back until her knees are by her head. The noises coming from her and the way she yanks my head even closer, like she can't get enough, has my thing pounding and steadily leaking.

When I feel her body slightly relax and I've licked away all of her liquid, I lift my head. Her eyes are open and she's staring up at the trees. Her lips are parted and her chest rises and falls with her heavy breathing.

I get back to my knees, situating myself between her legs. Her head tilts down and her eyes meet mine. The red on her cheeks has deepened and a light sheen of sweat covers her face. She's the best thing I've ever seen.

I grab my thing with one hand and move my other between her legs. I slip one finger between her lips and push it inside. Her walls are still spasming. I push in deep, until I can't go in any further, then pull it out and push in a second finger. I slide my hand up and down my thing at the same time I pump my fingers inside her. After a few strokes, I add another finger. She's tight around my fingers, but I push until I get the full length of them inside her.

Once she's loose enough, I curl my fingers and add a fourth. My thing is large, and it fits inside her snuggly, so I know she can take it.

Her arms lay beside her on the ground and she grips the dried leaves. She bites her bottom lip so hard, I wonder if she'll draw blood.

My hand moves faster around my thing and so do my fingers inside her hole. There's so much liquid coming out of her that it soaks my hand.

I look down and watch as my fingers disappear inside her. Only my thumb is sticking out. I want to push that inside her too. I want my whole hand inside her.

Tucking my thumb inward, I slowly start to press forward. My female scrambles up and grabs my wrist.

"Wait!" she shouts. I jerk my head up and look at her. "I can't... That's too much. It won't fit."

I tilt my head to the side, wondering why she thinks that. I have big hands, but it can't be much bigger than my thing.

"Yes. Fit."

Her fingers dig into my flesh and her eyes look like she's frightened of something. "No! It *won't* fit."

I grit my teeth and a growl comes from my throat. I don't say anything else, but I push her back down with my other hand. Before she can sit back up, I drop down and put my mouth back over the bump she likes to rub. I suck it between my teeth, and I get what I want from her. Her body relaxes and she stops fighting me.

My fingers are still inside her, so I pump them a few times while I suck on the bump. When I feel her relax even more, I tuck my thumb inward and push against her. It doesn't go in easily. I have to force my way past her outer walls. She tenses again, so I suck harder on the bump at the same time I go in deeper.

I'm not able to push my whole hand in—I don't want to damage her inside—but I get it past my knuckles. She grips me so tight, there's no room for me to flex my fingers. I hold still a moment, still playing with the bump, but letting her adjust to my hand filling her.

After several seconds, once her muscles have loosened even more, I slide my hand out past the knuckles and gently push it back inside.

It feels strange having my hand inside her. She's hot and slick and every few seconds, I feel her walls tighten around me.

Once I'm sure she's not going to pull away from me, I get back to my knees and reach for my thing. I look down at my hand inside her and pump my length. Her skin is so much lighter than mine. Seeing what I'm doing to her body, it doesn't look possible.

Both of my hands pick up speed. I shove my hand inside her over and over again, sliding in a little bit more with each one. The balls below my thing get tight and draw up to my body. I'm on the edge of releasing my seed when my female's walls close so tight around my hand that I can't move it. Her cry is louder than all the others.

I pull my hand from her and scoot up until the tip of my thing is at her gapping opening. It doesn't close all the way, so I easily push the head inside just as the first jets of my seed shoot out of me. I can feel the pulses of her walls around the tip as I coat the inside of her, mixing my seed with her liquid.

Once I'm empty, I pull out. Looking down, I see the creamy whiteness of my seed at her opening, attempting to leak out. I slide two of my fingers inside her, pushing back in as much as I can.

I look up when my female moans. Her eyes are closed and she has a satisfied look on her face. It makes me want to beat my chest and roar to the sky in triumph. *I* put that look on her face. Her male.

When her eyes slide open, they come to me. "Why do you do that?" Her voice is so low that I barely hear her.

I lean down and rest one of my fists on the ground beside her head. Two of my fingers are still at her opening, so I push them inside. I bend my arm until my face is close to hers.

"*Mine*," I grunt and her eyes widen. "My female. My babies in belly."

*eleven*

EVERLEE

The term 'mine' will always mean something differently to me now. People use it with such simplicity to claim their possessions. But just because you claim something is yours, doesn't actually make it so. Sometimes you have to fight, steal, barter, and connive to truly own it. And even then, someone else might come along and try to take it from you to claim for themselves.

People are not supposed to be possessions. They aren't meant to be owned by another.

The way Wild Man uses the word 'mine' gives it a whole new meaning. It makes me feel like a *'thing'*, not a living, breathing person. Not someone who has feelings and has the right to choose whether I want to be claimed.

But it also makes me feel something else. Important. Relevant. The center of someone's world.

It's not a good feeling to have in my current situation. I have a suspicion that when Wild Man calls something his, he'll fight to his very last breath to keep it. He's already said he would kill my family if they came for me, and I have no doubt he'd follow through with his threat.

And I know with certainty that if I did become pregnant, his possessiveness will only strengthen. Unfortunately, time is not on my side. I'm on birth control, but it's the stupid fucking pill, not the shot. It's been days—a week maybe? I've sorta lost track of time— since I took my last pill, so for all I know, I could be cooking a mini Wild Man inside me right now. I very well might be on my way to becoming a mother.

I shudder at the thought.

What in the hell am I going to do if I do get pregnant? I'm firmly against abortion, so that's out of the question. I can't imagine giving my child away, so adoption is a no. But raising a child who was created from a nightmare? I would love any child I birthed under any circumstances, but they would be a constant reminder of my time spent in the wilderness with a crazed man.

I need to get away from him before any of this becomes a reality.

A twig snaps to my left and the sudden noise jerks me from my thoughts. My head swings in that direction, only to see Wild Man stepping out from behind a tree.

He's wearing the cloth that covers his junk again, something I'm grateful for, but it also irritates the hell out of me. I'm still naked as the day I was born. Why does he get to cover his most private parts while I'm left flaunting mine for all the creatures in the forest to see?

"Asshole," I mutter quietly to myself.

It's not quietly enough, apparently, because Wild Man jerks his head my way, his eyes narrowing.

Oops. I forgot that I'm supposed to be quiet while the asshole hunts for food.

I don't know why he didn't just leave me at the tree hut. It's not like I'm helping him. Certainly not while I'm tied to another fucking tree.

The rope chafe's the skin around my waist, so I adjust it a little, shooting Wild Man a glare as I do so.

He ignores my look as he walks on silent feet toward me. He has a long stick in his hand. Both ends have been shaved down to pointy tips.

He goes to where the rope is tied to the tree and within seconds unties it.

How in the hell can he untie the rope so fast when I've been working at it for what seems like hours?

When I get out of here I'm Googling every knot known to mankind.

Using the rope, he leads me through the woods, thankfully going slower than his normal gait. I have to watch the ground to make sure I'm not stepping on anything spiky. Wild Man doesn't. It's like his feet are made of stone and can withstand anything.

"Where are we going now?" I ask because I'm sick of the silence. Screw him.

His answer is to jerk on the rope until I almost lose my footing. I don't let it deter me though.

I grab the piece of rope in front of me and give it a hard pull. "Hey. I asked a question. It's rude to not answer."

He abruptly turns, and I barely catch myself before I slam against his chest.

"Quiet," he says, his voice a deep, grumbly growl.

"I don't want to be quiet," I retort. "The silence is killing me."

He tilts his head to the side like people do when they're trying to understand something. "Not killing you."

My eyes roll heavenward before settling back on him. "Not literally. It's a metaphor." A line appears between his eyes. "I'm just saying, this silent business sucks."

"Sucks?" His eyes drop to my mouth, and I swear, I could slap myself for using that word. Of course, he's a man, so his mind goes immediately to the gutter.

I snap my fingers in his face and his gaze comes back to mine. "Eyes up here."

His lips form a firm line as he scowls.

"Quiet," he says again. "Hunt."

I throw my hands on my hips like an immature teenager getting ready to rant. "If you wanted quiet, then you should have left me at the tree hut."

"Tree hut?"

"Yes. Tree hut. Camp." I try another word. "Home."

I don't say *his* home because technically, although temporarily, it is *my* home at the moment as well.

"No."

My brows jump up. "No, what?"

"You stay with me."

Frustration has my back teeth grinding together. "But why?"

I need him to take me back to the tree hut and go hunt by himself so I can work on the stupid knots again.

"Mine."

I want to shove that godforsaken word down his throat and choke him on it.

"I already know you think I'm yours," I say in exasperation. "What does that have to do with taking me back to the tree hut?"

"You stay," he says stubbornly.

I throw my hands in the air and let them slam back against my sides. "Fine. Whatever."

He eyes me for a second before he spins on his heel and resumes walking. I watch my steps, but I don't keep them light like I was before. If he wants me with him, he can deal with me making as much noise as I want.

We walk and walk and walk. By the time we come to a stop, I've lightened my steps. Not because I'm trying to be quiet, but because all the stomping was starting to hurt my feet. Or that's what I tell myself. It's definitely not because the jostling was reminding me that I'm actually hungry and my noisy steps could ultimately harm our chances of getting food.

I lick my dry lips. I'm thirsty too, but I refuse to ask for the water pouch that's hanging from Wild Man's side.

My stomach rumbles loud enough for him to hear and he glances at me over his shoulder. I keep my lips sealed, but don't look away from him. His eyes move down my chest to my stomach, and it feels like a light caress.

He moves to a leafy bush. Squatting down, he begins plucking the purple berries. They aren't any that I've seen before. After he has a handful, he stands and holds out his hand.

I'm hesitant to take them. "What are they? They could be poisonous."

"No. Good."

Just because he says they're good, doesn't actually mean they're safe to eat.

When I don't take them, he tilts his head back and pops a few of them in his mouth. My breath catches, my first thought going to the possibility of him dying from poison. The ridiculous notion soon leaves my head. He's lived in the forest for years. Surely he's eaten them before.

I cup my hands together and hold them out. He drops the berries in my hand, waiting until I pop a couple into my mouth before seeming satisfied. I'm surprised at how sweet and tasty they are. Before I know it, I've eaten them all. Wild Man watches me the whole time.

He pulls the water pouch from his side and holds it out to me. Reluctantly grateful, I take it and swallow back several mouthfuls. When I give it back, he takes his own drink from it.

After he's reattached the pouch to his hip, he pulls the rope and we start walking again. My stomach is satisfied for now, so my mood has improved slightly.

After a while, we stop near a tree and he winds the rope around it.

"Stay," he grunts before walking off.

Jerk. It's not like I can go anywhere anyway.

I find a relatively soft spot near the tree and sit down. Drawing my knees to my chest, I wrap my arms around my legs. The position reminds me of yesterday and what I willingly let happen. I not only didn't fight Wild Man, but after the initial shock of what he wanted, I actually enjoyed it. My mind may have been screaming at me to stop, but my body apparently has a mind of its own, because it went along with everything Wild Man demanded.

Sitting close to him with my legs spread open, playing with myself while he touched his cock was the dirtiest, naughtiest thing I've ever done. I'm no prude, but I know my limits, and doing that, I would have thought, would surpass those limits. Not just the act itself, but the person I was doing it with.

And what he did with his hand....

I close my eyes at the memory. I never would have thought what he did would be possible, but I guess the body is more pliable than I imagine.

Afterward, I wanted to hate him for what he did to my body, but I only ended up hating myself. The tremors of my orgasm had barely faded , and I was already anticipating the next time he would do it again. All of it. Us taking our own pleasure while the other watched and him stuffing his hand inside me.

Why can't I feel disgust toward the man who's holding me against my will? My head knows right from wrong, but my body wants to play. I hate myself because Wild Man makes me feel things I never knew I could feel. He plays my body expertly, like he's perfected the art of seduction. This coming from a guy who was a virgin until I came along. How is that even possible?

Something rattles several feet away from me and instant chills form across my arms. I know that sound well and it sends terror through me.

I was seven years old when one of my brothers was rushed to the hospital after being bitten by a rattlesnake. Thankfully, he was given the anti-venom in time and there were no lasting effects. I remember crying so much it made me sick. I thought my brother was going to die. The summer before, there was a boy who was bitten by a rattler and he wasn't as lucky as Spencer. His body was found two days after he went missing.

Without making any sudden movements, I slowly turn my head. Sure enough, five feet away from me is a huge fucking diamondback rattle snake. The biggest part of his body has got to be the size of my forearm. He's coiled with his thick head sticking up, his tongue slithering, and his tail rattling its death beat.

Fear has me freezing, which works in my favor, because the best thing to do if you encounter a rattler is to stay still. What sucks is that I'm sitting down and can't even attempt to move away from it if given the opportunity. Sudden movements could startle the thing and it could strike.

Shit. I'm so damned screwed.

My nails bite into my thighs when, after several tense moments, the rattler uncoils starts slithering toward me, not away like it's supposed to.

Despite trying to stay as still as possible, my body begins to shake and my heart pounds so loud I'm sure the snake can hear it. There's no need to worry about getting away from Wild Man, because it won't matter anymore. I'm going to die from a snake bite.

That or a heart attack.

The snake is only a couple of feet from me now. If he so chooses, he's within striking range.

I stop breathing when he inches forward, the end of his split tongue slithering as he opens his mouth and shows me his long deadly teeth.

I've come to terms with my fate and are sending up my last prayers when two things happen at once.

The snake suddenly strikes, but it's not me that it sinks its teeth into. Right at the last second, a thick, tanned arm snaps in front of me and grabs the snake. Unfortunately, Wild Man's aim is off and he grabs it too far down its body to hinder it from attacking. The rattler twists around and sinks its sharp fangs into the meaty part of Wild Man's bicep.

Wild Man doesn't react to being bitten. He grabs the snake with his other hand just below its head and wrestles it to the ground. He snatches his stick, where he must have dropped it, and presses the pointy end to the top of the rattler's head. He jams it downward into the ground, puncturing the snake's skull. It twitches for a moment before going still.

I scramble on my knees and practically fall at Wild Man's side. Grabbing his arm with shaky hands, I lift it to look at the two puncture holes. They're about two inches apart and blood and a clear-ish liquid seeps from them both.

My stomach turns to knots and the back of my scalp prickles. I jerk my head up to look at Wild Man.

"Why did you do that?" I shout the question. My vision clouds as my eyes fill with tears.

His expression is fierce when he says only one word. "Protect."

# *twelve*

EVERLEE

S itting back on my heels, I look down at the man who's totally upended my life but alternatively saved it. I hate Wild Man for many reasons. All of them are valid. He's held me captive. He's raped me multiple times. He keeps me tied to him or a tree so I can't get away. He's threatened to kill my family. He doesn't allow me to wear clothes. And he's turned my body against me.

All of those reasons should have me rejoicing in the fact that he's currently lying in his bed, dying. He's so weak right now that I could easily leave him. It would take me time to figure out the knot on the rope or find something sharp to cut it—because of course, even after being bitten by a venomous snake, he still made sure to tie the other end of the rope around his wrist before he fell onto the pile of blankets in his tree hut—but from the look of Wild Man, I've got all the time in the world now.

So why am I sitting here by his side, wiping away the dampness from his forehead that never seems to go away. I should be picking at the knot or finding something I can use to saw through it.

I'm an idiot, that's why.

Within an hour of getting back to the tree hut, the symptoms started. His breathing became labored and a fine sheen of sweat coated his forehead. The site of the wounds is an angry red and is swelling. I look at the two holes now and notice several blisters forming.

I check the pulse in his wrist, and I don't know if I should be alarmed or relieved to feel a rapid beat.

Tears cling to my lashes as I stare down at him. He fell asleep a bit ago. His cheeks are flush and he's warm to the touch.

As much as I hate him, the thought of him dying tears jagged holes through my heart. I don't want him to die. I want him to let me go, but not at the expense of his life.

I pick up the piece of cloth I've been using to wipe his face and chest and dip it in the clay bowl holding water. Thankfully, the rope attaching us together is long, so I'm able to move around the tree hut.

While he laid in bed, soft grunts of pain leaving his dried lips, I left him long enough to search for supplies. I found a few decently clean pieces of clothes and another jug of water. I cleaned the wounds with the water and cloth as best as I could, but I don't know if it's enough. I don't think it matters anyway. Water and a questionably clean cloth isn't enough to fight sepsis and necrosis.

"You're so fucking stupid for doing that," I mutter past the thick clog in my throat.

Wild Man groans, but otherwise doesn't move or open his eyes.

I run the rag over his forehead and across his cheeks, wiping away the sweat that will only be replaced with more in a few moments. His breathing is labored and rattly, like he's sick with pneumonia. If only his illness was that simple.

I rinse and rewet the rag with fresh water and start washing down his neck and over his collarbones.

"Why can't I hate you like I'm supposed to?" I ask the silent man. "You've taken so much from me. I have every right to want you dead."

The hard muscles below the rag don't so much as twitch when I move it to his chest. Despite the dire situation, I can't help but appreciate the hard plains and deep valleys of his pecs.

"But I don't," I continue quietly, like I'm afraid some other person may hear my confession. "You make me so angry sometimes that I want to stab your eyes with rusty knives and cut off your hands with a dull blade, but I don't want you to die." I choke on the last word. A tear drops from my chin, landing on his chest right over his heart, and I wipe it away with the rag.

I move the cloth down his stomach, my eyes tracing each inch of skin that I wash. I linger on the two slash marks on his lower stomach, and once again, my curiosity piques. Sorrow fills my stomach when I think about everything this man must have gone through since he was a child. There are so many stories he could tell me.

But now those stories will die with him. No one will ever know how one small brave five-year-old boy managed to survive in the wilderness all by himself.

Using the back of my hand, I wipe away another tear before it has a chance to fall.

Once I'm done with Wild Man's chest, I run the rag over his face and neck one more time. I'm barely managing to hold onto my emotions and exhaustion has hit with the effort. I drop the rag in the bowl and curl on my side beside Wild Man with my hands tucked under my cheek. I keep my eyes on the side of his face until I can't keep them open anymore.

---

No matter how tired I am, I can't fall into a deep sleep. I'm terrified I'm going to wake up and find that Wild Man is dead. Each time I open my eyes to check on him, he's in the same position and his breathing and pulse is just as erratic as the last time. I wipe him down with the rag several more times, having no idea if it's helping him at all.

It's been hours since we made it back to his tree hut and he hasn't opened his eyes since he closed them.

I peel back the cloth covering the puncture wounds and find the blisters have grown in size. The swollen skin around the holes have turned to a deeper shade of red.

I get up and dump out the water from the bowl then pour in fresh water. Using a part of the cloth, I gently wipe around the edges of the wounds, trying to keep them as clean as possible.

I know my efforts are in vain. The chances of Wild Man surviving a rattlesnake bite are very slim, but if there's even a minuscule chance, I have to take it.

I clean his face and chest again before I lay back down beside him. All I can do is wait and try to make him as comfortable as possible.

So, that's what I do.

---

FOR THREE DAYS, I STAY VIGILANTE IN CARING FOR WILD MAN. CLEANING his wounds, keeping him as cool as I can by frequently running a cloth over most of his body, and dribbling water past his dry and cracked lips. He sleeps, his breathing labored and his heart racing.

I pray more than I ever have, hoping that by some miracle my efforts aren't wasted.

I've lain beside him and tried to sleep, but each time I drift off, I jolt awake. I've become intimately acquainted with fear. It's what I feel each time I check on Wild Man.

On the fourth night, I don't know how I manage it, but I must have fallen into a deep sleep. One filled with deadly snakes and wild animals screaming into the night. I'm naked, running in the forest, the rough ground slicing into my feet. I open my mouth to scream, but no sound comes out. I look behind me and see a huge snake, taller than me and the size of a tree trunk, with his mouth wide open. His huge fangs glow a bright white in the moonlight and they drip with bright yellow venom. All around me, I hear the howls of coyotes and the growls of wolves.

Just as the snake strikes forward, my eyes snap open.

At first, I'm disoriented because everything is dark, so dark that it feels like I'm still in my dream. I open my mouth to let out a scream, but immediately snap it shut when something above me moves. Not some*thing*, but some*one*.

Wild Man hovers above me, his face only inches away from mine.

"Wild Man," I croak.

"*Momor.*"

His voice sounds weak and scratchy, and I have no idea what he just said.

I lift my hands and lay them on his chest, pushing him back. It doesn't take much effort to get him to lie back down, which goes to show just how weak he really is.

I get to my knees so I can look at him. I can't see that well in the dark, but thankfully, there's enough moonlight that shines through the trees to offer me a glimpse of his face. His cheeks and forehead still glistens with sweat, but not as much as before. I press a hand against his chest and a wave of relief hits when I don't encounter the heat or a rapid heartbeat.

"How do you feel?" I ask, scooting on my knees closer to him.

His answer really isn't an answer, just a grunt. I hold the jug of water to his lips and help lift his head so he can take a sip. He swallows and a trickle slides out the corner of his mouth. I set it aside and put my hand back on his chest.

"Are you in pain?"

He places his hand over mine. "Stay."

My heart knocks around behind my sternum. Does he want me

to stay because I'm caring for him and he doesn't want to die alone, or is it because he simply wants me to stay?

My internal question is stupid. He's made it his mission to let me know that I belong to him.

The answer doesn't matter anyway. Regardless of the reason behind his demand. I'm obviously not going anywhere. At least, not until he's better. *If* he gets better, my mind whispers.

Of course he's going to get better. Him being awake and coherent is a good sign, right?

Please let that be true.

"I'll stay," I say, not adding the *for now* part at the end. That's another day's problem.

He blinks at me, like he's unsure whether to believe me or not.

"Sleep," I tell him. "You need to rest."

Using his good arm, he reaches up and wraps his fingers around my neck. His grip is surprisingly strong given his weakened state as he pulls me down beside him. He maneuvers my head, so it's lying on his chest and I'm plastered against his side. I want to protest, afraid of making him uncomfortable, but decide, for once, to let him do what he wants.

I close my eyes and let the sound of his steady heartbeat lull me into sleep.

*thirteen*

EVERLEE

I'm dreaming again. This one is a lot more pleasant and pleasurable than the last one.

I'm lying on a bed of purple flowers, staring up at a cloudless sky. The heat of the sun kissing my skin feels divine and welcoming. A smile tips up my lips, and I lift my arms above my head in a languorous stretch.

I suck in a sharp breath and let out a low moan when something delicious starts happening between my legs. Tucking my chin against my chest, I look down my torso and see a head full of black hair. Wild Man tips his head and his black eyes meet mine. I can only see his face from his nose up, because his mouth is currently devouring my pussy. The look in the black orbs is intense, like he's a starved man immensely enjoying his first meal after years of going hungry.

I slide my fingers through his hair, gripping the back and pulling his face tighter against me. His nose bumps against my clit and a spark of desire shoots through me, forcing a cry past my lips.

"Yes! Oh God, that feels so good, Wild Man."

His eyes flare with hunger and he bites down on my clit. My hips jerk up at the same time I shove his face against my wet folds.

"More," I demand huskily. "I need more."

He growls and it rumbles against my sensitive flesh.

He bites my clit again, and I screech to the heavens, the pain and pleasure mixed together making me feel something I've never felt before.

"My female," he growls. "Mine, always."

My eyes snap open at his growled declaration of ownership.

By the way my body is on fire, I'm not dreaming. My fingers cramp from the tight hold I have in Wild Man's hair.

I jerk my head down at the same time I release his hair. I try to scramble back on my elbows, but I get nowhere when Wild Man throws his arm over my stomach, holding me down.

"Stop!" I yell. My voice is so loud, I hear birds screeching as they take flight from the trees. "What are you doing?"

He doesn't answer, just continues his assault on my pussy. I suppress a moan when he jams his tongue inside me and pressed his nose against my clit, just like in the 'dream'.

I grab hold of his hair again, but this time to pull him away. "Wild Man, you have to stop. You're going to hurt yourself."

It's been five days since he was bitten by the rattlesnake. Three of those days he was in and out of consciousness. Three days of me wondering and worrying if he was going to die. It's been an exhausting experience, to say the least, both mentally and physically.

Yesterday was the first day I managed to get him to eat a few pieces of dried fruit. The wounds are still an angry red, but the swelling and blisters aren't as bad.

Wild Man ignores me and continues to, for all intents and purposes, eat me. There's no other word to describe what he's doing to me. He licks, bites, and sucks at every piece of flesh he can reach. I try to remember why he should stop, but what he's doing steals all of my common sense.

He releases me long enough to bite the flesh of my thigh, no doubt purposely leaving a mark behind. I've noticed he likes doing that; leaving marks on me like he's showcasing to everyone that I'm his. Even if there's no one here to see it.

My attempts to try to stop him are feeble. Wild Man may be the one who was bitten by a deadly snake, but I'm the weak one at the moment. Except for the first few times he's fucked me and I put up a fight, I've learned my willpower when it comes to his touch is non-existent. I *want* to stop him, to not give into the desire he stirs in me, but I simply don't have the will to follow through.

After an orgasm so strong that I see stars behind my closed eyelids and the tips of my fingers go numb, Wild Man sits back on his heels. He looks up my body until he meets my eyes. I should be embarrassed by the way his beard is soaked with my juices, but I can't muster the emotion. I'm still reeling from the aftershocks of my release.

My gaze slides to the wound on his arm, happy to see the swelling has gone down even more. His face is red, but I don't think it's from infection, but rather his excitement of him going down on me.

When he grabs my waist like he's going to flip me over to my hands and knees, I quickly sit up.

"Stop." I put my hands over his. "Wait."

He gives me his signature scowl. "No. You take my seed."

I ignore the apprehension the word 'seed' and what it could mean makes me feel and slap both of his hands. "I said wait," I demand resolutely.

"Female," he growls, digging his fingers into my skin.

Knocking his hands away, I scramble up to my knees. I point to the spot I was just lying. "Lie down." I see the argument waiting to come, so I add softly, "Please."

The scowl stays in place, and at first I think he's going to force me to do what he wants, but after a moment, he lays down.

I can't believe I'm getting ready to do what I am. My body may have turned against me when it comes to Wild Man fucking me, but I've never initiated the act. It's always been him.

He keeps his gaze on me as he settles down, his hands balled into fists at his sides. His cock is long and thick, lying flat against his stomach and leaks pre-cum.

Licking my suddenly dry lips, I throw one of my legs over his hips.

If he's so intent on fucking, I'll be damned if we don't do it in a position that's least likely to aggravate his injury. I didn't nurse him back to health only for him to relapse because he was horny.

He continues to watch me, his jaw clenched and his nostrils flaring, as I settle my pussy directly over the length of his cock. I don't sink down on him immediately. Instead, I slowly rock my hips back and forth, soaking his cock with my wetness.

It feels incredible. My eyes fall closed and a low moan escapes my throat. Wild Man is so hard, I feel each ridge and vein in his shaft. I gyrate my hips, enjoying the illusion of having control of my speed and the harshness in which I press against him. I'm still overly sensitive from the orgasm a few minutes ago, so I know it won't take me long to come again.

I dip my chin down and open my eyes, wanting to see Wild Man's expression. He's the one who's always in control. Taking me roughly and without constraint. Like an animal in the midst of a frenzy. I'm not under the mistaken assumption that I'm actually in control now. Even injured, Wild Man could take over at any second. I don't know why, but he's *allowing* this.

I expect to see him looking at my face, but he's not. His eyes are pinned where we're pressed against each other. The muscle in his jaw is so tight, it's a wonder he hasn't chipped a tooth. It's then that I notice the rapid rise and fall of his chest as he breathes harshly. It's his eyes though that has shivers of delight racing down my spine and my pussy clenching in need. They're pitch black and flare with the knowledge that he's barely holding onto his control. Why he's holding it back, I'm not sure, but I know he won't for long.

Leaning back and jutting out my chest, I rest my hands behind me on his thighs. A low rumbling growl comes from the back of Wild Man's throat, because I know his view just got better.

I'm depraved and should probably see a therapist for enjoying my captor's reaction so much.

I rotate my hips in circles, finding just the right rhythm to slide my clit against his hard flesh. Goosebumps rise on my arms and the muscles in my stomach contract at the sensations coursing through me.

I'm on the edge and want to fall over.

"Mmm... Wild Man," I moan deeply.

I don't know if it's my moan of pleasure or if Wild Man has just had enough, but as soon as the words leave my mouth, his firm hands are wrapped around my waist.

My head snaps down to look at him. His eyes are finally on mine. He looks enraged, but I know that's not what he's feeling. *He* probably doesn't even quite understand exactly what he's feeling. But I do. His want and need are overwhelming, almost more than he can handle.

"Inside... *now*." His tone is harsh and animalistic. The hairs on the back of my neck stand on end at his heated demand.

Sitting up, I wrap my small hand around his wet shaft and guide the head to my opening. His eyes fall back down to watch as I slowly sink down on him. I'm still not used to his size, despite the many times he's fucked me, so it takes me a few seconds to fully seat myself. I'm left deliriously full and strangely aching for me.

He hisses out a breath, his fingers digging into my waist, once I'm fully impaled on him. I lift up a couple of inches and glide back down. The tight scrape of his shaft against my inner walls has black spots dancing in my vision.

I keep my movements slow at first, taking advantage of Wild Man's temporary capitulation. I know it won't last long.

I slide up then black down, pressing my clit against the course hairs and the hardness of his pubic bone. Each time I do, the stimulation has my breath catching.

My control only lasts for a few strokes before Wild Man jack knifes to a sitting position and he takes over. His hands grip me so hard that I'll find bruises later. His growl has me shuddering. He lifts me up until just the tip of his cock is left inside. I don't have time to prepare before he pulls me back down roughly.

I cry out at the intrusion, but it's a cry of pleasure more than one of pain.

"Fuck me, Wild Man," I demand, latching my fingers around his shoulders.

He lifts me again, only to bring me back down even harder. My nipples scrape against his chest, adding to the sensations already racking my body.

"God, yes!"

I should be worried about him using his injured arm, but it's the furthest thing on my mind. All I can think about is how fucking good this feels.

Wild Man drops his head and pulls one of my nipples into his mouth. His teeth bite down, and I let out a screech. His manipulation of my body doesn't let up. He just continues to use and abuse it over and over again. He drives me up and down his cock, letting out grunts and groans as he grows closer to his release. My own release is balancing on the edge. One small push will tip me over.

It comes when he grinds me down, smashing my clit against his pubic bone.

"Wild Man!" I yell, tossing my head back with my eyes closed.

He growls, the sound sinister, savage and he stiffens below me.

If possible, I feel him grow bigger inside me seconds before the warmth of his seed fills me and he lets out a mighty roar.

---

SOMETIME LATER, AFTER WE'VE SETTLED BACK DOWN IN BED, I LAY WITH my head on Wild Man's chest. I run my fingers through the hairs over his pecs, my thoughts all over the place. The ends of my hair tickle my shoulder as Wild Man plays with the strands.

I adjust against him, and the scrape of the rope tied around my waist irritates my skin.

It's a stark reminder of why I'm here, even if my recent actions don't show it.

I'm here because Wild Man refuses to let me go. I'm here because of his unhinged obsession with me.

It makes me wonder if he would have done the same if another woman had wandered across his path. Is it *me* that he wants? Or would any female with working feminine parts do?

I feel rage when that thought crosses my mind. I want to take that stick Wild Man used to kill the snake with and jam it through an imaginary female's neck.

There are so many things wrong with that thought.

My eyes move to Wild Man's injured arm. It looks no worse for wear after our fucking. I run a fingertip just below one of the puncture wounds. The blisters are gone now and there's hardly any swelling. It still has a long way to go to fully heal, but it looks tons better than it did.

"Does it hurt?" I ask, breaking up the silence around us.

"No."

I doubt it really doesn't hurt, but Wild Man is the typical male and won't admit to it. Or maybe he just doesn't want to admit it because it might make him sound weak. Or maybe he's concerned it might worry me.

"Not first time," he says, his voice hesitant. Unless it's a one or two word sentence, his words always come out slow and stilted, like he's making sure he's using the right ones.

I tip my head down, looking past his, for once, flaccid cock, to the spot on his thigh where there's another pair of puncture wounds. I trace the small dots with a finger.

"Were your parents alive when it happened?"

"No."

My throat closes, and I blink back the tears welling in my eyes.

I clear my throat before asking my next question. "Was it the same kind of snake?"

"Yes."

*Jesus.* Twice he's survived a rattlesnake bite. Once when he was all alone with no one to care for him. Obviously, this man has a guardian angel.

I bring my hand back to his chest and run my fingers over the slash marks on his ribs.

"And this?"

"Big cat."

It takes me a moment to process what he said. Cougars and bobcats are known to be in this area. How in the hell could he have possibly survived an attack like that?

"How did you get away?"

"Big knife. Big cat became dinner."

I don't know why, but his answer nearly has laughter bubbling out of me. There's nothing amusing about the situation. It's actually quite heartbreaking and scary as shit.

"What does... fuck mean?"

The sudden change of subject and the question itself throws me for a loop. I tip my head back to look at him and find his steady black gaze on me.

How do I answer that question?

It takes me a few seconds to form a reply.

"It can mean many things." I slide my head back on his arm so I can see his face better. "An extreme reaction to something is one.

But the way I used it earlier, I was telling you to have sex with me."

"Sex? That's what we were doing?"

"Yes."

"Already having sex with you," he says, his brows pulling down.

"Yes, but I wanted you to do it harder and give me more."

"Why?"

I pause a moment. "Because fucking feels good."

This is the weirdest conversation to be having with a grown man. But then again, he was so young when he was left alone that I'm sure he never had the 'birds and the bees' talk with his parents.

"Hard sex is fucking."

Even though we just 'fucked', the way he says the word fucking has a small tingle forming between my legs. I ignore the need to rub them together.

"What is... soft sex?"

Again, his question gives me pause and it takes me a moment to come up with an answer. "Doing it slowly and softly is lovemaking."

He turns his head to stare up at the trees. "Lovemaking," he says slowly, almost with awe. He looks back down at me. "Next time we do lovemaking."

I don't know how I feel about making love to Wild Man. It's true that the term means soft and slow, but there's more that I didn't say. Making love is done with someone you care about. It involves tender emotions and done with reverence. It's looking deeply into someone's eyes while your bodies come together and feel an undeniable connection.

What I feel for Wild Man may not be the hatred I *should* feel, but it's certainly not the deep emotions that come with making love with someone.

Although, a small part of me wonders what he would be like as a gentle lover. Today was the first time he has taken me with us facing each other. All the other times have been while on my hands and knees or bent over. I hate to admit it, but I liked looking at him and seeing the way his eyes lit with desire and the tightening of his jaw when he found his release.

It's a dangerous thought to have and one I need to work at banishing from my mind.

I can't afford to develop feelings that will make leaving Wild Man hard.

Because one thing's for sure, I'm leaving the first chance I get.

*fourteen*

EVERLEE

I sit between Wild Man's legs with my back pressed against his chest. He's leaning against the log he usually sits on and we're in front of the fire as the flames cook our food. It's been a few days since I woke to Wild Man feasting between my legs, and while I know he's not fully recovered from the rattler bite and should probably rest more, he was insistent that we go find food. He chose fish this time, something I was grateful for.

Not only because I was able to bathe, but I wasn't ready to chance running across another snake. Before he went fishing, he bathed with me. Of course, bathing led to other things.

Since our conversation about lovemaking, Wild Man has tried doing it softly, but I've purposely made it impossible for him. He starts out slow, but I do something that drives the softness right out of him and he ends up taking me roughly.

He *fucks* me.

I'm not ready for soft and gentle yet. I'm not sure I ever will be.

I pick at the threads of the rope around my waist and hold up the loose part in front of our faces.

Earlier, when I came out of the tree hut after taking a nap, I found Wild Man sitting on the log. When I moved to sit across the fire from him, he ordered me to come to him. I expected him to have me sit in front of him on the ground like usual or to have me sit on his lap like I have a few times, but instead, he moved to the ground and had me sit between his legs.

"Will you take this off me?" I ask Wild Man, rolling the rope between my fingers.

He doesn't say anything at first, but I sense his eyes on the rope.

"No."

I don't know what I expected, but his flat out refusal wasn't it. I thought we had made at least a little bit of progress. You know, with me caring for him while he was practically dying. I could have easily left him while he was unconscious, but I didn't. I stayed by his side, took care of him, worried for him.

"Why not?" I ask, my tone tight from the anger slowly building in my veins.

"You leave," he grunts. He slides an immovable arm around my waist. "I won't let you go."

I smash my teeth together. There's no sense in telling him that I won't leave the first chance I get, because he probably wouldn't believe me. And leaving is exactly what I plan to do.

I may be softening toward him, and that's all the more reason to flee when I can. The longer I stay here, the deeper those feelings will root themselves inside me, and the harder it'll be to leave.

Instead, I repeat what I've already told him before and will probably repeat another hundred times. "You can't keep me forever."

"Yes," he answered resolutely. "You stay til I die. *Momor* is mine."

I don't say anything after that, because what's the point? It's obvious that when Wild Man comes to a decision, he won't be swayed from it.

It's not like the second the rope is off me, I'll take off. I won't leave until I know for sure I can get away. I'm just tired of it chafing my skin. But it would be useless to tell him that. Me being uncomfortable doesn't seem to bother him.

I keep quiet as Wild Man feeds us both the fish he cooked. He refuses to let me feed myself, preferring for me to take it from his hand with my mouth like I'm a toddler.

Whatever.

The water jug is passed to me and after taking a couple swallows, he takes it back, drinking from the same spot.

We sit for a while longer. The fire is far enough away that the heat isn't too much. The sun is still high in the sky and the birds overhead chirp. Every so often, something rustles in the brush surrounding us, and I jerk my head in the direction it comes from. I think I might have PTSD from the stupid snake.

As angry as I am at his refusal to remove the rope, I'm reluctant to admit, sitting with him like this, even in the silence, is nice.

After a while, though, I become restless, and I start squirming around. I've never been the type to sit idly by, and that's all I've been forced to do lately.

After adjusting my position for the fifth time, Wild Man grabs my hips and flips me around so I'm on my knees in front of him. I look at him wearily. I have no idea what to expect from him because he's always so unpredictable.

His legs are bent, spread out with me between them. Since he's not wearing the cloth covering, his dick dangles between his legs. He's not hard, but he's not fully soft either. His eyes trace over the features of my face, but then stops when they touch my lips.

He runs one of his hands up my arm and over my shoulder. When it reaches my neck, goosebumps erupt over my skin. His touch is caring and feather light, something a gentle lover would do. It has apprehension replacing the good feeling.

His fingers slide through my hair and he slowly tugs me toward him. With his gaze still pinned on my lips, I know what his intent is. At the last minute, just before his lips touch mine, I turn my head to the side, and they brush against my cheek. His fingers tighten in my hair, and I know he doesn't like my avoidance.

"Give me mouth," he growls, the rough sound filling my ear.

I shake my head against his tight grip. "No."

He growls again, using his grip to try to move my head where he can get to my lips. I hold steady, even when the strands of my hair threaten to snap and the sting of pain brings tears to my eyes.

"Mouth," he repeats.

I put my hands on his shoulders, digging my nails into his flesh. "No."

He's taken everything else from me and is keeping me captive. I *will not* give him something as intimate as my kiss.

"Female," he grates.

"No, Wild Man." I tug against his hold until I'm able to see his face. "You don't deserve my mouth."

His lips press into a grim line and anger tightens his eyes. I prepare myself for Wild Man to forcefully take my mouth. He could and there's really nothing I can do to stop it. I've underestimated his strength before, but I quickly learned how big of a mistake it was. What he wants, he gets, even if taken by force.

Surprisingly though, he doesn't force my head forward like I expected. Instead, after several tense moments, in which he spends looking at my mouth, he releases me so suddenly, I fall back on my ass. Thankfully, the ground is soft with crushed leaves, so I'm left no worse for wear.

He gets up from the ground and stalks through the opening, slapping the branches out of the way. It's almost comical to see his semi-hard cock slapping around his thighs with his movements.

I watch the opening with trepidation. Wild Man doesn't know how to give in, so I expect him to return at any moment and demand my kiss. But after sitting there for a while and he doesn't reappear, I finally start to relax.

I get up from the ground and look around me. I haven't gotten many chances to check out his living area. More often than not, Wild Man takes me with him when he leaves his tree hut. Or if he does leave me alone, it's not for long.

I rummage around a couple piles of stuff, finding nothing interesting. I do come across the clothes I was wearing the day he decided to keep me, and as tempting as it is to put them on, I leave them where they are. Wild Man will just take them off me. For some reason, he likes to keep me naked. Maybe because he's always naked. Or because it gives him easy access when he wants to fuck. Or maybe he just likes looking at a female body. Regardless, I make note of where they are for when I leave.

At the bottom of one pile, I come across a small stack of local newspapers. The thin pages are dirty and crumpled. I look at the date of the first one. Seven years old. I flip through it, not finding anything interesting. I look at the next one with an eight-year-old date.

*Where did he get these*, I wonder to myself as I flip through another.

When I reach the bottom of the pile, my brows jump up and my hand pauses on the cover. It's not a newspaper, but a dirty magazine.

What the hell?

The cover has a busty brunette sitting with her legs bent and spread open. She's sitting on a bed of black silk. One of her hands is holding a red popsicle that she's licking up the side. Her big perky tits with hard rose-colored nipples are on full display. Her other hand is cupping herself between her legs, hiding her goods from the viewer.

A heated flush coats my cheeks as I stare at the woman.

Why does Wild Man have this? I mean, it's obvious *why* he has it. He may have grown up in the wild, but he's still a man with working parts. But where did he get it from? And how many times has he looked at it? From the worn state of the pages, my guess would be a lot.

An image pops in my head and the heat in my cheeks gets warmer. Wild Man sitting on his log in front of the fire, one hand flipping through the pages of this magazine, while his other strokes up and down his cock. His breathing is heavy as his eyes eat up the images of carnal acts. Why that thought has my legs sliding together is a mystery I refuse to acknowledge.

I lift my head and peek at the opening he left through a bit ago. Curiosity gets the best of me, and I flip the magazine open to a random page. I've looked at nudie magazines before, and have even watched my fair share of porn, but it still feels erotic doing it now. I don't even know *why* I'm doing it. I guess I want to see what Wild Man has possibly gotten himself off to.

The picture is of a naked blonde woman lying in bed. Her head is hanging off the edge, her long hair touching the floor. A man, equally naked, is in front of her with his hard cock pointed at her lips. Her mouth is wide open as she waits for the man to feed it to her. Another man is on the bed holding her legs open. Her hips are lifted and his cock is nestled inside her. He stares down at where they're connected with a look of pure lust.

Warmth pools in my stomach at the erotic image.

I flip to another page.

This one is even kinkier.

A redhead woman, again wearing not a stitch of clothes, has her arms raised above her head where she's tied to a hook in the ceiling. She has on a blindfold and a ball gag stuffed in her mouth. There's a man behind her, his hips pressed to her ass, no doubt filling her back hole. One of his hands is on her hip and the other is pulling her head back by her hair. Another man stands in front of her, his hand wrapped around his impressive length. He looks like he's getting ready to stuff his cock in her clean-shaven pussy.

A rustling sound comes from behind me, and I snap the magazine closed. Embarrassment reddens my cheeks more as I spin around and face Wild Man. He stands just inside the opening, his pointed gaze on me. His eyes drop to the magazine in my hand before they lift back to my face. He shows no discomfort at my discovering his dirty magazine, not that I expected him to.

I drop the magazine when he starts walking toward me. Again, I don't know what to expect from him, and his face gives nothing away. He stops when he's only a foot from me, forcing my head to tilt back to keep him in view.

He grabs my hand and lifts it, and I feel something slide over my wrist. I look down, and I'm not quite sure what to think at what I find.

A delicate twig, no thicker than a piece of twine has been fashioned into a bracelet. Woven into the twig are tiny lavender flowers.

I lift my arm, a sudden pain scratching the insides of my chest at the kind gesture. In my boredom, I've made several twig bracelets. I used to do that all the time when I was out camping with my dad and brothers. While they were out fishing, hunting, or gathering wood, I'd sit and fashion bracelets. They were never really anything special, just something to do when I didn't want to join my family while they foraged the area.

This one is beautifully perfect though.

I tilt my head back up. Is this his way of apologizing after storming away from me earlier?

If so, he's definitely on the right track.

"Thank you," I say.

"Fuck."

The word is barely past his lips before he's grabbing my waist and lifting me up. My legs automatically go around his waist, and a moan slips out of me when his hardness encounters my softness.

Without another word, he carries me to his bed, and we do what he said.

We fuck.

*fifteen*

EVERLEE

As you can probably guess, Wild Man likes sex. He likes *a lot* of sex. Doesn't matter where we are, what we're doing, or the time of day. If he becomes randy, he pounces.

Take yesterday for instance, while we were out picking berries. I was down on my knees trying to reach a nice juicy patch of plump blackberries. Of course, I was naked—he still refuses to give me clothes, the bastard—so my wiggling bare ass was up in the air. The next thing I knew, big hands were gripping my hips and pulling me back, angling me where he wanted me. I knew what was coming, and I opened my mouth to tell him I wasn't ready— seriously, who would be while picking berries and getting poked by thorns—but my protest died on a cry of sharp pain. No prepara- tion. He just went for it as usual. And I was as dry as Sister Mary. So the sudden intrusion wasn't comfortable in the slightest, and I couldn't imagine it was much better for him. Did he care, though? Nope. He just kept going, banging me as hard as he could.

Thankfully—or not thankfully, depending on how you look at it—it didn't take long to get my juices flowing. That's what happens when you're unbelievably attracted to the man who's holding you captive. Your body gives your mind a big fuck you, along with the middle finger, and takes what it wants, even begging for more or to go faster, harder.

Another time, we were walking back from taking a bath. I was admiring a patch of pretty flowers and telling Wild Man a funny story about Rika. I was laughing and having a surprisingly good time, when my hips were suddenly caught in his hard grip. I was shoved over a large boulder, my breast pressed against the abrasive surface. Then he mounted me from behind and fucked me silly. That time, I was wet. He had just fucked me in the water, and I still had part of him leaking out of me.

Several times a day, I find myself on my hands and knees or bent over, and since the time I rode him after his snake bite, a few times he's demanded I repeat the act in the same position. That's the only position I get to see his face when we fuck. We never do it missionary, but I think it's because he doesn't know about that position. I have to admit, face-to-face is my favorite. I like seeing the intensity in his eyes as I move up and down on his cock or grind my pussy against his groin. The way they flare and heat, like having me like that is a wonder to him. It usually doesn't last very long though. When he gets to the point of losing control, he tosses me back, manhandles me so I'm on my knees, and rams his full length inside me roughly. It's those occurrences when I come the hardest. A sick part of me loves when he loses control and dominates me. I like seeing his handprints on my thighs and hips. I like when he slams inside me so hard my teeth jolt and blackness dances at the edge of my vision. I like when he bites my neck and squeezes my throat until my vision goes dim.

Maybe I'm a masochist.

Right now, we're both lying in his bed after having one of those intense fuckings. My heart has just settled down and my breathing is back to normal. Sweat coats both of our bodies. Wild Man is on his back and I have my head on his shoulder. His fingers slide through the ends of my hair. One of my hands is on his chest, and my eyes catch on another bracelet he made and gave to me a few days ago. I've gotten plenty of gifts from guys over the years. Some expensive and some not. It cost Wild Man nothing to make these bracelets and they're so simple, but they're honestly the sweetest gifts anyone has ever given me.

I tilt my head back to look up at Wild Man. His eyes are open and he's looking at the canopy of trees above us. The dark hair on his face is thick, tempting me to run my fingers through it. I have a couple of times and surprisingly, although coarse, the hair is also kind of soft.

"What's your name?" I ask. I've been wondering this since the first moment I met him. It's become normal to call him Wild Man and he answers to the nickname. But I want to know what his real name is.

He dips his chin into his chest so his eyes can meet mine. A line appears on his forehead, as if he's thinking hard about my question.

"Fey."

"Fey," I repeat the name, my brows dropping. That can't be right. It has to be a shortened version of something. Maybe his parents gave him Fey as a nickname and he can't remember his full name. I try to think of something that would constitute such a nickname, but come up short.

I say it again aloud, this time slower. "Fey."

The word has barely left my lips when Wild Man bucks up from his lying position and he hovers above me, his body wedged between my thighs. His face is so close, I have to nearly cross my eyes to look at him. Beneath his beard, his jaw his tense and a muscle works in his cheek.

He looks angry, and I don't understand why. Is it because he doesn't like me using his real name?

When he speaks, it's a low growl. "Again."

My brows pucker, and it's then that I realize he doesn't hate me saying his name. He likes it. And from the fierce expression on his face, he likes it a lot.

"Fey."

His lips tighten, and I swear if eyes could light someone on fire, I'd be a pile of ashes right now.

He drops his head, his eyes intent on my mouth. Right before his lips meet mine, I turn my head to the side.

Nope. Still not ready to give him that. The act of kissing is far too intimate. He hasn't earned the right to my lips, and I'm not sure he ever will. Not when he's still holding me captive, literally tied to him, and forcing me to stay naked.

Wild Man growls, the sound harsh. I couldn't care less if it angers him. He can go suck a big dick.

It's the same dog and dance as the other time he tried kissing me. When he grips my hair and tries to force my head where he can get to my lips, I hold steady, feeling a couple of strands of hair pop from their follicles.

"Mouth," he grunts.

"No."

He drops his head closer and his heated breath fans over my cheek. "Mouth."

"I said no," I reply forcefully.

I feel his glare on the side of my face, and I ignore it.

After a moment, his lips press against my cheeks, and I'm once again surprised he doesn't force his kiss on me. I don't know why, but it's like he wants me to give it willingly.

His lips slide to my ear and he pulls the lobe between his teeth. He releases it a second later.

"Your mouth, mine."

He can think my lips are his all he wants, but it doesn't change the fact that I will never willingly kiss him. Not in our current situation anyway.

After his words of possession, he uses his fists against the bed and jackknifes up. My eyes follow his movements as he stalks out of the enclosure. It takes me a few minutes to calm my racing heart. As much as I want to keep from kissing him, a small part of me wonders what it would be like to have his mouth against mine. I don't want that curiosity in my head. It would be so much easier to continue to deny him if it wasn't something I secretly crave.

I push those thoughts away and get up. I expect Wild Man to have left the tree hut, so I'm surprised when I find him near the fire pit. I eye him warily as I make my way over to the water jug. I adjust the rope around my waist when the coarse hairs irritate my skin. I've gotten used to having it around my waist, so for the most part, it doesn't bother me anymore. Is it possible to get calluses around your waist?

I pick up one of the mint leaves from a small stack and wrap it around my pointer finger. Opening my mouth, I gently rub it against my teeth. A few days after Wild Man first took me, he showed me how to use the leaves to clean my teeth. While it's not the same as brushing your teeth, I'll definitely take it over not cleaning them at all.

After I'm done, I take a mouthful of water and squish it around my mouth before spitting it out onto the ground, then swallow another mouthful. My mouth isn't as fresh as if using a toothbrush, toothpaste, and mouthwash, but I'll take it.

Once that's over, I walk over to Wild Man. He waits for me, an expectant look on his face. I flick the rope out of my way and sit on his thigh where he'll hand feed me. He still won't let me feed myself. I feel like a fucking toddler being fed by her parent. But seeing the enjoyment on Wild Man's face, I know how much he likes doing it—and for some asinine reason, I like giving him pleasure. At least in this regard—so I don't complain.

After feeding me several bites of fruit and dried meat, he picks up a piece for himself. Before he can bring it to his mouth, I reach out and snatch the piece of meat from him. I hold it up to his lips. He doesn't immediately open, so I look him in the eye with a raised brow. I watch in amazement when after several seconds, his lips twitch at the corners and amusement enters his eyes.

I don't know why he finds the notion of me feeding him amusing, but I can't think of that right now. All I can focus on is the pleasure lines by his eyes and the way the black orbs seem to sparkle with his amusement. I realize I want to see him laugh. I want to see a grin split across his face.

I give my head a little shake, not wanting, nor needing, those thoughts to fill my head. I push the meat closer to his mouth and he parts his lips. After I drop the food inside, I try to pull my fingers free, but Wild Man grabs my wrist. He holds my fingers in his mouth and swirls his tongue around the tips. Once. Twice. Three times before he lets me slip my fingers out.

My heart thumps in my chest and the muscles in my upper thighs twitch.

Jesus, the way this man can so easily get my motor running is pathetic.

Realizing the mistake I made by offering to feed him, I let my hand fall to my lap. When I don't reach for more of the food, Wild Man's brows pinch together and his arm tightens around my waist.

"More," he grunts.

I let out a small sigh, knowing it's pointless to deny him when he'll just make me do it anyway. I pinch a piece of fruit between my fingers and bring it to his lips. I try my best to not let it affect me, but I can't help the tiny thrill I get when his greedy lips pull it from my fingers, the glow of pleasure in his eyes growing.

This continues, him feeding me and me feeding him, for a while. We both watch the other, our expressions turning more and more heated. When I barely catch myself from squirming on his lap, I know I need a distraction.

"Do you remember your parents?" I ask after I swallow the berry Wild Man just popped into my mouth.

The lustful look in his eyes dims some with my question. He

brings his fingers to his lips and licks off the black juice from the berry before he answers.

"Little."

His words are coming easier and less stilted now that I've gotten him to talk more.

"Can you tell me about them?"

He doesn't say anything at first, his eyes appearing unfocused as he looks across the way. I follow his gaze to the pile of random things on the ground. A lot of it are regular things a person might have. A few books, the nudie magazines I came across the other day, some utensils and plastic containers, some small broken down cardboard boxes, an old boombox style radio that probably no longer works, and a few other odds and ends.

I get the feeling that all of it must have belonged to his parents.

"Noeny had long red hair," he says quietly. "She would—" he pauses for a moment, as if searching for a word. "—braid it. She liked when I played with it."

I smile. That must be why he likes touching my hair. His mother liked it, so he figured I would too, which I do. It's relaxing.

"Her eyes blue. When she laughed, she had bright stars in eyes."

A knot forms in my throat at the way he talks about her.

"And your dad?" I ask, having to clear my throat before I speak.

His gaze moves back to me. "He was big man. Very strong. Lot of muscles."

He says this with pride.

My eyes move to his chest. The dark hair covering his torso does nothing to hide the muscles beneath it.

"Muscles like you?"

At my question, he does the most normal thing I've seen him do so far. He grunts and rolls his eyes. "Mine bigger." As if to prove his point, he flexes his pecs.

I laugh. "You're such a typical man."

149

His expression turns serious as he watches my face. When his eyes drop to my mouth, I flatten my lips.

"Tell me more," I request, hoping to distract him. I don't want to fight with him right now, and from the intent look in his eyes, I know he's thinking about the kiss I refuse to give him.

Luckily, he takes the bait.

"Peepa was good mate. He protected Noeny and me all the time. Noeny was good mate too. She made him happy. Sometimes, they would stand with arms around each other and move around."

"Do you mean dance?"

"Dance." He says the word slowly. "Yes. Dance. Sometimes Noeny dance with me."

I move my arm around his shoulder and rest my side against his chest. "That's so sweet."

"Sweet. Noeny very sweet. Peepa said she sweet when he press his mouth to hers."

Despite the sore subject of kissing, I can't help but smile at that.

Wild Man gets really quiet and his arm tightens around my waist. His other hand lifts and his fingers delve through my hair. His palm is so big that the pad of his thumb swipes across my cheek, the tip close to the corner of my mouth. I can't help but stare at him. The way he's looking at me has my core clenching at the same time a knot of dread forms in the pit of my stomach.

"Are you sweet, *momor*?" he murmurs so quietly that I barely hear him.

There's that word again. *Momor*. I don't know what it means, but I like the way it sounds coming from his lips.

"I will know your lips," he continues, the tenor in his voice deepening, seducing me. "I will know your taste. You will know my taste." He swipes his thumb across my top lip, then my bottom. "These are mine." His eyes lift to mine, and fuck me sideways and upside down, the possessive look in them is harsher and more demanding than I've ever seen them. "You understand?"

My first reaction is to nod numbly, to agree without question due to the way he's fiercely watching and waiting for my acceptance. Anything to keep that look in his eyes. Like I'm the only thing he'll ever need to keep living.

But that's not what I do. I barely manage to stubbornly hold onto my resolve. I won't change my mind about this, no matter how fucking delicious he looks right now.

I hate that our easy, light-hearted moment is over and is replaced by something so controversial.

I keep my tone light as I lean toward him until only an inch separates our mouths. I pronounce each word slowly. "Fuck. You."

A salacious grins pulls up his lips, and I know he's taken my words for a different meaning than what I intended.

"No. *I* fuck *you*. Hard and fast."

*sixteen*

EVERLEE

As I squat with my ass inches from the ground, I try my best to ignore the man in front of me as he aims his pee stream to splash over mine.

I've lost track of how long I've been with Wild Man, but it has to be at least a few weeks. In all that time, I'm still not used to him doing this. It kind of freaks me out every time he does it, but it's also—and I'll carry this to my grave before I admit it out loud— kind of a turn on. I am in no way shape or form into the whole watersports kink—not dissing those who are, to each their own— so it's not like I want him to urinate *on* me. It's the reason *why* he does it that does shit to my body.

At least Wild Man affords me more privacy when I have to go number two. Of course, I gave him no choice in the matter the few times I had to go. There was no way I was shitting in front of him.

I stay squatted for several more seconds to let myself drip dry. Toilet paper is a luxury I'll never take for granted again when I get out of this place.

*If* I ever do, my mind adds.

Wild Man's expression is blank, but his eyes are watchful of our surroundings when I get up. It's like he's keeping an eye out for any predators.

"Why do you do that?" I ask.

He directs his gaze at me. "What?"

I throw my finger to the spot we just peed.

"To cover scent," he replies, giving me the answer I assumed. See? Who wouldn't shiver at such protectiveness? I bet you just did. "To keep others away," he adds.

He turns, keeping his eyes on me until I fall into step beside him.

"What others?"

"Creatures."

"So, not people then? Just animals?"

He looks at me, his eyes flinty. "People too."

I stay quiet for a moment. Wild Man's steps are silent. Mine, not so much. I still haven't perfected the art of walking light-footed.

"You do realize that masking my scent won't work on people, right? It doesn't work that way with humans."

Surely he has to know that. People don't have super sniffer noses like animals do.

Wild Man abruptly stops and faces me. "*I* keep people away. *I* protect."

I take a step back from him at the look that enters his eyes. It's a hard look. One that shows just how dangerous he can be if he or something that belongs to him is threatened.

I don't reply, and he doesn't wait for me to, before he's turning around and resumes walking. I wait for him to take a couple of steps before I follow him.

We just left the waterfall. One good thing about Wild Man? He likes to bathe a lot. I'm a shower every day type of girl, sometimes twice, so my little heart is happy that he bathes every day as well.

Instead of leading me back to his tree hut, we head in a

different direction, one we've never taken before. The growth gets denser and denser, which makes it harder to avoid stepping on pointy things. My feet have toughened up, but it still hurts like hell when I step on a hidden pine cone.

"Ow," I mutter, glaring down at the prickly thing.

I lift my foot, seeing the little indents through the dirt. So much for taking a bath and having clean feet.

Wild Man stops and glances at me over his shoulder. When he sees my lifted foot, he walks back to me. He bends and scoops me up like a husband would his new bride. I always found the gesture romantic and swoon-worthy when a man does that to his woman.

I would have never pegged Wild Man as the romantic type, but in many ways, he is. It's just his type of romance is more raw, rougher.

I wrap my arm around his shoulders and lay my head on his chest, my face close to his throat. I take a deep breath and his earthy musky scent fills my senses.

"Thank you," I say and lay a kiss against his neck.

"Foot hurt?" he asks.

He carries me so easily, like I weigh next to nothing.

"I'm okay." I finger a lock of his hair. "Where are we going?"

"You see."

I sigh and relax more in his arms. It's amazing how safe I feel with him. The man who's hurt me in unimaginable ways makes me feel protected and adored. Who would have thought?

After trekking through the thick forest for a while, I lift my head when it starts to clear. My breath catches in my throat at the beauty that comes into view. I would have never guessed that something like this would exist in this part of the wilderness.

We're in a field with hardly any trees. The ground is covered with a multitude of brightly-colored wildflowers. Purples, oranges, blues, yellows, almost every color under the rainbow.

"Wow," I breathe, my head moving to and fro, taking in the magnificence of it all. "This is beautiful."

Wild Man keeps walking. I want to tell him to stop because I know with each step he takes, he's trampling the flowers beneath his feet. There's a big tree with low hanging branches about fifty feet away and that's where he's headed. As we get closer to it, I notice something on the ground. It's not until we're under the canopy of branches that I realize it's two piles of rocks. The rocks are about the size of two of my fists combined.

Wild Man sets me down on my feet. My gut twists when I step closer to them, instinctively knowing what they are.

Wild Man confirms my suspicions when he says gruffly, "Noeny and Peepa."

My throat closes, and I blink back the tears wanting to form. I walk to the bottom of one pile and set my hand on a rock. I feel Wild Man behind me.

"Peepa."

Wild Man is the strongest man I know. While he's shown his strength physically, the mental strength he has is astronomical. I don't know of a single person who could have endured what he has and come out on top. To have witnessed his parents gruesome death by a wild animal, somehow survived the same animal, buried his parents, all at such a young age, and then to have continued to survive in the wild is a feat I'm not sure anyone else could have accomplished. I am in complete awe of the man.

After gently running a finger over a rock on the second pile, I come to a stand and turn to face Wild Man. His gaze is focused on the pile of rocks where his mother is buried. His expression is blank, but I can see the pain lurking in his black gaze. No matter how many years have passed and how old you get or how strong a person is, the death of a parent will forever remain painful.

I walk up to Wild Man and slip my arms around his waist. Turning my head, I lay it against his chest. His strong and steady heartbeat meets my ear. He wraps his arms around me, holding me against him. I feel the telltale tug of my hair that tells me he's fingering a lock, Again, I have to work hard to keep my tears at bay.

I press a kiss on the center of his sternum and tilt my head back so I can look at him. "Thank you for bringing me here," I say quietly. "You know your parents would be so proud of you, right?"

He grunts and says nothing else.

"They would," I insist. I run my hands up and down his back. "What you've done, survived out here on your own, is amazing. I don't know of anyone else who could have. Not someone so young."

He looks over my head at his parent's graves, a frown pulling his brows down.

"Why did you keep their skulls?" I ask and he gives me back his attention.

"Keep them with me. Watch over me." His voice is gruff.

Between his emotional tone and his words, my heart breaks anew.

"I bet they're up in Heaven right now looking down at you. I bet they both have smiles on their faces as they watch over their brave boy."

"Heaven?" he asks with curiosity.

"The place where people go when they die. They go to Heaven and watch over the people they've left behind. And sometimes they send people to their loved ones so they aren't sad anymore."

He's silent as he processes my words, but his fingers continue playing with my hair. Then his expression turns thoughtful as he gazes down at me. His next words change my life irrevocably and seals my fate.

"They sent you to me. Noeny and Peepa gave me you, so I won't be alone."

## seventeen

EVERLEE

After that life-altering statement, I forced myself to look away from him. I didn't want him to see what his words did to me. The magnitude of their meaning and how it destroyed the rest of my resistance against him. And I knew if he looked into my eyes, he would see it.

We stayed at Wild Man's parents' burial site for a while. He found a spot against the tree beside their graves and he pulled me down between his legs. We didn't talk much. Just a few words here and there.

When we do leave, we do so with our hands locked together. Wild Man walks slowly so I'm able to easily keep up with him without shredding my feet. I kind of want him to carry me again. I liked being in his arms.

We're not far from the tree hut when a branch snaps to our left. Hearing random sounds in the forest isn't uncommon, but I've grown accustomed to knowing what to listen for. A twig snapping isn't a bird flying off or a little harmless critter scurrying away.

Wild Man and I both spin around at the same time, and I'm shoved behind him. I peek around his shoulder. Something thick wedges in my throat and fear spikes through my veins when I see a big dark-gray wolf standing not ten feet away from us. He's standing on all four legs and the sides of his mouth are raised, showing off long gleaming white teeth. Although the growl coming from the thing is barely discernible, the sound is ominous.

My first thought is to grab Wild Man's hand and start running, which is stupid, right? I mean, the wolf would catch us and maul us to death with his huge teeth in two-point five seconds. I'm pretty sure there is no outrunning a wolf.

I don't know what to do when faced with a wolf. Do you run? Stay still. Drop to the ground in a submissive position? Try to intimate it?

My first instinct is to not move. Wolves are alpha creatures. I would think intimidation would anger them.

I grab Wild Man's hand in a death grip, scared down to my bones.

We stay that way for several moments. Us eyeing the wolf while he continues to stare at us. Surprisingly, the wolf stays where he is and even stops growling.

Then the idiot at my side does something stupid. He peels my fingers from his hand and takes a step forward.

I want to screech at him and ask what he's doing. Maybe living in the wild really *has* made him crazy.

I don't yell, but I do hiss. "What are you doing?" I'm desperate to reach out and snatch him back to me.

For all the attention he gives my question, it's like he doesn't even hear me. He just keeps walking. I look from him to the wolf, and my eyes turn to saucers when I find him sitting on his haunches, no longer in a threatening pose.

Wild Man doesn't stop until he's right in front of the wolf. I tense, unsure of what I'm preparing to do. Part of me wants to run toward Wild Man and drag him back—which is asinine because the animal could finish me off with one bite and still attack Wild Man. The sane part, the part that has a hole wanting to rip through my chest because it means leaving Wild Man to fend for himself, urges me to run in the opposite direction.

Instead of doing either, I stand there in stupefaction as Wild Man reaches his hand out and lays it on top of the wolf's head. And the wolf does *nothing*! He just sits there and allows it.

*What in the ever-loving hell?*

Wild Man steps aside to stand beside the wolf, his eyes coming to me. "Come meet Teeja."

I swallow through a dry throat, trying to gather some saliva to coat my mouth. I slowly shake my head, still afraid to make any sudden movements. "No thanks."

Wild Man's lips twitch behind his beard. "It's okay. He won't hurt you."

I eye the wolf wearily and find his bright blue gaze on me. If I didn't know any better, I'd say he's watching me with curiosity.

I shake my head again. "Still no thanks."

"Come, *momor*." He leaves the animal's side and walks to me. He grabs my hand and begins tugging me forward. "Teeja is curious about you."

I dig my heels into the leafy ground and try to pull my hand free. "I really don't want—"

I cut myself off because the wolf begins walking toward us and my fear has mounted to epic proportions. He seems friendly enough with Wild Man, but that doesn't mean he won't try to bite my head off when he gets close enough.

The wolf stops right in front of us. I lock my shaky legs in place and hold my breath when he tips his head back and his eyes meet mine. I'm reluctant to admit, the wolf has beautiful eyes, crystal blue like the sky. They look too inquisitive to belong to an animal.

Teeja drops his snout and the first place it goes is to the juncture between my legs. It wouldn't be as bad if I had clothes on, but I'm vulnerably naked. I let out a little squeak and my hand in Wild Man's tightens, my nails digging into his skin. I clench my thighs together, feeling really fucking uncomfortable in more ways than one at the moment.

The wolf's snout twitches, and I feel a blast of warm breath fan across my thighs and other parts.

"Relax," Wild Man says beside me. "He's scenting my mark."

Scenting his mark? Like I'm some fucking animal or something.

Thankfully, the wolf only gives me a couple more sniffs before he moves his attention away. His nose moves down my legs to my knees before moving upward. He sniffs my stomach, and the animal is so large his head almost reaches my breasts.

After a moment, his wet nose butts against my balled-up fist and he lets out a huff of air. I hold still, not daring to move a muscle in case he wants to chomp my hand off and use it for a chew toy.

"*Momor*." I hear Wild Man speak, but I don't tear my focus off the wolf. Teeja is what he called him. "He won't hurt. Wants your touch."

My touch? I'm not touching a fucking wolf. A *wild* wolf at that.

Teeja nudges my hand again and tips his head back, looking at me like he's expecting something.

"You want Teeja to think you don't like him?"

I grit my teeth at Wild Man's manipulative cajoling.

It's not out of fear of offending the animal that has me eventually slowly lifting my hand. What softens my heart is when Teeja's tongue slips out the side of his mouth over his long teeth and he begins panting. It almost looks like he's smiling at me, which is ridiculous. Animals don't smile, but I swear Teeja is.

My muscles are solid as I lift my hand and cautiously slide my fingers through the hair on top of his head between his ears. It's surprisingly soft and very thick. I relax a little when Teeja seems to enjoy my caress.

Never in a million years would I have thought I would ever pet a wild wolf.

I feel Wild Man come closer, his naked body—except for the cloth covering his groin—pressed against the side of mine. I look at him, a small smile sliding across my face.

"He's beautiful," I state. "Is he... your pet?"

Lines form beside his eyes, showing his amusement at my question. "Teeja, a pet? No creatures in forest are pets. Especially Teeja. Too wild and free."

I look back down at the wolf, my fingers still gliding through his thick hair. Teeja still watches me inquisitively, and I have to agree with Wild Man. This animal would never allow himself to be a person's pet.

After a few moments of me petting Teeja, he suddenly stands and turns away from us. He takes several steps before he looks over his shoulder.

"Come." Wild Man grabs my hand. "We follow."

Teeja trots ahead of us and we trail behind him. It's not long before we round a small group of trees surrounded by thick bushes. Remember me mentioning my heart melting a few minutes ago? Now it's a soggy puddle of goo sloshing around in my chest.

Right in front of us, only a few feet away, is another gorgeous wolf. Solid white, as bright as snow, except for a jet black patch surrounding the wolf's left eye and ear. What makes her more unique are her eyes. One is just as black as the patch, while the other is a blue so light it almost looks clear.

But it's not that wolf that brings a silly grin to my face. It's the four bushy-tailed pups that are playfully sniping at each other. They look to be no more than a couple months old.

My hand goes to my chest. "Oh my, God. They're so precious."

I look over at Wild Man, but he's not looking at the pups. His gaze is on me. I quickly move my eyes away. The way he's looking at me makes things happen in my stomach. Like he's just as mesmerized with me as I am with the pups.

"Teeja's been gone. I thought this why."

"What's her name?"

"Vena."

"Vena," I murmur the name.

My eyes move back to the pups. I laugh when one wiggles his butt, his bushy tail swaying, before leaping on one of its siblings.

I want to run my fingers through their thick pelt of hair, but I'm not sure Teeja or Vena would appreciate it. Wolves can be very protective of their mates and offsprings.

As if sensing my thoughts, Teeja trots to one of the pups, a dark gray with a few lighter gray stripes, and latches his teeth into the scruff of his neck. He picks the pup up and carries it over to me, dropping the small bundle of fur right at my feet.

I look at Wild Man expectantly, hoping I'm not reading the situation wrong and Teeja is giving me permission to touch his pup.

"Go ahead."

I move slowly as I get down on my knees. I don't even notice when the rough ground scrapes against my skin. I hold my hand out first, letting the pup take a sniff. A small laugh escapes me when its tongue darts out to swipe across the back of my hand.

The pup's fur is soft when I lay my hand on the top of his head. It jumps up so its front paws are on my legs, lifting its head to peer up at me. I scratch it between its ears, which it seems to like.

Two of the other pups come bounding over, nudging the one I'm touching out of their way, as if saying it's their turn for some attention. I can't help but laugh, feeling lighter than I have in weeks.

Wild Man squats down beside me, lifting his own hand for the pups to smell before petting them.

One of them stays back, sitting on its haunches between Vena's legs. It looks smaller than the others and its coat is almost identical to Vena's, except its black patch of fur is a line between its eyes. I hold my hand out toward it, but it doesn't move closer. Vena looks down at the pup, and after a moment, drops her head and nudges her. It falls forward, and when it still doesn't move toward me, Teeja walks over and gives it a nudge with his nose. As if reluctant, the pup takes slow steps toward me. My heart softens even more. I want to scoop the poor thing up and cuddle it against my chest.

It stops just within reach, as if scared to get too close. I keep my hand steady and let the pup touch its nose to the back of it. After what seems like minutes, it finally moves closer. I gently lay my hand on top of its head, right over the black patch of fur.

"Did you give Teeja and Vena their names?" I ask Wild Man. The pup loses its weariness and flops to its back. With a laugh, I begin scratching its belly.

"Yes."

One of the pups starts attacking Teeja's legs, letting out tiny growls.

"Can I name the pups?"

"If you like."

Happiness swarms in my stomach.

"First I need to figure out who the males and females are."

Wild Man pats the head of the pup closest to him. "This one male." He points to the one trying to gnaw off Teeja's back leg. "That one male." He points to one who's attacking his own tail. "And that one."

I look down at the no-longer skittish one. "And this one?"

"Female."

"So, three boys and one girl," I comment and look down at the little female pup staring up at me with curious eyes from her back. "I believe I'll call you Devika."

"Devika?"

163

I glance up at Wild Man at the inquisitive note in his voice. "Yes. It means little goddess."

The corners of his eyes crinkle and a small smile curves his lips. "Good name."

For unknown reasons, his praise has pleasure coursing through me, and I can't help but grin at him.

My attention is stolen when I hear a high-pitched yelp. The pup who was attacking Teeja is down on his stomach. His tail wags a mile a minute as he stares up at his father, who's also on his stomach, staring back at him as if daring him to attack. I laugh when the pup suddenly bounces up and jumps on Teeja's back. Teeja rolls, taking the pup with him until the pup is on his back with Teeja's front paw on his stomach. He playfully nips the pup's ear.

"And his name is Drefan, which means trouble."

Wild Man chuckles as we both watch the two playfully fight. "Good."

I look at the gray pup who's still chasing his tail. "He will be called Khelan."

"Which means...?"

"Playful."

"This one?" he asks, stroking the ears of the gray and black wolf pup who's fallen asleep.

It takes me a moment to find the right name, but then it pops in my head. "Nemu. It means sleep."

Vena trots over to me, and I run my fingers over the top of her head. Teeja watches, paying no attention to Drefan, who's currently chewing on his father's tail.

"Such a pretty girl," I murmur softly to the female.

After a few pats, she goes to Teeja and plops down beside him, resting her head on her front paws.

I bring my attention back to Devika and smile down at the little pup.

LATER THAT NIGHT, WE'RE BACK IN WILD MAN'S TREE HUT. HE SITS ON the log, and I'm between his legs on the ground with my head resting on his thigh. Our bellies are full from the meat and fruit we just ate. My eyes drift closed from the relaxing way Wild Man softly sifts his fingers through my hair. I love when he plays with my hair.

The leaves rustle across the fire and my tired eyes open to find Teeja laying on the other side with his family. They came back with us and we shared our food with them. The meat, at least.

Wild Man slides his fingers more fully through my hair, and I lift my head to look at him. I immediately recognize the look in his eyes.

Blatant desire and need.

It doesn't surprise me since he's only taken me once today, and that was hours ago when we first woke up.

His fingers flex in my hair and he tilts my head back. His other hand, which I only now realize is stroking his cock, angles the head toward my lips.

"Open, *momor*," he demands huskily. "Suck."

I open my mouth. Not because he ordered me to, but because I *want* to taste him. I *want* his cock to slide between my lips. I want to feel the head nudge the back of my throat. For him to grab my hair and guide my movements. I haven't taken his cock in my mouth yet, but I've thought about it often.

A pearly drop of pre-cum clings to the tip, so I stick my tongue out and flick it across the slit. Giving head has never been high on my list of things I like to do during foreplay, but it's different with Wild Man. I liked the way he tasted the few times I've sucked his cum off his fingers. Maybe it's from all the fruit he eats, but there's a slight sweetness to him.

A deep rumble comes from him and his fingers tighten in my hair. "More," he groans. "Take more."

I open my mouth wider and he slides in a couple of inches. I turn on my knees so I'm fully facing him and lay one of my hands on his thigh. I move my other hand to cup his balls, lightly scraping my nails over the sensitive skin. He grunts and his hips lift.

"Good mate," he growls.

I grow slick between my legs at his praise. A psychiatrist would have a field day with me if I were to ever sit down in front of one.

I take him deeper. He's so big that my lips are stretched around his girth as wide as they'll go. I slide my mouth off his shaft until just the tip is inside and flick my tongue over the slit, pressing against the little hole.

"*Momor,*" Wild Man growls, shoving his hips upward, trying to force my head down to take more of himself inside. "Fuck mouth. Hard and deep."

His words have a flood of liquid seeping out of me.

I dig my nails into his thigh and lightly squeeze his balls, my actions telling him I'm the one in control at the moment. I want to tease and torment him. To drive his need so high he loses control and forces his will on me.

Desperate for some type of touch between my legs, I shift my bottom half over until I'm straddling one of his outstretched legs. I sink down and moan around his shaft when my pussy makes contact with his shin. The coarse hairs on his leg adds to the stimulation. I rock my hips up and down, soaking his leg with my juices.

I hum when the head of his cock hits the back of my throat. When I tighten the muscles, attempting to swallow, he lets out a low hiss.

I wrap my hand around the base of his cock that's not in my mouth and slide it up and down the exposed part. I take him in fully and slide him back out over and over again. Slobber slides from between my lips and coats my chin. I keep up a steady rhythm against his leg as I continue to fuck him with my mouth.

Wild Man's hands in my hair become painful when he suddenly shoves my head down, wedging his cock in my throat. He groans and grunts, the sound barely discernible over the gagging sounds I make.

His thrust become brutal and savage. He pulls my head down at the same time he thrusts upward. Tears leak down my cheeks and slobber slides out the edges of my mouth. Both hands are in my hair now and he uses the strands to pull my mouth away until just the head is left inside. I tighten my lips around his girth, flicking the slit with the tip of my tongue. I'm rewarded when another drop of pre-cum seeps out. I greedily swallow it down.

"Love mouth," Wild Man snarls. "More, *momor*. Deeper."

He pulls me down his shaft while lifting his hips. More of his length slips inside my throat, activating my gag reflex again, which only makes him thrust faster and his growls of pleasure to become deeper, more animalistic.

It fuels my own desire, and I fuck my pussy harder against his leg.

This time when he pulls my head back, I let his cock fall out of my mouth. I immediately go for the twin balls below. I lap at them, then pull one in my mouth, sucking gently.

"*Momor*," he grates.

I suck the other in my mouth and move my fingers down to his perineum, where I gently massage the sensitive muscle. His thighs tense and he lets out a deep groan.

I move back to his cock. I look up at Wild Man as I slip the tip back in my mouth. His jaw is tense and his eyes blaze fire. As I take him all the way to the back of my throat, I move my finger at his perineum further back. My fingers are soaked with my slobber, and I use some of it when I press my finger against his anus. He stiffens and his fingers tighten in my hair, but he doesn't stop me. I apply light pressure and the tip slips inside.

I've never played with a man's asshole before, but Rika says some men find it highly erotic and can have one hell of an orgasm with the correct stimulation.

When I push more of my finger inside, Wild Man pulls my mouth off his cock then forcefully jams it back inside. His eyes appear wild and crazed, like he's past the point of reason.

I add a second finger. Wild Man's viciously fucks my mouth. His grip in my hair slams my mouth down while his hips thrust up. Over and over again. I continue taking his ass with my finger and grind against him, soaking his leg with my juices. I'm close, only seconds away from coming.

Wild Man goes to the back of my throat and he holds me there. The growl that leaves him has my insides liquifying.

I love when the madness hits him, as if he's lost all control and will go insane if he doesn't get every inch inside me that my body will allow.

I feel his shaft growing harder, and if possible, fatter, and I know he's close. I want him to flood my mouth with his cum so much that he leaks out the edges, so I tighten my throat muscles around him.

Just when I think he's going to find his release, I'm suddenly jerked away by my hair. In a daze, my watery eyes peer up at him.

"Whaaa?"

I'm pulled to my feet, but only long enough for Wild Man to spin me around by my hips. He pulls me down to his lap so my legs are spread wide open and resting on either side of his. My eyes immediately go to Teeja, who has his bright blue gaze on Wild Man and me. I have no clue if Teeja understands what we're doing, but regardless, I don't feel comfortable fucking in front of the wild animal and his family. At least when I was sucking his dick, I was facing away.

I try to get up from Wild Man's lap, but he holds me in place with a firm grip.

"Wild Man," I start, but it ends on a moan when he places the length of his cock between the lips of my pussy. I shake my head of the daze. "Stop. I don't want to do this in front of them."

"Why?" he asks. Shifting his hips and sliding his cock against me. I close my eyes and release a low moan. "It's nature. Teeja fucks Vena. You played with offspring today."

He presses his cock right over my clit while his other hand comes up and palms my breast, tweaking one nipple between his fingers.

"I know," I say breathlessly. "But that doesn't mean I want to watch them do it anymore than I want them to watch us. It just feels... weird." My eyes slide open, and I see Teeja still looking at us, his head tilted to the side as if in curiosity. "Teeja is watching us."

"He's curious," Wild Man grunts. "Let him watch."

"Jesus," I moan when his cock hits a particularly sensitive spot. My nails dig into his thighs where I'm gripping him to stay balanced.

Wild Man wraps an arm around my waist and he lifts me.

"Wild Man, please..."

I try to protest some more, but my words die a quick death when I'm suddenly being shoved down on his cock. I let out a low cry, partially from pain, but mostly from pleasure.

"Oh, god," I moan. My legs hooked over his shift and the muscles in my calves tighten.

Why does being full of him have to feel so damn good?

Teeja and his family are soon forgotten, and I let myself go. With his hands still around my waist, Wild Man lifts me and lets me fall back down, repeating the movement so fast and furious that my boobs bounce.

I lean my weight back against his chest and throw one of my arms behind me. I find his hair with my fingers, and I thread them through the thick strands. His face goes to the crook of my neck and his teeth latch onto the skin presented before him. He always goes for the same spot. He bites and sucks the skin, renewing the mark that's still there.

The whole time, he flexes his hips and uses his arm around my waist to lift me up and down on his cock.

He hits a spot inside me that has me seeing stars. I bite my lip so hard to stifle the scream wanting to break free that I taste a tinge of copper in my mouth.

"Yes!" I hiss, rotating my hips. "Right there, Fey," I say, using his real name.

His gravelly growl in response has my stomach muscles spasming.

One of his arms is locked around my waist as he continues to fuck the hell out of me. His other hand goes down my stomach and his fingers slide on either side of his cock.

"So wet," he groans against my ear. "I like your wetness. Does my thing feel good for you, *momor*?"

"Cock," I moan, barely able to get the word out. "Your thing is called a cock. Say it."

"Cock." I shiver at the rough note in his voice. "Does my cock feel good?"

"Yes. *So so* good."

He bites the side of my throat. "What is this?" He shoves his fingers deeper inside me, sliding them along his cock.

"Pussy."

"My cock feels so good feeding my pussy."

I ground myself down on him. "My pussy," I whimper.

He lifts me up and slams me back down hard, digging his fingers in deeper.

"*My* pussy, *momor*. Always mine."

He puts his palm over my breast, cupping it fully. "What is this?"

I can barely form the words past the intense pleasure consuming me. "Breasts. Or boobs. Or tits. Whichever you prefer."

"*My* tits, *momor*." He squeezes the plump flesh. Not enough to hurt, but just enough to emphasize his point. "*Mine.*" He jams his hips upward.

He shifts his hand over until it lays over my pounding heart. "This mine too. Tell me."

I don't want to say the word, but whether I refuse him or give him what he wants, I'm afraid it's too late.

I can deny it until I'm blue in the face, but it won't change the fact that his claim is true.

I am his. Every single inch of me.

"Yours."

*eighteen*

WILD MAN

I stand close behind my female, my attention focused on the look on her face. Her expression is serious, as if she's really concentrating on what she's doing. Her eyebrows are a straight line and her lips are parted with the tip of her tongue touching the bottom one.

I desperately want to take that tongue between my lips and taste her, but she's still keeping her mouth from me.

But that's fine. She'll eventually give me what I want.

*Momor* suddenly straightens, her back going stiff and her eyes tracking movement in the knee deep water we're in. A moment later, her hand darts forward, the spear she's holding dunking beneath the clear surface.

She pulls it out and spins to face me, grinning so big her cheeks puff out.

"I did it!" she shouts, holding up a wiggling fish speared on the end.

I chuckle. "Good, *momor*." I still struggle with finding my words, but they're coming easier with each day. "Dinner for you." I pluck the fish from the spear and toss it on the bank. "Again. Dinner for me."

She turns back, lifting the arm holding the spear, poised and ready to stab another fish.

My eyes slide down her back and over the roundness of her backside. I want to go to her and shove myself inside her tight hole. To rut in her wetness until she squeezes me, and I shoot my seed in her womb.

Cock and pussy. That's what she called my thing and the place between her legs. I like the words, and from the way my female's breathing picks up when I use them, she likes them too. Or she likes when I say them.

My cock twitches, but I push my need down. Mostly, when the need to take *momor* hits, I take her wherever we are, no matter what we're doing, but I'm enjoying watching her hunt for our food. There's no need for her to do this—I will always provide for her—but when she came to me and asked if I would teach her, I couldn't deny her. And from the smile on her face, this makes her happy.

She told me of the ways her people hunt for fish. It seems complicated and more work than necessary.

A few minutes later, Ever spins around and holds up her spear, another fish with beady eyes stuck on the end. She angles it toward me, her eyes glowing proudly.

"Dinner for you, and it's a big one." She grins.

I grin back, snatching the fish off the end. "Now we clean."

Her full pink lips curve downward and her little nose wrinkles. "I caught the fish. You get to clean them."

We walk out of the water, and I grab the other fish. She follows me to a rock that's flat on top. I plop both fish down while she sits on a smaller rock beside the bigger one. She eyes the fish with disgust when I begin cutting off the head.

"My dad tried his best to get me to clean the fish we would

catch, but I could never stomach it," she says, turning her face away.

"Did you fish much?" I ask, running the knife along the side of the fish to scrape away the scales.

"We were outdoors a lot. My dad took me and my brothers camping several times a year and we either hunted or fished for our food."

She sits with her arms behind her to prop herself up and her legs lay in front of her, crossed at her feet. The new position pushes out her tits. The tips—nipples are what she called them—are pointed and hard from the cool water. I'm tempted to lean over and suck one into my mouth.

I look back down at the fish and flip it over to scrape the other side. "Did you like camping?"

"I loved it." I can hear the smile in her voice. "Most of the time anyway. Until I got older and wanted to hang out with boys and my friends more."

I jerk my eyes to her, my lips pressed into a line. "Boys?" I ask, my voice deepening.

Her eyes slide to me and she looks like she wants to laugh. "Yes, boys, Wild Man."

"You were with boys?" The hand I have wrapped around the knife tightens. "Did you fuck them?"

Her chin moves upward, like she's looking down her nose at me. "Yes, I did. With a few of them anyway. I had a life before you took me."

"Did you give them your mouth?"

"Some of them, yes."

My mood darkens. I want to take the knife I'm strangling and jam it down the throat of every boy she gave her mouth to. "How many?"

My face must give away the anger I'm feeling because my female sits up, brushing her hands against each other before placing them on her thighs.

"Wild Man," she starts, but I cut her off.

"How many, *momor*," I growl.

Her brows fall and she catches her bottom lip between her teeth. "Five."

I drop the knife and put both hands on the rock, leaning toward her. She tilts her body back, as if I would ever let her get away from me. "You gave five boys *my* lips, but won't let me have them?"

A fire starts in her eyes, which only makes my anger hotter.

"Yes. You don't get them after everything you've done to me."

I want to wrap my hands around her slender throat and squeeze until her eyes water and she begs me to let her go. To shake her until she gives in.

"You wanted what I did."

Her brown eyes flash again and the muscles in her jaw move. "I may want it *now*, but I didn't at first. I'll never forget the pain you caused me."

Remembering the first few times I took her and the way she fought me, has my cock filling up and growing hard. Then the expression that was on her face comes to mind. The pain that was in her eyes and the screams she let out when I entered her. I don't regret taking my female. She needed to know she was mine. My only regret is the pain the act caused.

"You're mine, *momor*," I growl between my teeth. "You belong to me. As your male, it is right I fuck you. It is nature for a male to mate with his female. To dominate her and show her who the alpha is. To show her how strong he is so she knows he will protect her."

"You're delusional." I frown, not understanding that word. "You may think the world works that way, and maybe it does out here, but I'm from a different place where it doesn't. We aren't animals to be dominated. There are no alphas who need to master or intimidate their females. Where I come from, what you did in the beginning is called rape."

The way she says that last word, it sounds like something bad. "Rape?"

"It means fucking someone who doesn't want it. People are put away for the things you did to me." At my questionable look, she explains in words I'll understand. "They're put in a small room with bars for years, and they're only let out when people say they can, and only for a little while before they're put back."

My fingers dig into the rock when I think about being put into such a place.

"You would put me there?"

Some of the anger falls from her face. "No," she says softly. "I wouldn't."

"Why?"

Her eyes fall to her lap and her hair slides forward. Her voice is just as soft when she answers. "I don't know. Maybe because I'm just as delusional as you."

I still don't know what that word means, but I get the feeling it's not good either.

She looks up and her eyes look sad. "Even if I do want you to touch me now, you're still hurting me every day you keep me here. I miss my family and friends."

"Boys," I growl.

She shakes her head. "You mean men. I stopped being with boys a long time ago." I scowl, knowing what she means and not appreciating being corrected. "No, Wild Man, I don't miss other men, except my dad and brothers."

My eyes narrow. "You would leave me?"

Her answer doesn't come right away, but when it does, my anger comes back doubled.

"Yes, Fey. I would. I don't belong here."

My hand flashes out, and I wrap my fingers around her throat. I drag her toward me until our faces are so close I can feel her breath on my lips. "Mine, *momor*. You never leave."

I can tell she wants to fight me on this. The black circle in the center of her eyes gets bigger and the line of her lips goes straight. But she doesn't argue. She doesn't agree with me either.

Our mouths are so close, I could easily bring her lips to mine. I don't. She'll give them to me on her own.

We stare at each other for a moment. When her face turns red from my tight grip, I release my fingers from her throat.

We both notice the blood at the same time. While I was leaning my hands on the rock I must have cut myself on the knife. My anger was so hot that I didn't notice.

As soon as *momor* sees the blood, her temper changes, and a frown appears between her eyes. She picks up my hand and flips it over. There's a large gash that's still oozing blood.

Uncaring of the cut, I watch her face, liking when I see the worry in her expression. My female may want to leave this place, but I don't think she wants to leave *me*.

"Oh my, god." Her voice is low. "What have you done to your-self? You stupid man."

The fish are forgotten as she scrambles up from the rock. I let her drag me back to the water. Once we're waist deep, she dips my hand under the surface, and I barely feel the sting.

"Does it hurt?" she asks, looking up at me past the hair that's fallen in her face.

Water drips from my other hand when I lift it to push the hair away. "No."

The lines beside her eyes tighten. "I don't believe you."

I flex my fingers in hers to prove my point. I hardly feel anything. A cut from a knife on my hand is nothing compared to some of the other things I've been through. And nothing compares to the pain of thinking about her leaving.

She grips my hand tighter, holding my fingers together so I can't move them. "Don't do that."

"Tell me about family," I say as she continues to inspect my hand. "Why would you leave me to go to them?"

She answers without looking at me. "Because I love them."

"What makes you love them?"

"They care about me, and I know they're worried about what's happened to me." Her small finger gently slides over my palm, tracing the outside of the cut. "I hate knowing I'm putting them through that. My father and brothers are very protective of me." She looks up, meeting my eyes. "You know how you get angry if you think something might happen to me?" I give her a jerky nod. "They are the same. They're like you when it comes to something hurting me. They'll find me, Wild Man, and take me away. And when they do, I worry what they'll do to you. I don't want to see you hurt any more than you want to see me hurt."

It's not the first time she's told me this. I'd like to see her family try to take her from me. No one, man or creature, will come near my female. I'll slaughter anything that comes between me and her.

For now, I ignore her warning. "Tell me about father and brothers. What are they like?"

A smile curves her lips. "You actually remind me of them a little." I raise my brow at that and she laughs. "They go crazy when they think I'm in danger. I can't count how many times my brothers have threatened boys if they came near me."

There's that word again.

*Boys.*

I'll kill them all.

Before my temper rises, she continues, rushing her words as if she knows her mistake.

"It was a headache having them around sometimes. I couldn't go anywhere without at least one of them with me. But as much as I hated it, I also loved the closeness we all share."

"How many brothers?"

"Four."

She takes my hand and pulls me out of the water. Grabbing the cloth I use to cover myself, she attempts to rip a piece off. I take it from her when she has trouble and easily tear off a strip.

"Thanks."

She wraps the piece around my hand and ties it off on the back. Once she's done, I grab her hand and pull her to a fallen tree. I sit with my back to it and pull her down between my spread legs. She leans back against me, a small breath leaving her.

She continues talking without me asking.

"My oldest brother is Maddox, but we all call him Mad for short. He's eight years older than me and takes his role as big brother very seriously. I feel horrible for the people around him right now because he's cranky on the best of days. I'm sure by now he's a beast to be around because he doesn't know what's happened to me."

Her gaze drips off to the water.

"Next is Ethan, who's six years older. He's the black sheep of the family."

"Black sheep?" I ask, not understanding this term.

"The rebel. He does the opposite of what my father says. Something happened between them years ago and neither of them will talk about it. Whatever it was caused a rift between them and it's never healed. Ethan lives to piss off our dad."

I pick up a lock of her hair and twist it around my finger. She watches the movement with a small smile

"Spencer is five years older. He's the nerd and can tell you everything there is to know about computers and technology." She sees my confused expression and explains. "Computers are metal boxes that can store, retrieve, and process information. When Spencer was thirteen, he hacked into the Pentagon's database— the Pentagon is the government and a database is where they store information. I thought Dad was going to have a heart attack when he found out. Luckily, Spencer was able to hide his trail so the government could never locate where the hack came from."

The outside world seems confusing and too big.

"And then there's Joseph, or Joe," *Momor* continues. "He and I are the closest because there's only three years between us. He's more sensitive than my other brothers, and likes to fuck with our older siblings. But he has a short fuse. When he gets angry, people around him know to stay away.

"One girl with many boys. Like Devika."

She lays her arm on top of mine that I have wrapped around her waist. Her fingers play with the dark hair. I see from the side of her face that she's still smiling.

"Mom really wanted a girl, so they kept trying until I came along."

"What about Noeny?"

Her expression turns sad. "Mom died when I was two. She got sick and never got better."

I tighten my arm around her. Using my chin, I brush away the hair on her shoulder and kiss the side of her neck over my mark.

"I remember Noeny and Peepa talking about having baby. She had one in stomach when she died, but her belly wasn't round yet."

One of the few memories I still have of Noeny and Peepa was when they told me I was going to be a big brother. I was so excited. That was a few days before we came to the forest. It was supposed to be our last adventure before Noeny had the baby.

"Oh, Fey." *Momor* turns around and scoots close so her knees touch the inside of my thighs. I like when she uses my name. I like when she calls me Wild Man too. One of her hands goes to my cheek and the other lays on my chest where my heart is. Her eyes glisten, like she's about to cry. "I'm so sorry."

I like this side of my female. The one who shows she cares for me. She's fought me so much since I claimed her, but her fights are coming less and less.

I'll make her love me like she loves her family, so she'll never want to leave.

"It was long ago," I say, placing my hand over hers on my chest.

Her smile is sad when she gives it to me. "I bet you would have been a great big brother."

I don't know if she's right, but when I was a boy, I liked the thought of having a little brother or sister.

*Momor* leans forward and presses her face into my neck. I grab her by the waist and pick her up so her knees are on either side of my hips. The position puts her pussy right over my cock. I'm hard, because I usually am when she's this close, but I don't try to enter her.

Now's not the time for fucking. Right now, I just want to hold my female close.

*nineteen*

EVERLEE

I snuggle deeper into the warmth at my back and the arm around my waist tightens, pulling me even closer. The nights are getting cooler, but the blankets that cover us and Wild Man's big body always pressed against mine keeps me nice and toasty.

I slowly blink open my eyes and it takes them a minute to focus. One of my hands rests on the pallet in front of my face, and my gaze snags on the bracelet around my wrist. Wild Man must have made me a new one and slipped it on my wrist last night after I fell asleep.

I'm still wearing the other two he made me. The lavender flowers have long since died, but the handmade bracelets are still just as pretty. This new one doesn't have any flowers, but the vines he used are delicate and fine. The way he intricately wove them together is beautiful.

I roll to my back and turn my head. Wild Man's on his side with his dark gaze on me. I always get caught up in his eyes when looks at me. They're so dark, I can't tell where the pupil stops and the iris begins.

"Thank you for my new bracelet. It's beautiful."

My gratitude pleases him, if the smile he gives me is any indication. I don't think I'll ever get tired of seeing him smile. Through his thick beard, I notice two dimples.

"You're welcome."

Lifting my hand, I run my fingers through the coarse hair of his beard. "How do you keep this so short?"

"Scissors."

I roll my eyes, because his answer is obvious. "I know that. I've seen you do it. But how do you know how to do it?"

"Peepa hair on face. Let me cut when it got long."

I can just imagine a little Wild Man standing in front of his kneeling father with a big pair of scissors in his little hand. He'd have a look of concentration on his face as he slowly snipped away the hair.

That image has a smile lifting my lips. "I bet your mom enjoyed watching that."

"She did. She would sit and watch with smile like you."

Unbidden, another image forms in my head of another little boy standing in front of Wild Man on his knees. He'd have dark hair like his father. Just as Wild Man trimmed his father's beard, this little boy does the same to Wild Man. Without thought, I place myself in the image standing a few feet away. I'd watch them with a smile, just as his mother did with her husband and son.

I don't like imagining Wild Man in the future with me still with him, but they keep coming more and more. And the kicker is, I'm there willingly, and I'm happy. I can't imagine staying in the wilderness like this. It's uncomfortable during the best of times and utterly horrible and frightening during the worse. The only enjoyment I get out of this situation is being with Wild Man.

His finger tracing the space between my eyes pulls me out of my nonsensical thoughts.

"Why stop smiling?" he asks, a frown forming on his face. "What are you thinking?"

I force the smile back in place. "Nothing important."

He looks like he doesn't believe me, but he lets it go.

He knocks the covers off of us, and I open my legs so he can slide between them. We always have morning sex, so I expected that's what he wanted.

The cool air hits between my legs, and I feel wet. I'm aroused, anticipating what's to come, but it's not the normal wetness. I look down and see red on my thighs.

Horror and embarrassment has my head jerking up to look at Wild Man to see if he noticed. His eyes are on my face and not what's going on down there.

"Off," I say, pushing against his chest.

Of course, he's unmovable.

"What's wrong?"

When he begins to dip his chin, I latch my arms around his shoulders and tug him down. The last thing I want is for him to look down and see all of the blood.

The only reason I'm able to pull him down is because of the surprised movement. He plants his fists on the pallet beside my head and lifts his chest off mine. I don't let him go, so I'm forced up with him.

"*Momor*?"

"I started my period," I blurt to distract him when he tries to pull away from me again. "I'm bleeding."

His brows slam down and his body jerks back. "Bleeding?"

"Yes." I feel the heat of embarrassment coat my cheeks. "I started my period," I state again. "Most women go through this every month."

I began to worry because my period was late, and I always start on time like clockwork. I've lost track of how long I've been with Wild Man, but I'm positive I should have started my cycle well before now, especially since I haven't been taking my birth control. I was certain the inevitable had happened, and I was carrying Wild

Man's child. Now, relief mingles with my embarrassment. Getting pregnant by this man cannot happen.

That thought slides through my head, followed by a little niggle of regret. It's a stupid and irrational thought to have, but I can't help but wonder what Wild Man and my child would look like. It hurts knowing I won't get to see him as a father. There's no doubt in my mind that he would make a wonderful dad.

Wild Man reaches back and unlocks my arms around his neck and begins to lean back.

"What are you doing?" My voice comes out loud and panicked.

He doesn't answer. He just continues on his merry way and gets to his knees. I try to close my knees to block his view, but his hands land on top of them, stopping me. When I reach for him, frantically grabbing at his hair, arms, *anything*, to pull him back down, he grabs my hands in one of his big hands and places them down on my stomach, trapping them.

His eyes drop down, and I close mine in mortification. I'm not ashamed of my period. I just don't want Wild Man to see the evidence. I mean, come on, what woman would?

His frown deepens into worry when he sees all of the red on my thighs. "Why do you do this?"

Mortification doesn't even begin to describe what I'm feeling right now, but I push the feeling away. I can't imagine what he must be thinking. He was too young when he was left alone to understand the workings of a woman's body. Blood usually indicates an injury, so for him to see so much without me withering in pain must confound him.

"It's part of the cycle of life for women," I tell him, his rapt gaze still locked between my legs.

How embarrassing!

"Women have something in their stomach called a uterus. During the month, if the woman doesn't get pregnant, the lining of the uterus sheds away, which is what's called a menstrual cycle. That's the blood."

His eyes lift to mine, and I can see them working as he absorbs what I've just told him.

After a moment, he asks, "So if woman sheds blood, she doesn't have baby in her belly?"

"Usually."

His brows slant down as if he doesn't like my answer.

"Wild Man—"

My words are cut off when Wild Man suddenly grabs my hips and pulls me downward. My ass is pulled up so it lays on his thighs. I know the look in his eyes, and his intent, before he even spreads my legs so they wrap around his waist.

"Oh, no." I try to slap his hands away. "We are not doing this right now."

I know some people are into having sex while the woman is on her period, but I am not one of them. Even the thought of it has my stomach churning with revulsion.

Wild Man stops my attempts to shove him away by grabbing both of my hands and clamping them together into one of his big ones. He presses them down on my stomach, his dark gaze meeting my frantic ones.

"Stop, *momor*," he grates, his voice dropping several octaves.

Against my better judgment, I do stop, but I look up at him pleadingly. "Please. I don't want to do this."

After the first few failed attempts, I stopped fighting Wild Man when he wanted to have sex. It took me a while to admit it, but I enjoy the way he makes my body feel. But this is different. I'm on my period for fuck's sake.

"Why?" he asks with genuine curiosity.

How could he not know? Even with his lack of knowledge of such things, how could he possibly think I would be okay having sex while bleeding between my legs?

"Because it's...." I can't think of the appropriate word to voice my thoughts, so I go with, "dirty."

His expression doesn't change, but his eyes darken. "Dirty sex."

186

The hand not holding mine in place moves up the inside of my thigh and my legs stiffen. "Sounds like fucking."

"It's not the same."

I try to worm my hips off his thighs, but his hold doesn't allow me to go anywhere.

"Not the same," he says huskily. "But can feel good like fucking."

His hand travels further upward, moving over the wetness covering my thighs. I swallow the lump that's formed in my throat.

How could he be turned on right now? More importantly, how is it possible that his hand getting closer and closer to my pussy is turning *me* on right now?

I try again to tug my hands from his grip. In return, he tugs on my wrists until I'm scooted further up his thighs.

"No! Stop, Wild Man!"

"I feel your heart beat here." He squeezes my wrists to show he's talking about my pulse. "You like this."

I shake my head. "No!"

I jolt when his finger grazes over the lips of my pussy, and I can't tell if it's more from mortification or desire. My head swims with so many emotions. I want to demand he stop, at the same time I want to beg him to touch me harder. I feel disgust at myself at the same time I feel my skin heat sensually.

His finger slips between my lips before he skims them up and over my clit. My back bows and a little whimper slips out of my mouth.

Later. Later I'll let the reality of what we're doing have the light of day. Right now, I just want more of what he's doing.

He dips his finger back down to my hole, and I ignore the fact that he's wetting the digit with more than just my arousal. Two fingers go in while his thumb presses against my clit. I bite my tongue to keep from crying out, but a low moan still manages to escape. My eyes close in blissful delight.

He fucks me slowly with his fingers for several long agonizing moments. I need more. I need to be stuffed full of him. My period is now the last thing on my mind.

When his fingers leave me, my lids snap open. It's on the tip of my tongue to beg him to put them back. My hands are now free, so I reach for his wrist.

I pause when he lifts my hips and grabs the base of his cock. He stares down at me, his expression full of dark desire, as he lines himself up to my opening.

"My *momor* doesn't carry my baby in her belly," he grates between clenched teeth. "I will fuck her 'til she does."

The last word has just left his lips when he's forcefully pulling my hips down at the same time he surges forward.

The pain is sharp, but it's mixed in with a delicious pleasure I know I'll never get with anyone else.

I've barely had time to recover from his first brutal thrust before he's pulling out and slamming back inside. I throw my arms over my head, grabbing the cloth in a tight grip, and arch my back.

"Oh God, Fey! Yes!"

Several more thrusts follow, his grunts filling the space around us with each one. His fingers wrap around my waist, and I'm hoisted up so I'm straddling him with our chests pressed together. He grabs a handful of my hair and yanks my head back. His black eyes filled with heat stare down at me.

"Ride, *momor*," he growls. "Fuck my pussy with my cock."

My walls clamp down on him as the filthy words leave his mouth. I love when he talks like this to me. And what's even hotter is when he calls my pussy his. Because it is. It has been since nearly the beginning.

I dig my nails into his shoulders for leverage and angle my hips upward, sliding off his shaft. With only the head left inside, I let myself fall back down on him. He hisses out a breath while a low moan leaves my lips. I move up again and repeat the movement, going faster with each stroke.

"More. Harder," he grunts. One palm moves to my butt where

he grabs a cheek. His other wraps around my throat, squeezing hard enough to nearly block my air. "This is your cock." He emphasizes his point by pulling me up and yanking me back down. "Take like you own. Your cock, *momor*."

I don't know where it comes from, but the need overwhelms me, and I couldn't ignore it even if I wanted to.

I slide my fingers through his hair, fisting the thick strands and pull his head back like he's done to me so many times. I stare down at him, letting him see the truth in my next words.

My voice doesn't sound like my own when I say, "It *is* my cock, Wild Man." I ground down on him, smashing my clit against his pubic bone and hitting a spot inside that nearly leaves me dizzy. "*Mine*. Only *ever mine*."

I don't realize how true those words are until I say them aloud. Just the mere thought of someone else touching Wild Man or his hands on another has an anger growing so hot inside me it scorches the sides of my brain. I've never been the possessive type, but this man brings it out in me. I feel just as crazed about him as he does about me.

His eyes move down to my lips, and for a brief moment, I wonder if he's going to try and kiss me again. The thing is, I'm not sure I have it in me to stop him this time. Each time he tries, it gets harder and harder to deny him.

One moment I'm sitting on his lap and the next I'm tossed on the bed, flat on my stomach. I haven't had time to register the new position before Wild Man's big body is mounted over mine from head to foot. He doesn't pull me to my knees like I expect. My legs are spread and his cock is spearing my pussy once again. One of his hands sneaks beneath and up my body to wrap his fingers around my throat. His grip is so tight he steals my air. But, god, does it feel good.

He rams his hips forward over and over again, growling and snarling. His head dips and his teeth latch onto his usual spot. I've grown to love the marks he leaves on me. I want him to leave more all over my body.

"My *momor*," he snarls against my neck.

His pace picks up, his thrusts becoming harsher, like he's trying to insert himself so far inside me that he'll never get free. The whole time, his possessive hand stays around my throat.

I let out a hoarse cry when my orgasm hits. My release spurs his own. He lets out a roar and his hips buck so hard against my ass, I wouldn't be surprised if I have bruises from his hip bones later. More marks for me to admire later.

---

HOURS LATER, AFTER ANOTHER ROUND OF SEX AND AFTER WILD MAN TOOK me to the pool of water to wash—because there was blood all over us, something that didn't seem to bother Wild Man in the least, but it sure as shit did me—I'm lying in bed.

The cramps started an hour ago, and they hit with a vengeance. My period has always been light, but I've had bad menstrual cramps since I started my menstrual cycle at twelve years old. They've gotten so bad in the past that my doctor prescribed pain meds. Obviously, I don't have them with me, so dealing with the pain now is not a good time.

Thankfully, after explaining in more detail to Wild Man that I'll be bleeding for a few days and demanding I be allowed something to cover at least my lower half, he found some cloth for me to use. My top half is still bare, but at least I have something for my bottom half to staunch the flow of blood.

I'm curled on my side with my hand pressed against my stomach when Wild Man walks into the bed area. He carries a bowl and a jug of water. When he sees my huddled form, a slight frown appears between his eyes.

When I told him I was lying down earlier, I didn't tell him why, only that I was tired. It was the truth. The pain hadn't hit yet, but I knew it was coming.

He stops near my head and drops to his knees, setting the bowl and jug beside him.

"What's wrong? Do you hurt?"

His concern touches a place near my heart. I reach out and grab his hand, thankful the cramps have resided for the moment.

"Cramps," I say.

"Cramps?"

"A pain in my stomach. A lot of women have them with their period. It's normal."

He scowls. "I don't like it."

A light laugh leaves me. "I don't either."

"I brought food and water."

At the mention of food, my stomach growls.

I smile at Wild Man. "Good call. Thank you."

When I place my hands behind me to sit up, he stops me. "Stay."

His hand dips in the bowl, and I open my mouth for him to slip the small piece of fresh fruit in my mouth. The juicy flavor has my mouth watering for more. We're quiet as he continues to feed me.

I've just taken a sip of water when I feel a cramp starting. I grimace in pain when my lower stomach tightens.

I feel Wild Man's eyes on me as I take in a slow breath and let it out through my lips. I feel like I'm in fucking labor.

"What do you need?" he asks, his voice gruff.

I slide my hand down to my lower stomach and my fingers get caught on the rope. Frustration has my teeth gritting.

"Take this fucking rope off me!" My voice comes out louder than I intended, but I don't apologize. I am so tired of feeling it around my waist, like I'm an animal that needs to be leashed.

I expect Wild Man to deny my demand or at the very least ignore it, so I'm surprised that after a moment of hesitation, he begins to work on the knots.

I'm lying here with my mouth hanging open, staring at his hands when the rope falls away and he tosses it near the entrance.

A huge weight lifts off my shoulders and it feels like I've shed a hundred pounds.

Does this mean he trusts me to not run away? The more pressing question is, *will* I try to run away if given the chance?

Of course, this could only be a temporary reprieve. For all I know, he plans to put it back once the pain is gone. Only time will tell.

Another cramp begins, but I ignore the pain and grab his hand, bringing it to my cheek. "Thank you."

He doesn't say anything to my gratitude, but simply gives a jerky nod. "Is there anything else I do?"

I shake my head, wishing there was, but unless he can make my pain meds magically appear, I'm going to have to suffer for the next few hours. Luckily, I typically only have cramps for several hours each cycle.

"Roll over," he says, setting the bowl and jug on the floor.

Once I'm facing away from him, I feel his warm body move so he's pressed against my back. His arm comes around my body, the weight settling on my hip so it's not pressing on any squishy parts of me that might cause discomfort. His big hand presses against my lower stomach, moving in slow, soothing circles.

The hair on his face gets caught in my hair, so he uses his chin to push it off my shoulders. He presses a light kiss against my neck. It's not a sexual kiss, more like a calming gesture.

I snuggle into his chest, the muscles in my stomach finally relaxing.

Who knew being wrapped in the warmth of a man's arms and having him lightly rub your stomach could be so effective.

# *twenty*

EVERLEE

L ife with Wild Man has its perks.

For instance, I've been meaning to start a diet to shed some of the extra weight around my middle. I've always wanted to be the type of woman who could sit in a bikini and not have that little roll in my stomach that pushes out past the bottoms of the bathing suit. Unfortunately, I'm not one of the types who can eat anything and still pull that off. I have to work hard at the gym and count calories. I hate counting calories. I love food too much.

Living with Wild Man in the wilderness, I still don't count calories, but I don't need to because the food we eat doesn't contain many. I've finally accomplished that flat stomach, and I didn't even have to work for it.

I look down at my midriff and rub my hand over it, snickering in glee to myself. The lack of rope doesn't escape my notice. It's been several days since I was released from that cursed thing. I've been half expecting Wild Man to leash me again, but so far he hasn't.

Another benefit of living in the wild with no rules and societal expectations, you don't have to worry about what anyone will think of you. I'm a people pleaser, and I like to be liked. Not because I want to be noticed—I actually don't like to be the center of attention—but because I want people to be happy when they see me. I like for everyone to be happy, and when that doesn't happen, it stresses me out. It's exhausting to try to please everyone. Out here, I only have one person I need to keep happy, and it takes almost nothing to achieve that goal.

Wild Man is a simple man.

He eats. He hunts. He cares for me and fucks me. He sleeps. All with a few variations of other things thrown in between those top things.

He also makes *me* happy.

I never thought I could be happy in a place like this with a man like Wild Man, but I am.

I miss my old life. My family and friends the most, but also modern conveniences like a toilet and toilet paper, fresh brewed coffee, a soft bed, electronics. Clothes should be one of the top things on my list, but surprisingly, I've gotten used to walking around naked. It's kind of freeing not having material constantly rubbing against my body. I'm not saying I would shun clothes if they were presented before me, but not having that option isn't as irritating as it used to be.

I'm pulled from my ruminations when Teeja, who's trotting ahead of Wild Man and me a few feet away gives a small yelp at Drefan, the rambunctious one of the siblings.

Teeja and his family have visited us several times since I was first introduced to them. I love having them around. The wolf family has become my entertainment over the last couple of weeks. The way Teeja is with Vena and their pups kind of reminds me of the way Wild Man is with me.

Protective and willing to do anything to keep them safe.

It's strange to compare a man to an animal, but it's also not so strange. Wild Man grew up in the wild surrounded by wild animals. It's not so unusual for him to have picked up on some of the wild life's mannerisms. Like marking my urine with his own to mask my scent. While it won't keep humans away, it would animals.

Teeja stops in front of us. He lets out a low growl and the hair along his spine stands up. His head jerks to our right, but I don't see what's alerting him. He gives a deep snarl before he yelps in the direction of Vena and their pups. Then the six of them take off in the opposite direction.

Wild Man, who's been next to me, steps in front of me, his back ramrod straight with tension. His hand tightens around the spear he's holding as he faces the direction where Teeja sensed danger.

I grab his arm and peek around his body, curious to know what's out there.

Without looking at me, Wild Man hisses, "Stay."

I'd bristle at the command if my nerves weren't currently being frayed. There are any number of predators that it could be. Some Wild Man could handle, some I'm afraid he couldn't.

What comes through a thick briar of bushes is the last thing I expect.

An old man, probably in his late sixties, dressed in tattered jeans and a green and black plaid shirt, topped with a ratty straw hat.

I'm even more surprised when I see the tension leave Wild Man's shoulders. I would have thought the opposite would happen.

This man could equal my escape.

He could also be more dangerous than an animal. He looks like a stiff wind could blow him over, but looks can be deceiving.

The man's hair that's sticking out of his hat is completely gray. He's tall and nearly skin and bones. It's a good thing Wild Man doesn't view him as a threat because he could easily break him like a twig. He has straps over his shoulders from what looks like some kind of pack he's wearing on his back.

"Boy," the man says in a smoker's roughened voice. The hint of a smile can be seen through his thick unkept beard.

When Wild Man starts walking toward him, I cling to his back. He stops and looks over his shoulder at me. "No threat," he says. "Ben safe."

I still don't let him go. I peek around his arm before lifting my eyes back to Wild Man.

"I'm naked," I say, keeping my voice low.

He looks at me like he doesn't understand the problem with me being unclothed in front of another man.

It's sort of funny if you think about it. Only in the wild would an alpha and possessive man like Wild Man be okay with other men seeing his woman naked. If he grew up in civilization, he'd be spitting mad and raging.

"In my world, it's not normal to walk around naked," I tell him. "You could actually go to jail if you did it in public. Only in someone's home are they allowed to go without clothes."

I'm not sure if he truly understands or not, but after a moment, his chin jerks up.

He looks back at the man. "Shirt."

The man seems momentarily surprised as his eyes flicker from Wild Man to me. He slips a pack that looks too big for him to carry on his frail shoulders from his back and shrugs off the flannel shirt before he tosses it to Wild Man, leaving him in a black t-shirt.

I try to keep myself hidden when Wild Man turns around to face me. My cheeks warm because I know the old man must have at least gotten a peek.

When Wild Man slips the shirt up my arms, it smells like tobacco and earth. It feels weird to have the material covering me. Thankfully, the man is tall, so the tail of the shirt goes to mid-thigh.

Once I've finished buttoning up the shirt, Wild Man turns back to the man.

"I see you found a lady," the man says, interest lighting his eyes. Wild Man doesn't say anything to that.

I step to Wild Man's side to get a better look at the old man.

"I'm Ben."

I don't know why, but I'm nervous. Besides Wild Man, this is the first person I've seen in weeks.

"Everlee."

Ben smiles. "Nice to meet ya."

I don't say it back. I'm not convinced yet that this meeting will be a good one. It's apparent the two know each other, but the question is how? And why is he here now? Wild Man seems to be comfortable around him, so that's something.

"Come," Wild Man says, grabbing my hand and turning us toward the tree hut.

Ben follows. I can feel his eyes on the back of my head and it makes me want to rub my neck. For Wild Man to have his back turned to the man must mean he really trusts him.

When we make it home, Wild Man lets my hand go, and I stand off to the side, feeling weird having someone else in our private space. Teeja and his family have been here a few times, but this is different.

Ben takes a seat on the opposite side of where Wild Man and I usually sit, like he's done this a dozen times. I watch the man with weary eyes as he sets the pack beside him on the ground.

Wild Man brings him a bowl and he trades it for the pack. Then he comes to me, grabs my hand, and brings me to our usual seat where he pulls me down on his lap. I make sure the shirt fully covers me.

With his arm wrapped around my waist, his hand laying possessively over my stomach, Wild Man says, "My woman."

Ben looks up from his bowl of meat, his bushy brows raising. "I see she got you talkin', so that's good."

Wild Man grunts.

"How do you know each other?" I ask.

"Oh, boy here and I go way back." He pops a chunk of meat into his mouth and doesn't wait to finish chewing before he continues. "Gotta be ten years now."

I lift my brows, surprised at his answer.

"I bring him supplies when I'm in the area."

"How did the two of you meet?"

Ben's chuckle is rusty. "Purely by accident and divine intervention. I was out trekking in these parts and stumbled across a coyote. He was a mean sumbitch. Saw my life flash 'fore my eyes. Right before the animal attacked, this hulkin' man comes running out of nowhere, naked with his dick swingin' in the breeze, and took that coyote down. Slit his throat from ear to ear." He grins, the teeth he flashes behind his thick beard are surprisingly bright white.

"Wow."

"Yup. I was grateful to the boy for savin' my life. I tried talkin' to him, but I couldn't get nary a word from him. He just tied a rope around the coyote's neck and started dragging him away. I followed cause I was curious about him, and he didn't seem to mind. Took me here, cooked that coyote, and shared it with me."

I look at Wild Man. He's not paying attention to either of us as he starts digging into the pack. He pulls out a tooth brush and tosses it into the pile of junk he's accumulated over the years. I'll be digging that out later. Then he pulls out a tube of toothpaste. Before he can toss that, I snatch it from his hand. He pauses his exploration of the pack to glance at me.

"Toothpaste is your friend," I tell him.

He's been keeping his teeth relatively clean by the mint leaves, but this will do a much better job.

He goes back to digging in the pack, and I look back at Ben.

"How often do you come?"

"I figured prolly once a month or so." He spits a piece of gristle into the fire. "'Bout the time he would be needin' more. I'm a bit late this time cause my gout was givin' me hell." His weathered hand rubs over one of his knees. "I left here that first day leavin' everything I had. Owed it to him for what he did. Told him I'd be back, but I don't think he understood. He was a might surprised when I did come back with more supplies."

"Did you ever try to get him to leave with you?" I ask curiously.

"I asked, but again, he just ignored me."

"Did you tell the authorities or anyone else about him?"

From all the rumors I've heard about the wild man in the woods, none of them could be confirmed. As far as everyone knew, no one had ever actually met the mysterious man and communicated with him. Everything was just speculation. Most people thought the rumors were just stories people told, but I always believed them.

"Nah." Ben shrugs, tossing another chunk of meat into his mouth. "Boy seemed alright out here by hisself. Seemed like it was the place he wanted to be, and if he wanted to leave, he could have easily followed me. Who was I to bring people 'round he may not want to see?"

His answer is reasonable, but it's also sad. Wild Man was never given the opportunity to make the choice of living in civilization or alone in the wilderness. However, if an eyewitness, someone who actually met the wild man, had come forward, curious people would have flooded the area. Not to mention, the authorities would have probably gotten involved. I shudder to think about what would have happened to Wild Man if he were discovered.

"Fey."

Ben looks up from his bowl. "Wuz that?"

"His name," I reply.

His eyes slide to Wild Man. "Huh." He brings them back to me. "It's a strange one, ain't it?"

"I figured it's probably a variation of his name. He hasn't heard the name in so long, he probably remembers it wrong. Or maybe it's a nickname his parents gave him."

"S'pose so."

"Thank you for lending me your shirt."

"Don't mention it."

Finished with the meat, Ben sets the bowl down and picks up the jug of water. He chugs half the contents before he wipes his mouth with the back of his arm.

I continue to watch the curious man. When he first came upon us, I didn't know what to think of him. To a man like Wild Man, anyone could be a threat, and I've grown protective of my savage lover. But after sitting with Ben for just the little time I have, my worries have faded. Ben seems to really care about Wild Man. He was grateful to him for saving his life, but I get the feeling it's grown to something more over the years he's been coming out here. Something that resembles paternalism.

"Don't reckon he'll be needin' those anymore," he says with a chuckle.

I look down at what Wild Man just pulled from the pack. It's another nudey magazine. He briefly glances at it before he throws it into the smoldering fire pile. My cheeks heat when I glance back at Ben, who has a knowing smirk on his face.

So that's where he got the others from. I guess it makes sense for Ben to have brought them to Wild Man. Wild Man is a viral male in his prime with needs. Until recently, he had no sexual experiences to visualize. I bet those magazines came in real handy over the years.

"How did you come to be here with him?"

How much to tell him?

And more importantly, should I use this opportunity to try and get away?

Those two questions play around in my head on a loop as I think about my answer. Ultimately, the very last thing I want is for Wild Man to get hurt. My time spent with him may have started out painful, but I've grown to care for the man. More than I want to admit at the moment. Who knows, maybe it *is* Stockholm Syndrome, but it would devastate me if something were to happen to him. Just the thought sends a sharp pain to the center of my chest. And just as painful is the thought of leaving and never seeing him again. He's become a vital part of my life. When I think about the future now, I see him there.

If I were to leave now, I'd be stripping a part of myself and leaving it behind. And my father and brother's would hound me until I told them where I was. They'd no doubt come for Wild Man. A chill races up my spine to think about what they would do to him. My family can be irrational and down-right dangerous when it comes to protecting our family. Especially me, the only female in the bunch.

Since Wild Man removed the rope from my waist, I get the feeling that he now trusts me. Trusts that I won't leave him. He's not even concerned that I'll try to enlist Ben's help. It hurts me to contemplate breaking that trust.

Now *I* have to trust in myself and Wild Man that I'll eventually talk him into letting me go. Not permanently. I don't believe leaving him forever is an option for me now. He's become too important to me. But I refuse to believe I'll never see my family again. They're just as important. Besides, eventually, my family will find out where we are. I'd rather head them off and go to them before they come here. Maybe I can talk Wild Man into coming with me. Introduce him into society and slowly show him the world he's been missing.

It's strange to imagine Wild Man wearing clothes, eating with utensils at a table, him walking the streets or driving a car. But I think if given the chance, he would enjoy those things.

I pull my thoughts from those possibilities and look back at Ben.

"Like you, I happened to be walking in the woods when I came across Wild Man," I tell him. "Instead of leaving, I decided to stay."

"Wild Man?"

"It's what I call him. Seemed like it fit."

Ben eyes me like he doesn't believe me. I hold his stare with unblinking eyes. It doesn't matter if there's a lot more to the story than that, that I've omitted the more gruesome details. The only thing that matters is that I won't be utilizing him to try to escape. That I'm here now of my own free will.

"Okay, girl. If you say so," he says.

I lift my arm and wrap it around Wild Man's shoulders, looking at Ben. "I do."

## twenty-one

EVERLEE

"Come sit." I pat the space between my legs on our pallet of blankets.

Wild Man walks over and drops to his knees, scooting toward me, a predatory look in his eyes.

I laugh. "Not for sex, you savage."

"Fuck my *momor*."

I hold my hand up and press it against his wide chest, stopping him from moving over me. "There's time for that later." I smile up at him as he looms over me. "Now turn around and sit."

He gives me a sexy disgruntled look before he turns and drops to his butt. I scoot up until my legs hug him, and he lays his hands on my ankles. His long mane of blue-black hair falls down his back. It's so thick and luscious, surprisingly healthy since he's not taken care of it. I love running my fingers through it, but they often get tangled in the strands. I was ecstatic when Wild Man pulled out a brush from Ben's pack.

Speaking of Ben, he left about an hour before the sun went

down, which was a couple of hours ago. He told Wild Man and me that he would be back in about a month.

Would we still be here then?

Once Wild Man is settled in front of me, I pick up the length of his hair, separating it into several sections. I grab the brush and start working on the bottom first.

When I told Wild Man earlier what the brush was for, he didn't seem surprised. One of the few memories of his mother is of him playing with her hair, so he probably remembers what it's used for. But apparently, he never felt the desire to use one.

"You have such beautiful hair," I say wistfully, carefully running the bristles through the strands.

"I like your hair," he says.

I know he does because he's always touching it. My hair is great, but his is fabulous.

"Do you want to brush mine after I'm done with yours?"

His thumbs start moving over my ankle. "Yes."

I smile as I set the first section away and start on another.

"Ben seems like a good guy. It's nice that he brings you things."

"Good, yes."

"Why did you save him all those years ago?"

Wild Man tips his head back, like he's enjoying the attention I'm giving him. "Wanted coyote dinner."

I snort out a laugh at his reply. That may be the case, but I also believe it was because he simply wanted to save Ben.

"You must really trust him to allow him in your home."

"*Our* home."

I roll my eyes, but my lips twitch with a small smile. "Fine. *Our* home."

"Hmm...," he hums. I peek at the side of his face and find his eyes are closed.

"Why did you never go with him when he offered to take you to town?"

His eyes open and he looks across the space. "Liked where I was. Didn't want different."

That's understandable. Anyone would be leery of such a big change. Especially when those changes are so drastic and you don't fully understand what those changes would be.

I carefully work on a knotted section. "Do you ever regret not going? Do you ever wonder what life would be like away from here?"

"No." His thumbs move circles on my ankles. "Maybe now."

My fingers pause in his hair, and I look at him. "Why now?"

His eyes flicker to the side, meeting mine. "Is *momor* happy?" he asks instead of answering.

"With you, yes," I reply with the truth. I am happy with Wild Man. More so than I ever thought possible. "But out here," I use the brush to gesture around us, "only sometimes. It's much different than what I'm used to. It's harder to live in a place like this. And I miss my family and friends."

His brows drop, but he doesn't say anything else. I want to know what he's thinking. Is he mulling over the possibility of leaving the wilderness? Taking a chance in civilization? For some reason, that thought makes me a little sad. I don't want Wild Man to change because of me. I love the way he is. His savage nature is what drew me to him. Living in civilization will eventually force that out of him.

But should *I* have to totally change to be with him? Upend my life and forget about the people I love? Living without him is something I can't even comprehend now, but I don't want to live without my family and friends either. In order for us to be together, one of us will have to make sacrifices.

"Do you trust me, Wild Man?" I ask.

I drop the section of hair and pick up another as I hold my breath and wait for his answer. The absence of the rope and his willingness to allow Ben into the tree hut proves he does, but I want to hear him say the words.

"Yes." There's no hesitation in his voice.

"I'm glad." His answer pleases me, and I can't help the silly grin that slides across my face.

As much as I want to broach the subject about us leaving, I decide to wait. I don't see Wild Man being very receptive to the idea at first, and I don't want to ruin this moment.

Once I'm done with his hair, I run my fingers through the strands, amazed at how soft it is. It reaches just past his shoulder blades and is the prettiest color I've ever seen. His mom had red hair, so I wonder if his dad had the same blueish black hair or if he got it from someone else in his family.

I drop the brush by my hip and push Wild Man's shoulders. "Lay down," I tell him. His head twists around and he looks at me. I lean forward and press my lips against his shoulder. "Please."

I move out of the way as he gets to his knees. When he starts to move around to lie on his back, I stop him. "No, on your stomach."

His brows drop, but he doesn't argue as he leans forward on his fists and lays down. I hike a leg over him and settle my weight down on his butt. Leaning forward, I press my hands against his lower back, digging my fingers into the muscles. I smile when Wild Man lets out a deep groan.

I work my hands in circular motions, hitting all the hard muscles. I can't imagine how good this must feel for him, having never had someone give him a massage.

I slowly move up his back, kneading his lats with my knuckles, then switching to my fingers when I get to his deltoids and shoulders.

Wild Man lifts his hips, one of his hands going under him, and a little thrill goes through me because I know he's adjusting himself. Is what I'm doing turning him on?

I suck in a breath when the movement has his ass pressing against my core.

Jesus, when did I become so wet and why did that feel so good?

Wild Man's head is turned to the side. His eyes have been

closed during my massage, but now they slide open. His hair is out of the way, so I have a clear view of his face. The heat I see in his black gaze has more moisture seeping from me.

I lean forward and lay my lips against the crook of his neck, licking the spot and then sucking the skin into my mouth. He's marked me so many times, it's about time I do the same.

His hips lift again, putting pressure against my pussy, and I can't hold back a moan. I lower my torso, letting my breasts skim across his back.

"My Ever is *wet*," he growls.

He's definitely not wrong. I'm soaked even as more leaks out of me.

"Rub pussy on me. Let me feel how wet you are."

*Jesus.* It was a mistake teaching him naughty words.

Maybe I should be embarrassed to consider rubbing myself on his ass, but that doesn't stop me. I push my pussy down, smearing myself on his asscheeks.

"Ah... god," I moan.

I sit up and look down my body to Wild Man's butt and notice the amount of juices I've left on him. Again, shouldn't I be cringing?

"More, *momor*," he grunts, his voice grating. "Harder. Fuck it against me."

I don't know what turns me on more; his filthy mouth or what I'm doing.

I rotate my hips back and forth, up and down, getting lost in the erotic and down-right dirty way I'm getting off on grinding against him. My lips part, and I pant, losing my breath at the intense sensations. Who knew humping a guy's ass could feel so erotic and good.

I press harder against him, needing a firmer touch. My clit hits the perfect spot, and I let out a low cry.

*Good god almighty.*

Suddenly, Wild Man spins below me. Before I can lose my

balance, his arm latches around my waist and he takes me down to the bed, so now I'm the one below him. The look in his eyes is feral, like he's just as turned on by our naughty play and he's on the verge of madness.

He grabs the back of my legs and lifts them, spreading them wide and pushing them back so far that my knees nearly touch the pallet beside my head. My pussy and ass are open, and his eyes lock on both. I bite my lip in anticipation as he dips his head with a needy growl rumbling from his lips.

"Yes, Wild Man!" I scream when he slides his tongue through the folds of my pussy.

He snarls against me, and the sound sends my desire soaring higher. He sucks at my clit, grazing his teeth against the bundle of nerves. His tongue moves down to spear my sopping hole, then he flattens it and moves back to my clit to torment me some more.

He braces his forearm against the back of my legs to keep them in position and uses one hand to poise a finger at my entrance. As he continues to drive me insane with his mouth at my clit, he shoves a finger inside. I reach between my legs with one hand and fist his hair, smashing his face against me.

"That's it, *momor*," he growls, thrusting a second finger inside me. "Fuck my face. Smear your juices on me. Drown me."

I cry out, my eyes snapping closed and my head thrashes back and forth. When he adds a third finger, I think I might pass out from the overload of pleasure.

Then, with three fingers fucking my pussy and his mouth still devouring my clit, he presses another finger at my back entrance. The juices leaking from my pussy makes it easy for him to slide the digit inside. He doesn't stop until his knuckles prevent him from going any farther.

"Wild Man!" I shout his name over and over, smashing his against me.

"I fuck this hole, momor," he growls, shoving his finger deeper in my ass. "This mine. All of you mine."

He snarls and growls, sucking my clit like it's the last dinner he'll ever have. His fingers fuck me deep and fast in both holes, until I hit a peak so high, I slide over the edge and my orgasm slams through me.

I scream and buck my hips, calling out his name, begging for more even when I know I can't take anymore.

My legs are boneless, and I feel like I'm floating by the time my release dwindles to little lingering spasms.

My eyes slowly slide open, my breaths coming in pants with little mewls of pleasure. Wild Man peers down at me from his kneeled position. He wipes the back of his arm across his mouth, but his beard is still wet with my release. He fists his cock, the head an angry red with a clear pearl of precum clinging to the slit, angling it down toward my entrance.

Before he can plunge inside, I press against the bed to sit up enough so I can grab a handful of his hair. I tug him down and meet him halfway with my lips.

*twenty-two*

WILD MAN

The moment my *momor's* lips press against mine, I know every single inch of her is and will always, forever, be mine. This female was the reason I was born. She's the reason I breathe and is the reason I fought so hard to stay alive after Peepa and Noeny were taken by the big bear. I claimed her before she gave me her kiss, but after this moment, there is nothing that will ever keep me from her.

She is my female.

My woman.

The Noeny to my babies.

My Ever.

My *momor*.

I groan and thrust my tongue inside her mouth. Her taste is better than I ever expected, and is one I'll crave for the rest of my life.

I grab her hair and force her head back at a better angle. I fuck her mouth the same way I'll fuck her pussy.

"*Mine*," I growl against her lips. "My lips. My kiss."

"Yours," she moans.

I want to beat my chest and roar to the sky that this female is mine, and I'll kill anything that tries to keep her from me.

"You taste like dreams," I tell her, licking at her lips. "Sweet dreams and sunshine. Never stop kissing."

"Fuck me, Wild Man. Take *your* pussy and show me I'm yours while you kiss me."

I almost lose my seed at her words. Only my wants and needs give me the strength to hold it back.

My *momor* doesn't carry my baby. I need to see her belly get big and round with my child.

*Momor* would be a good mother. Protective and loving and fierce. Like Vena is with Teeja and her pups.

I grab my cock and point it at her pussy, letting just the tip slip inside. Little sounds leave her, her breath whispering across my lips.

I thrust my tongue inside her mouth at the same time I ram my hips forward. I swallow her scream. Pulling out of her tightness, I thrust back inside.

I lift my head and look down at *momor*. Her brown gaze looks dazed as she gazes back at me. Fitting my hand around her throat to hold her in place, I drive my hips forward, seating my cock fully inside her. She cries out again, her voice straining. Her ankles lock around my lower back and her hips lift off the bed, meeting my powerful thrusts. When her nails dig into my thigh muscles, I hiss at the bite of pain. I know my *momor* feels good when she uses her nails on me. My back has her marks from the last time I took her. I like her marks on me almost as much as I enjoy leaving mine on her.

At my hiss, she relaxes her grip. I bare my teeth and bend down low until I'm in her face. "Do it again. Mark me, *momor*."

I feel the muscles in her throat work, and her face turns a deep red. I loosen my grip slightly, and she sucks in a sharp breath.

"More," she pants. Her tongue darts out to lick her lips. "Harder, Wild Man. Take your pussy harder."

I drop my mouth to hers and kiss her savagely as I work my cock inside her in a merciless frenzy. My Ever wants it harder, and she'll get everything she wants.

I use my grip on her throat and one at her waist to pull her down while I punch my cock in and out of her tight pussy. I make sure to hit the spot at the top of her pussy with each forward motion. I know she likes when that spot is touched.

It's still not enough. I need to go deeper. Releasing her throat, I grab behind one of her knees and lift her leg over my shoulder. It tilts her ass up, and I manage to go in further. I lean down, dropping my fist beside her head.

"Yes," she hisses.

She grabs my hair and pulls my mouth back down to hers. I thrust my tongue in her mouth as my hips power back and forth.

"Mine," I growl against her lips. "Say it, *momor*."

"Yours," she cries. "Oh, God. I'm yours."

Her walls grip me tight and she rips her mouth from mine to let out a hoarse scream. My own release follows right after. I tip my head back and roar to the trees. Birds take flight, scattering into the sky, as if fleeing a crazed predator.

I am a crazed predator. Crazed for my female and the life we'll share. And god help anyone or anything who dares to threaten to take her from me.

# twenty-three

EVERLEE

I jerk awake when an unholy roar fills the night air. My eyes snap open and dart around looking for the source, but instinctively, I already know.

Wild Man. And he sounds like he's in pain.

With the new moon, it's too dark to see anything. A shuffling sound comes from outside the sleeping area and another roar nearly pierces my ears.

I scramble up from the bed, feeling around the floor for the spear Wild Man always keeps near while we sleep. I don't feel it, so I try to find something else to use, but come up empty.

"Wild Man!" I scream, fear knotting itself in my stomach.

His answering bellow has those knots doubling in size.

Uncaring that I don't have a weapon, my only thought is to get to him. What in the hell is happening? Has an animal made its way into the tree hut? My thoughts are frantic as I run to the opening.

I still can't see shit, but I can barely make out shadows across from the fire pit. There are several of them. Not animals, but people, and they're wrestling another shadow to the ground.

Before I can even think about finding something to hit the people with, arms wrap tight around my waist from behind and lift me up from the ground.

"Let me go!" I scream, thrashing against the hold.

Wild Man roars again. "*Momor*!"

"Ever, it's me. We've come to rescue you."

My struggles stop at the familiar voice and my breath gets stuck in my throat. "Joe?" I croak.

"Yeah, baby sis. We're so fucking sorry it's taken us so long," he says against my ear. "Come, I'm taking you out of here while they finish with him."

"No!" I renew my struggles, scratching at his arms, desperately trying to break his hold. "They've got to stop! They're hurting him!"

"Damn right they are," he growls.

Fear tightens the band around my chest at the sinister note in his voice.

Grunts and groans coming from my dad and brothers mix in with the deranged roars coming from Wild Man.

"You've got to stop them! Dad! Don't hurt him!"

"Joe, get her the fuck out of here!" Dad barks, sounding out of breath.

I still can't fucking see in the dark, so I can't tell what's happening. I can't tell how badly Wild Man is hurt. Or if one of my brothers or Dad is. I can't stand the thought of Wild Man in pain, but I don't want my dad or brothers hurt either.

I buck and kick back against my brother's hold. "Joe, please! You've got to let me go so I can save him!" Wild Man and my family are more alike than either knows. Both will fight until one isn't breathing. Wild Man is fierce and the strongest man I know, but it's four against one, odds I doubt he can defeat. My dad and brothers won't stop until he's dead, and if by some chance Wild Man manages to get the upper hand, he won't stop until they are. "They're going to kill each other!" I yell.

"No, *they* are going to kill *him*," Joe says, skyrocketing my fear.

He starts dragging me backward. I screech to the top of my lungs and fight harder than I have in my entire life. I try to kick back, but I only meet air. But Joe is just too strong and overpowers me. He pulls me through the leafy opening, and I desperately grab onto branches. My fingers slide down the stiff stalks, cutting into my skin. I ignore the pain.

"Let me go! Let me go!" I scream over and over again.

Wild Man isn't yelling anymore. All I can hear is Joe's heavy breathing in my ear, grunts coming from the tree hut, and the heavy sound of flesh hitting flesh.

Joe keeps dragging me backward, further and further away.

My heart feels like it's being sliced from my chest with a dull blade. I can't get enough air to breathe and my head feels dizzy with dark spots dancing in my vision. My struggles taper off when my arms feel too heavy, even as my mind screams to *fight*! To get to my dad and brothers before they kill the man that I love.

I let my body go completely limp in Joe's arms. He sets me to my feet and my legs nearly buckle, but I force the muscles to work. As soon as his grip on me loosens, a rush of adrenaline fills me, and I take off blindly for the tree hut.

"Everlee!" Joe calls behind me, and I hear his thundering footsteps as he chases after me.

I brush the hair out of my face, hardly registering the blood I'm smearing on my cheeks from the gouges on my palms. I can barely make out the tree hut entrance just up ahead.

I'm only a few feet away when my foot hits something hard. I don't have time to register the pain before I'm flying forward. A sharp pain shoots through the side of my head when I collide with something solid.

The blackness comes fast, but before it fully takes me under, I hear another roar of rage.

And this one, I know, is the sound of death.

# twenty-four

EVERLEE

The first thing I notice is the smell. Apples and spices. Dad says my favorite food when I was a child was cinnamon applesauce. I'd always choose that over any other sweets. Even in adulthood I do the same. Instead of Ben & Jerry's being my comfort food, I always grab a jar of applesauce. I love the smell of apples so much that every room in my house has at least two apple scented candles.

The next thing I notice is the silence. There are no birds chirping or insects buzzing or leaves rustling. The only sound I hear is a light hum of some sort. It's far too quiet, and I don't like it.

And why is the bed so soft? I've grown used to sleeping on a pallet on the ground. I feel like I'm laying on a pillowy cloud. The blanket lying atop me is too heavy, as well.

What I notice the most is the lack of warmth at my back and the muscular arm I've grown used to having around my waist. The hard length that's usually wedged between my butt cheeks is absent. Wild Man always wakes me up, demanding sex, before he gets out of bed. I never complain, because I love having him inside me. I don't remember him doing that this morning, and my body isn't deliciously sore like it normally is when he does, so why is he not in bed with me now?

I crack open my eyes and immediately regret my decision. Pain explodes in my head the moment my eyes encounter the bright light. Why in the hell is it so bright? The trees above us shade the tree hut, so where is the light coming from?

A moan leaves my lips, and I lift my hand to the side of my head where most of the pain is centered. My fingers encounter something soft right above my ear on my temple. I poke it with my pointer finger and wince at the sharp ache I get in return.

"Ever."

The muffled voice sounds like it's coming from far away, like through a long tunnel. The deep timbre sounds familiar, but it's not Wild Man, and I can't place it.

"The light," I croak. My mouth feels like cotton was shoved inside it.

"Ethan, close the shades." The voice sounds closer, and I'm still struggling to remember who it belongs to. "Ever, can you hear me? Open your eyes for me, honey."

Seconds past before the light I see through my closed eyelids finally dims. The relief is instant. There's still pain in my head, but it's not as profound.

I slit open my eyes and a blurry picture tries to focus in front of me. I blink several times before it begins to clear enough for me to see the man hovering close to my face. Dark brown hair and hazel eyes. He has a shadow of hair on his cheeks and chin, which seems strange. Dad shaves every day, so to see that he obviously hasn't in a few days is out of the ordinary.

"Dad?" I rasp. Jesus, why does my throat feel so raw and dry?

I open my mouth to ask for some water, but a glass with a straw is presented in front of me before I can. A hand goes behind my head to lift it from the pillow and my greedy lips latch around the straw. I pull in several deep pulls. The water is good and cold and feels wonderful against my throat, but it tastes different.

"That's enough for now." Dad pulls the glass away before I'm finished. "I'll give you more in a few minutes. I don't want you to get sick."

Why would I get sick from drinking water?

"Wha—" I cough and clear my throat. "What happened? Where am I?"

I try to look around, but the movement sends a wave of dizziness through me. I close my eyes and breathe in deep through my nose and out through my mouth.

"What do you remember?" comes Dad's voice.

I open my lids, my brows pulling down. Another sharp pain pierces my skull when I try to think back to the last thing I remember. I come up blank. "I don't remember."

Dad frowns, his gaze moving across the bed to something on the other side. I turn my head, moving slow in fear of setting off my head again. My brother, Maddox, is there, looking down at me with a worried expression. It's then that I realize all of my brothers are here. Ethan is over by the window, Joe is sitting in a chair in the corner, his elbows resting on his knees, and Spencer is leaning against the wall by the door. They all look at me wearily, like I'm on my deathbed or something and they don't know how to react to it.

I bring my gaze back to Dad, just now noticing the bruise on his jaw and the split that cuts across his right eyebrow. The area is slightly swollen. I swing my gaze back to my brothers, see past the dizziness that follows, and note they aren't in much better shape. Maddox's bottom lip is swollen and there's a gash down the middle. Ethan has a black eye and a cut on his cheek. Spencer's nose appears to be broken, and even through the dim light, I can see the darkness that's developed just under his eyes. Joe's the only one who seems to be uninjured.

"What in the hell?" I demand, attempting to push my hands into the bed to sit up.

"Lay down," Dad orders as he pushes on my shoulders. "That knock on your head has had you out for two days. The doc said you'll be feeling the effects from it for a few more, so I know you're still in pain."

As if my head agrees with Dad's words, the pounding comes back with force, and I slump back down. Nausea churns in my stomach, so I take in a deep breath, praying that I don't get sick. I'm sure the pressure of throwing up would feel fantastic for my head.

"Doc?" I ask. The blanket I'm under is down to my waist and I'm wearing a lavender t-shirt. Below the blanket, I have on a pair of cotton shorts. The material against my skin feels annoying. "Dr. Neilson was here?"

"Yes," Dad answers. He sits forward in his chair, resting his elbows on his knees. He clasps his hands together and lays them on the bed. It kind of looks like he's praying, but Dad isn't the praying type. "I figured it was better he treat you here since your injuries weren't life threatening. Just a nasty bump on your head. Once the word gets out that you were found, which we all know wouldn't take long, everybody and their cousin would swarm the hospital."

One bad thing about living in a small town is everyone is in everyone's business. There's no such thing as privacy or keeping secrets here.

My mind catches and sticks on one word.

"Found? What do you mean?" My brows pucker, and even that small move has a small niggle of pain radiating through my head.

Dad licks his lips and his eyes drop to his clasped hands. The muscle in his jaw twitches when he lifts them back to me.

"You've been missing for six weeks, Ever. Your brothers and I just found you two days ago."

"Gone?" I choke out.

All of a sudden, a searing pain stabs at my skull, and I slam my eyes shut. The pain is so great that I clutch my head, expecting to feel blood seeping from my ears.

Behind my closed eyelids, visions flash. They come so fast and are so brilliantly vivid that I can't comprehend them before they're gone and another takes its place. They repeat over and over again. But then they start to slow, and I get a better understanding of what they are.

Memories.

Of my time in the forest with Wild Man.

My fascination the first time I saw him while he bathed in the water.

Him confronting me afterward.

Sitting in front of the fire and eating.

Trying to leave afterward.

The first time Wild Man fucked me and the pain I felt during that experience.

Wild Man standing above me as I peed and him masking my scent with his own.

The first time he took me, and I didn't fight back.

Hunting with him and the sickening worry I felt when I thought he was going to die from a snake bite.

Meeting Teeja and his family.

Wild Man teaching me how to fish.

The way he always gave me the bigger pieces of fruit.

Falling in love and realizing I didn't want to live in a world if Wild Man wasn't in it.

The night I was taken from him.

His roars piercing the night as my Dad and brothers beat him.

My eyes flash open. My hands are covering my face and when I pull them back, my gaze is caught by my wrists. The woven bracelets. They're gone.

"Where are they?"

Tears prick my eyes when I look at Dad. He looks haggard, like he's aged twenty years since I saw him before I left to find Wild Man.

"What?" he asks, his voice hoarse.

"My bracelets." I rub the skin around my wrist. "Where are they?"

I hear a scraping and look over at Mad as he opens my bedside drawer. He pulls out three familiar bracelets and holds them up with a finger. "These?"

I lean over, uncaring that the move brings on another wave of dizziness and pain, and snatch them from him. Some of the weight that's gathered on my chest eases when I slip them over my wrist.

My throat closes, and I bring my eyes to Dad. I'm so fucking scared to voice the question that's pounding through my head. The answer is either going to kill me or save me. Tears prick my eyes, and I let them fall.

"Is he dead?" My voice is raw and filled with so much profound heartache.

"God fucking willing," Ethan mutters from across the room.

I ignore him and keep my gaze trained on Dad, waiting for his response with my heart firmly lodged in my throat.

The line of his jaw twitches and something that looks like hatred enters his expression. "He wasn't when we left him, but he probably is now. If not from his injuries then the wild animals probably got to him. Either way works fine for me."

A sob escapes before I can stop it and tears flood down my cheeks. My lungs feel like they're being constricted by an imaginary fist and if it weren't for the pounding I hear in my ears, I'd swear my heart actually stopped beating.

"No," I moan, refusing to believe even the possibility that Wild Man is dead. He *can't* be. He promised me that he would always protect me. That nothing would ever hurt me. But I'm hurting now. I'm hurting so much that I know I'll never recover. My heart, my life, my very soul will never be the same. I need him to take away that hurt.

"Ever," Dad says, reaching for me. "Everything will—"

I don't let him finish. I knock his hand away and start throwing back the covers. I don't hate Dad or my brothers for what they've done. They didn't know that I fell in love with my captor and essentially destroyed my heart when they beat him to death. Or beat him so badly he couldn't defend himself against the predators who roam the forest. All they knew was that I was missing. Had no clue what had happened to me. My family loves me and I love them for searching for me.

I don't hate them, but I can't look at them right now. I don't want to see their faces and the damage that Wild Man inflicted on them before they took him down. I can't look them in the eyes and not break down, knowing that, because of them, I'll never be whole again.

"What in the fuck are you doing, Everlee?" Dad asks when I slide my feet to the floor and try to get up from the bed. I'm forced to close my eyes when the room starts to sway.

"I'm going back out there," I say. I open my lids, grateful when the room stays where it's supposed to. "I have to find him."

If there's a slim chance he might still be alive, I have to go to him. Even if he's not—I press my lips together when they start to wobble—I need to find him before the animals get to him. He deserves to be buried and not eaten by wild animals.

"Like hell you are," Dad growls, getting up from the chair.

I press my hands against the mattress, intent on getting to my feet so I can dress. Before I can though, Dad is in front of me, pushing me down by my shoulders.

"You aren't going, Ever," he says, using his firm dad voice. "Your ass is staying in bed where it belongs. You have a fucking head injury for fuck's sake."

I tip my head back, straightening my spine, and meet his gaze. "I'm going."

"Why? Why in the hell would you want to go back out there? We just rescued you."

"Because I love him." I give him the truth.

Dad has a temper, but he doesn't show it often. You always know when he's about to lose it when the veins in his forehead start poking out. Like it is right now. I get his anger. For weeks he's worried about his daughter, not knowing what happened to her. If she were alive, dead, or suffering.

But he's not swaying me on this. He can rant and yell to his heart's content. It won't change my mind. Nothing short of death would keep me from finding Wild Man.

I start shoving at his chest, my moves becoming frantic. "Move!" I yell.

Desperation fills my mind when he doesn't move an inch.

"Ever, stop," he barks, reaching for my arm.

I pull away. I can't stop. I won't ever stop. Not until I get back to Wild Man.

I start kicking out at him, scratching the hands reaching for me, yelling at the top of my lungs to be let go. I know what I must look like. A crazy person on the verge of hysteria. But I don't care and they don't understand.

"Mad, Spencer," Dad grates between his teeth, capturing my wrist when I lash out toward his face. His eyes are hard as he stares down at me.

I watch in my peripheral vision as Mad and Spencer approach us. I don't like the look in Dad's eyes right now. He's in his alpha protective mode and there's no telling what he'll do.

"Hold her down," he tells my brothers in a firm tone.

I'm so shocked by what comes out of his mouth that it takes a second to register the words. And in that second, Mad and Spencer go for my arms, and I'm forced down on the mattress.

"Dad!" I yell, pulling on my brother's grips. "What in the hell are you doing?"

He walks to the nightstand and grabs something. He holds it up, and I realize it's a syringe. He snatches the cap off and tosses it on the nightstand.

"Dad?" I croak.

He comes to sit on the bed by my hip. I've stopped struggling because it hurts my head too much. Mad and Spencer's grips loosen, like they're afraid they'll leave marks on my wrists.

"I'm so sorry, honey," he says. The anger has drained from his eyes and a look of remorse replaces it. I know from that expression that he really is sorry. That this is eating him alive. "But I have to do this."

"Please don't," I beg, tears sliding down my cheeks.

"You'll see things more clearly when you wake up."

I shake my head. "I won't. I'll still love him."

He doesn't say anything else as he sinks the needle into my arm and pushes the plunger. I move my eyes away from him and stare up at the ceiling, a steady stream of tears still sliding from my eyes.

"I'll always love him," I whisper, the last word falling from my lips right as everything goes dark.

## *twenty-five*

WILD MAN

I clench my jaw and suck in a short breath of air as I try to force my body up off the ground. A grunt of pain blows through my teeth when a sharp pain pierces my side. It feels like I'd been stabbed between two of my ribs and the knife is still wedged inside. Even the lightest of movements has my vision going blurry. My whole body hurts, like a big bear chomped on me with its teeth and aggressively shook me, banging my body against trees.

It doesn't matter though. I have to get to my feet and go after her.

They took my *momor*.

I know it was her family. Her father and brothers. Even if one of them hadn't whispered in my ear that I would die for hurting his sister, I would have still known.

And now they're going to pay for taking her away from me.

When I told *momor* that I would kill her family if they attempted to take her, it was the truth. At the time, at least.

Now, they'll pay, just not with their life, but with a lot of pain. I want to rip their heads from their necks. To use my knife and gut them like I do the animals I kill for food. To filet their skin from their bones and toss their carcasses to the side to let the other animals feast on them. But I can't kill them because *momor* loves them. It would hurt her, and I know killing them is something she would never forgive.

I try to open my eyelids, but I can only crack them open into slits. It's barely enough for me to make out that the sun is either going down or coming up.

I don't know how long I've been laying here, which means I don't know how long *momor* has been gone. I've woken up a couple of times, but each time I did, the slightest movement had blackness swallowing me up again.

Slowly, I lift my arm, testing the movement. When the blackness doesn't fill the little vision I have and the pain is barely tolerable, I bring my hand to my face. The skin around my eyes feels different, puffy, which is why I can't open them. There are also several deep cuts on my face. The blood from them is sticky and not fresh, which means they're are no longer bleeding.

There's a rustle of movement over where I think the opening is. My first instinct is to get up and defend my home, but that'll take more strength than I have right now. So I lay there, tracking the creature by its movements. I can tell by the sound of their steps it's an animal and not *momor's* family coming back to finish me off.

I feel warm breath on the side of my face. Before the whine comes, I know who it is.

"Teeja," I grate between my teeth.

He answers by swiping his tongue on my cheek. The lick stings, and I want to push him away, but what little strength I woke with is going away.

"Teeja, no," I say. Even talking is painful.

Familiar black spots move into my vision and my hearing sounds muffled, like something is covering my ears. Little pricks poke along my scalp, almost like something is crawling around on my head.

I decide to close my eyes for a moment until the feelings go away....

I DON'T KNOW HOW LONG MY EYES ARE CLOSED, BUT THE NEXT TIME I open them, I can see a little more. The sun is directly above me, shining through the trees way up in the sky. My body feels like it's on fire, the pain different than it was before. Each breath I take in sends a sharp pain in my side, but I force the air into my lungs anyway.

I turn my head to the side and see Teeja only a couple of feet from me. He's laying on his stomach with his head on his paws.

"Teeja," I grunt and the wolf's head pops up.

He doesn't get up, but stays lowered to the ground as he scoots forward on his paws until his face is close to mine. He whines, flicking his tongue out to lick across my forehead.

With effort, I test my legs, the muscles tensing as I try to lift them. I can move them, but it makes the pain in my side worse. I try my arms next. Those are easier to lift, but it's still not enough to get me off the ground.

My mind screams at me to get up and go after *momor*, but my body won't allow it. Anger coats my insides, making my skin feel hot.

I have to be strong to get her back, and right now, I'm as weak as a baby and can barely move.

I know her family won't hurt her. She's safe with them.

And that's the only thing that gives my mind peace.

But once I heal and get my strength back, I'll be taking back what's mine.

# *twenty-six*

EVERLEE

W ild Man and I are in the bathing pool. The bright sun
shines down on us, making the clear water sparkle brilliantly. Water falls down on us from the small trickle sliding over a
rock's edge, mimicking a shower. It feels cool and refreshing.

But what feels better is the way Wild Man is holding me. I have
my arms and legs wrapped tightly around his shoulders and waist.
His big hands are on my ass, holding me up. We look deeply into
each other's eyes as he slowly slides his cock in and out of me,
hitting spots inside that feel incredible.

"*Momor*," he whispers in a tone I've never heard from him
before. It's filled with reverence and devotion.

We're making love. He fucks me softly and slowly and with
care. It's just as I knew it would be.

When Wild Man fucks me, using his strength to slam inside
me, his hands gripping me to hold me in place, a feral look in his
eyes, he always makes me feel things I never knew were possible.
He brings my body to life in a way that's life altering.

But making love with him has me seeing a galaxy worth of

stars. He makes me feel loved and adored. Like I'm the only thing he'll ever need. The only thing he'll ever see. Like I was put on this earth for the sole purpose of being with this man, just as he is the same to me.

It's a complete contradiction from what I'm used to from this savage man.

He leans forward and gently presses his lips against mine. His tongue slides out and licks across the seam, and I immediately open to let him inside. He makes love to my mouth just as sweetly as he does with the rest of his body.

"My *momor*." He swivels his hips and presses against my clit, eliciting a low moan from me. "Are you mine?"

"Yes. Oh god, yes."

"Tell me, Ever," he rasps in a low voice. "Tell me you're mine."

I tighten my arms around his shoulders and dig my heels into his ass, getting him deeper inside me. "I'm yours, Wild Man."

"Always and forever," he adds.

"I love you, Fey."

His name has barely left my lips when everything goes bad. Wild Man is ripped from my arms and is pulled beneath the water's surface. I open my mouth and let out a shrill scream.

I jerk awake and jolt up in bed, the sound of my piercing scream still bouncing off my ear drums. It sounds so real that I cover my ears, trying to block out the noise.

"Ever."

I snap my head to the side, wincing when the sudden movement sends a dull ache through my temple.

My best friend sits in a chair pulled close to the bed. Her eyes glisten with tears and her bottom lip trembles.

"Rika?" I ask, my throat dry and scratchy.

She's off the chair and on the bed on her knees in the next instant. I barely have time to brace before she's got me wrapped tight in a hug. My own throat constricts as I sling my arms around her.

"You scared the shit out of me, Ever," she says, sobbing against my neck. "Don't ever fucking do that again." She pulls back, furiously wiping at the tears sliding down her cheeks. "Swear it to me."

I slap away my own tears. "I swear."

She pulls in a deep breath and blows it out through her mouth on a loud exhale. She swivels and settles her ass next to my hip.

"How are you feeling?"

Truthfully? I feel like my world has been turned upside down and inside out. I feel like I'll never be able to take in a full breath, nor feel my heart beat properly again. A part of me is missing, one in which I'll never be able to get back.

But I don't tell Rika that. She'll think I'm crazy just like my dad and brother's do. There's no way I can keep my feelings for Wild Man from her, but I need to tell her in a way she'll hopefully understand.

"I'm okay."

Rika eyes me like she knows I'm lying. We've known each other long enough for her to recognize all of my expressions.

"How long have you been here?"

I still can't believe dad and my brothers drugged me. They're ruthless and protective to a fault, but I would have never thought they would be capable of something so drastic. I feel betrayed by my own flesh and blood.

"A couple of hours," Rika responds. "I would have been here sooner, but the Horde wouldn't let me. Jesus, Ever." Her eyes close and her lips form a straight line, like she's trying to hold back more tears. "The last six weeks have been hell." She opens her lids. "We didn't know if you were alive or dead." Her voice cracks on the last word.

I reach over and grab her hand, bring it to my blanket clad lap. "I'm so sorry," I say with sincerity.

I would have been freaking the hell out if the roles were reversed.

"Tell me what happened," she demands.

I don't want to open my mouth and let the words out. It's going to break me to talk about my time spent with Wild Man. I still don't know if he's alive or dead and not knowing is killing me.

Even so, I tell Rika everything. From the fear I felt at the beginning. The anger toward Wild Man for holding me captive. The pain of the rapes. The terror when he insisted I was his and his insane need to get me pregnant. How he kept me tied to a rope and forced me to feed from his hand. The story of his parents and their skulls he keeps by his bed. The snake bite and me caring for him.

Her brows rise when I tell her I began to enjoy his touch and even initiated it. I watch the disbelief on her face when I tell her that I fell in love with the wild man in the forest.

By the time I'm done, she looks at me as though I've lost my mind. Maybe I have. Who in their right mind would fall in love with their captor? A man who's hurt me in unimaginable ways.

If that makes me insane, I honestly don't care.

"I love him, Rika," I say simply.

"Ever—"

"And I don't care if that sounds crazy. I *love* him." I stress, imploring her to understand. "He's hurt me in so many ways. In ways that are a woman's worst nightmare. In spite of that, I still fell in love with him. It's not Stock Holmes syndrome," I add before she can say it. "What I feel for him isn't fake or imaginary or a coping mechanism. It's pure and real and deep. It consumes my mind and body." I press a hand to the center of my chest. "He makes my heart beat stronger."

"Wow," she says, shock and awe in her tone. "I honestly don't know what to say. What my mind is telling me to say is you really need to go see a psychiatrist, but I'm not going to suggest that because I don't think it would do any good." She pauses a moment, her expression turning thoughtful. "No matter what details you give, I can't truly imagine what you went through because I wasn't there. I know *you* believe you love this man, but how can you be so certain?"

Tears come to my eyes, and I let them course down my cheeks. "Because I feel like I'm barely alive right now. Like a huge part of me is missing. There's a hole in my heart and that piece is with Wild Man. I never got to tell him that I love him."

"Oh, Ever," she says softly. When she scoots forward, I fall into her arms.

"I don't even know if he's alive or not." I pull back from her. "I need to know."

"You know the Horde isn't going to let you go back out there. And quite frankly, I don't blame them."

I sniff and bring the cover up to wipe my nose. "Oh, I know they won't. Did they tell you Dad drugged me to knock me out?"

"They said you were given a sedative when you became hysterical."

I grit my teeth. "I only became that way because they refuse to let me go. They have no right to keep me from him. I told them I wanted to go find Wild Man. They weren't onboard with the idea."

"Can you blame them? You were missing for six weeks, and then when they find you, you want to go back to the same place you were held captive. Try to see things from their view."

"I do, and I understand." I take a deep breath. "Believe me, I know how all of this sounds, but can you try to understand where I'm coming from? Whether it's logical or not, the man I fell in love with could be hurting or even dying. He could already be dead." I swallow thickly, refusing to let more tears loose. I've cried enough already. "I don't care if Dad and my brothers like it or not, I need to go back."

"Even if they did give in, you know they won't let you go by yourself."

I nod. "Yeah, I figured that, and I'm okay if they come with me."

If Wild Man is still alive—and I refuse to believe he isn't—the meeting between him and my family won't be a pleasant one. Actually, it'll probably be down right ugly, like it was the last time. But if taking one or all of them with me is the only way they'll allow me to go, then so be it. I'll stop any altercation before it starts.

"So, how are you going to talk them into it?" she asks skeptically. "I don't see them giving in."

"By giving them no choice. They can't keep drugging me and they can't always keep watch. They'll either agree to go with me, or I'll somehow go by myself."

---

"How did you find me?" I ask Dad, running my tense fingers through Mr. Bones fur where he's laying in my lap.

I'm still angry with him and the others, but I've calmed down enough to realize acting frantic will get me nowhere, except maybe another shot in my arm. I need him to see I'm completely rational, of sound mind, and can make sensible decisions. Like going after Wild Man because I actually love him and not because he believes I've attached myself to him because of a sick bond.

Rika is still with me sitting crossed legged at the end of my bed. Dad barged in when he heard us talking and knew I was awake. Of course, with him came Mad and Ethan. I don't know where my other brothers are, and quite frankly, I don't care. I'm pissed at them too, because they let Mad and Spencer hold me down while Dad injected that fucking sedative.

"Ethan and Spencer were out scouting the area, looking for clues, when they came across boot tracks. He called in the rest of us from where we were tracking twenty miles away."

It had to be Ben. He's the only person that could have led tracks back to the tree hut.

"How in the hell did you end up in that part of Black Forest?" he asks. "The last we talked, you were in the northern part."

233

I fiddle with the bracelet on my wrist. "That next morning, at the last minute, I decided to change my location. The section I was in wasn't producing any results, so I moved south. I had planned to call you that night and tell you of the new location."

As expected, Dad's eyes flash with anger. "Goddamn it, Everlee!" he spits between clenched teeth. Mr. Bones jumps from my lap at the tension in the room and scurries from the room. "This is why you should have brought one of you with us."

"Yeah, well, I didn't." I glare at him. "And you know what? I'm glad I didn't. I'm glad I ended up where I was and who I was with."

"And just fuck all to your family and we went through?"

I close my eyes and try to pull in a calming breath. I know they all went through hell, and I hate that they did, but if it wasn't for the decisions I made, I never would have found Wild Man. I never would have experienced a love so deep and consuming. I won't ever regret that or wish it didn't happen, even if it meant I could take away the pain they went through.

"I'm sorry you went through that." I open my eyes and look at Dad. "But if I could go back and change things, I wouldn't."

"Doc examined you while you were out those couple of days." My gaze switches to Mad. His hands are shoved into his pockets, and I see the lumps of his fists. He looks just as upset and angry as Dad. "He said there was evidence of intercourse. Were you fucking him willingly?"

I flinch at his crass words.

"Maddox!" Rika shrieks, shock on her face. "Don't be an asshole!"

I wait for Dad to intervene, but he doesn't. He looks slightly uncomfortable, but his eyes say he's waiting for my answer.

Maddox's hard eyes move to Rika. "My sister. Not yours. You have no say in this." His gaze moves back to me. "Well?"

"Not at first, but it wasn't long before I was," I reply truthfully. I won't sugarcoat the facts, but I won't lie to them either.

After shooting me a disgusted look, he storms from the room, slamming the door behind him. Ethan's expression doesn't appear much better than Mad, but at least it's only disappointment on his face and not revulsion as he follows behind Mad.

Dad looks murderous. His jaw works back and forth and his hands are fisted by his sides. I don't know if he's angry at me because I wasn't a willing participant at first or that I did become willing.

He says nothing as he continues to look at me for what seems like forever. I expect him to explode again or for him to approach and try to offer me comfort of some sort. He scrubs a hand over his face before he turns and walks out of my bedroom. The silent click of the door when he shuts it sounds louder than when Mad slammed it.

I angrily brush away my tears.

Disappointing my family is something I've always tried to avoid. Seeing that disquiet on Dad's face as he left hurts worse than any words he could say. I feel like a failure of a daughter.

But they just don't understand. Nothing I say could make them understand.

And it changes nothing.

My dad and brothers are tenacious and stubborn, but I'm of their blood, so I have the same traits.

Rika eyes me doubtfully, her expression sorrowful. "I don't see you getting your way in this."

"Then you'd be wrong," I reply confidently. "But first, I need you to pick something up from the store for me."

# twenty-seven

WILD MAN

I think something inside of me might be broken or at least cracked. The stack of bones that are on either side of my chest ache, especially on my right side. I have to take shallow breaths since deep ones feel like I'm being stabbed repeatedly from the inside. Even when I do, it still hurts to breathe. Not from my injuries, but because *momor* is gone.

My eyes aren't as puffy, so I can see out of them now and the blackness that likes to put me to sleep hasn't come back for a while. I think it's been days since *momor* was taken because I've woken up several times with some of them being during the day and some at night.

Teeja has been there each time I open my eyes. Lying the length of his warm body by my side at night when the coolness in the air leaves little bumps all over my body. He keeps Vena and the pups away. I think it's because he doesn't know if whatever attacked me is coming back. If he understood my words, I'd tell him not to worry. *Momor's* family won't be back. I'm sure when they left, they believed I was either dead or dying. Maybe I should be. Maybe if they did this to someone else, they would be. But I'm not letting go of my female so easily. I'll fight even death to get back to her.

Teeja has brought me food. Small animals he's killed. When I was first left on my own as a boy, I ate berries and bugs to stay alive. I was older the first time I killed an animal. I was so starved and sick of eating berries and bugs that I ripped into the small animal with tall ears, not caring what parts I ate, only that I wanted to fill my caved-in stomach. When I learned how to make a fire, I remembered Peepa putting food on top of the flames, so I did the same to the animals I killed. I had gotten used to eating meat raw, but I found I liked it much better over the fire. Since then, I can barely keep meat down if it's not heated by flames. I've barely been able to move, so I haven't been able to make a fire to cook the meat Teeja brings me. But I still eat it. To rebuild my strength so I can get to *momor*.

Food isn't the only thing I need to consume though. Luckily, as uncomfortable as it's been, it's rained a couple of times. There was a small bowl on the ground near where I laid. With a lot of grunts and pain barely tolerable, I managed to drink the small amount of water gathered in the bowl.

Thankfully, the pain in my side isn't as great today, and I'm able to move a little better.

I look down at my body and see all the dark spots on my chest and stomach. Most of it are marks under the skin where it looks like blood has come to the surface and can't escape, but I do have a few cuts. They don't look bad though.

I've managed to partially prop myself up against the log near where I make fires, and doing just that takes all of my breath, which makes the pain in my side worse.

Teeja whines close by, and I look at him. He's sitting on his hind legs, his head tilted to the side. If he were human, I'd imagine he'd have a worried expression on his face.

Teeja first came to me years ago. I was out hunting and was just getting ready to kill a fox for dinner when I heard a yelp off in the distance. The sound startled the fox and he took off. When the yelp came again, I could tell whatever it was, was in pain. I went searching for the animal, thinking it would be my dinner instead since it scared off the fox. I came across a pup wolf that had gotten stuck in a tangle of vines. He was so young that he was probably still feeding from its Noeny.

Instead of killing the pup, I freed it from its trap. Most of the wild animals in the forest keep to their own kind and don't mingle with other creatures. I expected the pup to take off as soon as it was free, but it walked up to me, sat on its hind legs, and stared right into my eyes, like he was thanking me for freeing him. When I left the area, it followed. I didn't know where its Noeny was. I had seen other wolf families before, so I knew females usually had more than one pup. This one was alone though. Maybe the family had died.

I didn't shoo the pup away when he followed me back home. I had been alone for so long that it was nice to have another life near. I shared the little bit of meat I had left from the day before with the pup. He stuck around for days, following me everywhere I went, before he left. But he kept coming back.

Teeja walks up to me now and nudges my arm. With effort and searing pain, I lift my arm and lay my hand on top of his head between his ears. I once saved him all those years ago and now he's helped save me.

"Go to family, Teeja," I tell the wolf. My voice is deep and scratchy. "I'm good now."

He licks the underside of my upper arm then looks at me like he's asking if I'm sure.

I scratch the top of his head. "Go to Vena."

He looks at me with eyes that look like the sky before he turns and trots away.

I slump against the log, my eyes feeling like something heavy is trying to pull them closed. The pain in my side is getting worse again since I sat up, so I let myself slowly fall over on the side that doesn't hurt as much.

Every time I wake up, I feel a little stronger and it's a little easier to move. As much as I want to force my body up and make it work properly, I know I can't. I need to sleep and heal.

I don't know where *momor's* family took her. When I was a boy living in the wild, after Peepa and Noeny were eaten by the big bear, I wandered around for days and days, looking for a way out or for someone to find me. I was scared and lonely. I cried and screamed, but I learned fast to keep quiet, because there were animals nearby that I knew would eat me too. I never found a way out or another person. By the time I was older, grew stronger, and knew I could find my way out, I no longer wanted to. The thought of leaving this place was frightening. My memories of the world beyond the wild were faded. I liked where I was. I felt safe here, so I stayed.

Now it's time I leave. My female is in the big world, and somehow, I'll find her and bring her back.

## *twenty-eight*

EVERLEE

I f looks could kill, Dad would be spazzing out on the floor right now. I love the man, I really do, but I do *not* like him right now. In fact, I'm teetering on the edge of loathing him, something I've never felt for him before. And my brothers, each are lining up behind Dad, walking a thin line, barely balancing on my 'like' meter.

It's been ten days since they found me and none of them have relented on letting me go find Wild Man. I never expected they'd let me go on my own, but I was hoping they'd eventually agree if one or more went with me. I truly understand their refusal. Their reasons are valid. But I'll be damned if they'll stop me from going, so their wisest choice would be to let me go with an escort, because if they don't, I'll find a way to go on my own.

"You can hate it all you want," I tell Dad, straightening my spine and putting steel in my voice. "But you won't stop me. I *will* be going. Nothing other than death will keep me from finding him."

From over to my left, Mad takes a step toward me. I swing my gaze his way and point my finger at him. "You stay the hell away from me."

He stops, his brows raising at my aggressive tone and the fire spewing from my eyes. I'm still pissed at him and Spencer for holding me down on the bed that day.

They. Fucking. Drugged. Me.

Like I was a mentally unstable patient in a hospital.

"This right here goes to show how foolish you're being, Ever," Dad says, and I whip my gaze back to him. "For you to think, even for a moment, that I would allow you anywhere near that man again. You're not in your right goddamn mind."

"*Allow* me to?" My tone is deceptively calm when on the inside, I'm fuming so hot I feel the flames of my rage heating my skin. I am so fucking over them keeping me from doing this. "And how exactly are you going to stop me? Tie me to my bed? Lock me in my room? Put bars on my windows?" I lean forward. "Hold me down and force a needle in my arm again?"

Something flickers in his eyes. They skitter from me for a brief moment before coming back. I've never doubted Dad's love, and I don't now, so I know what he did bothers him. Just not enough to let me go. And I'm not sure if it's enough to not do it again. I want to say he wouldn't, but I wouldn't have thought he would do it the first time either.

"I won't apologize for what I did," he says unrepentantly. "You needed to calm down and that was the fastest and safest way to do it."

I ignore that. Not because I believe it's true, but because it's a moot point. The deed has been done and nothing either of us can say will change it. All it proves is what Dad and my brothers are capable of.

All of a sudden, my anger and animosity drains out of me. I deflate and the weight on my shoulders feels too heavy for me to carry. The stress of the last week has sucked so much of my energy. My thoughts of Wild Man and the condition he's in—if he's even alive—has consumed my every waking moment. And the longer I don't know the answer, the bigger the hole in my heart gets. Any time my brain tells me there's a real possibility he's dead, I snap the doors closed to those thoughts, refusing to entertain the idea. He can't be dead. He's lived in the wild for over twenty years, fought deadly animals much stronger than my family, survived two rattlesnake bites and a cougar attack at a young age. He *has* to be alive.

"I love him, Daddy," I say, my voice much lower now that the strength has left my body. "I love him so much that it feels like my soul is shriveling up and dying and my life force is fading. I know you can't understand that, but it's the truth."

"You can't love him."

"Why not? Because you say so?" My smile is flat and lifeless. "You may be the smartest man I know, but right now you're incredibly stupid. You know love works in mysterious ways. It doesn't let you pick who you or I choose. It picks you and matches you with the person who's perfect for you. Wild Man may not be the typical man and our time may have started out rough, but there is no other man out there that I would choose over him. He's the only man I would ever choose."

"He raped you, Ever." It takes a lot for Dad to say that out loud. I can hear the struggle in his voice.

"In the beginning, yes," I admit. As much as it paints a very nasty picture of Wild Man, I won't deny what he did.

"How can you stand there and openly admit that and still think I would be okay with you going back to the man who forced himself on you? Who held you captive and kept you naked for six fucking weeks? Who left marks on you that you're still healing from." At that remark, the spot on my neck that Wild Man always likes to bite and suck tingles. The mark is almost gone and that makes me incredibly sad. "Our lives were hell. Utter fucking hell,

Everlee. I've never felt so goddamn helpless in my life when I couldn't find you. Can you not understand why I'd sooner saw off my limbs before I let you anywhere near him?"

"I do understand. I can't imagine how hard it was for you." I look at each of my brothers, all with their dour expressions and tense stances. They look like they want to shake some sense into me. My gaze lands on Rika, who's sitting on the couch to my left. She hasn't left my house since the first time I woke up to her sitting beside my bed. She had a better understanding of my feelings, but I know she still doesn't fully grasp them. There's no way she could. I look back at Dad. "But you're not understanding me. *I* was the one who was taken. It was *me* who endured something horrific and fought to get back to you all. I suffered. I screamed and cried, begged and fought so damn hard. Some days I felt like I'd never get free. Some moments, I even thought death would have been a better alternative. For a time, all I felt for Wild Man was hatred."

I pull in a shaky breath. Tears have long since gathered in my eyes and have found their way down my cheeks.

"I lived through all that, and I *still* love him. Even though our beginning was a nightmare, I still fell in love. And what's more, I know he loves me too. I know he does because he made me feel it. He made me feel cherished and protected and adored. Like I was the most important and precious thing in his life." I plead with my eyes for him to understand. "I get that it's hard for you to believe and goes against every protective bone in your body. If it weren't for our beginning, wouldn't you want someone like that for me? Someone who would treat me like the most treasured gift? Who would give anything just to see me smile and laugh. Someone who made all those terrible feelings worth it because, in the end, the joy and happiness I felt far outweighed those bad times."

Dad's voice is rough when he says, "I'd give anything for you to have that, Ever. But I can't forget that beginning."

My legs feel like jello as I walk to him. I wrap my arms around his waist and lay my head on the center of his chest. He's well over six feet, so my ear lays perfectly over his steadily beating heart. He wraps me up and hugs me tight, like he'll never let me go again. I've always felt so safe and loved in Dad's arms.

I pull back moments later and tip my head up to look at him. My Dad, despite being in his late fifties, is still very handsome, and because of his daily work out regimen that he rarely misses, he's stacked with muscles and has the body of a man in his early forties.

"I don't expect you to forget it," I tell him quietly. "I never will because, even painful, it's a part of our story. But what you must do is accept my decision. You don't have to like it, but you have to learn to live with it."

"Ever—"

I lean up to kiss his cheek, cutting him off. "I'll always be your little girl and will always be okay with your need to protect me, but your little girl can make big girl decisions. And this is one thing I don't need your protection for. I'm safe with Wild Man. He would protect me just as fiercely as you or the others would. You have to let me do this."

"But he's hurt you."

"He's also protected me."

His jaw clenches and I can tell he wants to say more, but he keeps his mouth closed. For once, sensing that no matter what he says, my mind will not be changed. I feel the restless energy coming from my brothers and know they want to continue the argument, but they won't go against Dad. Well, Maddox might, just because he's a big asshole and doesn't know when to stop.

The tense moment is interrupted when there's a knock at the door. I step back from dad and go to the entryway. I don't doubt for a moment this conversation isn't over, but for the moment, Dad seems to be on the verge of relenting. I just need to keep working at him. He'll never fully be on board with me finding Wild Man, but I don't need him to be. I just need one toe.

I feel eyes following me to the front door, but I ignore the stares. I'm honestly surprised they're letting me answer the knock. A couple of reporters have shown up over the last few days, wanting the gossip from the girl who was held captive by a savage wild man. My only guess is that their thoughts are too consumed by the possibility of Dad letting me seek out Wild Man and trying to come up with other reasons why he shouldn't.

I look through the peephole and see a woman on the other side. I can't see much of her through the warped hole, but just by the shirt she's wearing, she doesn't appear to be a reporter. I flip the deadbolt and pull open the door.

The woman startles, like she didn't expect me to actually open the door. She looks to be several years older than me, closer to Maddox's age. She has long, wavy dark hair and navy blue eyes. She's taller than the average woman, standing several inches above me. Her clothes, which still makes me believe she's not a reporter now that I can see her full outfit, is a t-shirt with a rock band logo and a pair of worn jeans with holes in the knees.

"Hi. Can I help you?" I ask.

A line forms between her eyes as she looks me over. Not in a weird judgemental way, just with curiosity. Her teeth latch onto her bottom lip like she's contemplating what to say.

"Are you Everlee Adair?" she inquires, her voice hesitant.

I feel someone walk up behind me, probably Dad or one of my brothers. Her gaze moves behind me before they come back.

"I am. And you are?"

I can visibly see the flash of relief enter her eyes. "My name is Camille Salone. I'm looking for my brother."

"Your brother?" My brows furrow, not comprehending why she would be here looking for him.

"Yes. His name is Phenix. He's been missing since he was five years old."

"Why would—" My words trail off, and I swear my world tips

upside down. I grab the door jam when I feel like I might list over sideways. A hand grabs my waist, helping to support me.

"Oh Jesus," I mumble.

The woman steps forward and my eyes dart back to her.

Her expression is filled with concern when she asks. "Are you okay?"

I can't answer. My brain is overflowing, trying to fathom the impossibility.

Fey.

Could it mean Phenix?

Wild Man never mentioned he had a sister. Only that his mother was pregnant when they went to stay in the wilderness for one last foray.

I look at the woman in front of me. Really look at her. Hair dark enough that it looks like there's a hint of blue. Eyes so dark, they almost look black. And they're slightly slanted, just like Wild Man. While Wild Man had a full beard, his full red lips always caught my eye because they were such a contrast to the darkness of the hair on his face. This woman has the same lips.

"H-he never said he had a sister," I say, barely getting the words past my dry throat.

Sadness enters the woman's eyes and she looks down at her hands. She's twisting them together. "It's been over twenty years and he was so young when he went missing. I'm not surprised he didn't remember me." She looks up and a world of pain is in her gaze. "I wasn't home much the last couple of years before our parents took him on that last adventure. I had an autoimmune disease that had me in the hospital more often than I was at home."

Something in my chest fractures, splits right down the middle, and I suck in a sharp breath, hoping to relieve the pain.

I reach out and grab one of her hands. "Please, come in."

I tug Camille inside and turn to the rest of the room. It must have been Dad who was behind me because he's standing close by.

My brothers are scattered throughout the room, eyeing the newcomer as if they aren't sure what to make of her. All except Maddox. He looks like he may want to kick the woman out. I glower at him, daring him to even try, and I pull Camille over to the couch. Rika scoots to the end, making room for me to sit. Camille sits on the other end.

"How old were you when they left?" I ask, turning my body to face her.

I'm still having trouble believing this woman is Wild Man's sister, but the evidence is right in front of me. They look too much alike for it not to be true. I'm surprised I didn't notice it when I first opened the door, because it surely smacks me in the face now.

"Seven."

"And they just left a sick seven-year-old girl in the hospital while they went gallivanting in the forest? Sounds like great parents to me." Maddox says with a hostile tone.

"Maddox!" I snap, not believing my brother could be so heartless. It's a good thing he's across the room, or I'd leave my handprint on his face. "How dare you!"

I glare at him, but his eyes are focused on Camille.

"You really believe this woman?" he asks, switching his gaze to me.

"I do actually," I say. "If you saw Wild Man, you'd believe her too. They look too much alike not to be related. And besides, why in the world would she lie?"

"Media attention. Fame. Money. Those are just a few reasons."

"Jesus, brother. Not everyone is jaded like you." I shoot him a hard look. "Either keep your trap shut and play nice or get out of my house."

Camille touching my hand pulls my attention back to her.

"It's okay." Her eyes slide sideways to Mad before coming back to me. "Really."

"No, it certainly is not. This is my house and while people are in it, they won't be assholes to my guests."

Mad wisely clamps his lips shut, but doesn't lose the animosity in his eyes.

"Now," I pat the top of Camille's hand. "Tell me more."

I'm ridiculously curious to learn more of Wild Man and his life before he and his parents went into the wilderness.

## twenty-nine

EVERLEE

L ater that night, I'm in bed staring up at the ceiling, my thoughts all over the place, trying to process everything I learned today.

After more heated words, some pleading, and me ultimately putting my foot down, I finally managed to get dad and my brothers to leave and go home. Well, most of them anyway. They only agreed to leave if one of them could stay. Thankfully, it was Joe who was nominated for babysitting duty. Joe may be hot headed when pushed, he's also the most level-headed and the one I'm closest to. I'd much rather it be him than any of my other brothers.

Of course, this still doesn't mean I can sneak away. Just because they aren't in my house anymore, doesn't mean they aren't around. I'd bet my last dollar that at least one of my brothers is parked somewhere outside on the street keeping watch. They know me too well. When I set my mind to something, there's nothing that will keep me from following through with it, and I'm dead set on going back into the wilderness to find Wild Man.

Joe's sleeping on the couch since Rika, who flat out refuses to leave, has taken up residency in my spare bedroom. It's been nice having her around, but I'm sick of peopling. I'm tired of pretending that I'm okay when I'm far from it. I'm heartbroken not just because I'm not with Wild Man, but also because I have no idea what condition he's in. I've kept myself from thinking of the worse case scenario, but sometimes those thoughts sneak in. When they do, I want to curl up into a ball and cry until there's nothing left inside me.

I roll to my side and hug my pillow to my chest. Tears slide down my cheeks, soaking the cotton material.

I've played nice to dad in my demands he let me go find Wild Man. That changes tomorrow. If he doesn't agree, I'll take drastic measures. One way or another, I will be leaving tomorrow.

Making that decision, my thoughts drift back to Camille. I found out through her that Wild Man is twenty-eight years old. He's been living in the wilderness for a little over twenty-three years. His birthday is in a couple of months on December thirteenth.

Camille didn't have to answer Mad's question on why her and Wild Man's parents decided to leave her in that hospital and take that last trip into the wild, but she did anyway. Apparently, Gabriel and Josie Salone were avid outdoors people. They loved spending time in nature and living off the land. That's how they met thirty-four years ago. They were both backpacking in Hawaii and stumbled across each other. Camille says it was love at first sight for them both. They met, fell in love, and never left each other's side.

When they found out Josie was pregnant with their third child, they decided to hang up their adventure hat by taking one last trip. They wanted to take Camille with them like they had previously, but with her being so sick the last couple of years, they felt it best for her to stay behind. She was left in Josie's sister's care. They were only supposed to be gone for a week in the Appalachian Mountains in upper New York state. When they didn't come back after that week and they heard no word from them, they scoured the mountains. The Appalachian Mountains are over two-thousand miles long and spans from Canada all the way down to Alabama. No matter how many people were searching, there was no way they could cover every square foot.

It wouldn't have mattered anyway. Gabriel and Josie weren't in the Appalachian mountains. They were in Black Ridge National Forest in west Texas. It's anyone's guess why they ended up there and not where they originally planned, and there's no way to get those answers now.

Camille and I both cried when I told her what happened to her parents and the things I knew about Wild Man. What he endured and how hard he fought to stay alive. I told her how strong and brave her brother was, that he was a true survivor. A protector.

She asked why I called him Wild Man, and I explained that the folks in town gave him the moniker years ago when they first heard of the man who lives in the wild. I didn't give her the more gruesome details of Wild Man and my first meeting. I could tell Maddox wanted to enlighten Camille, but he wisely kept his trap shut. She didn't need to know those things about her brother. I smiled a little when I told her I used the name because Wild Man acted... well, wild when we first met. She smiled when she told me the name Fey was indeed a nickname for Phenix. It was the one she gave her baby brother when he first came home from the hospital after being born. She was only two years old and had trouble pronouncing Phenix, so she called him Fey. I could tell that she really loved that, although he didn't remember his big sister, she was still with him, even unconsciously.

It was by pure luck that Camille heard of the story of what happened to me. She and her two-year-old twin boys live in Oklahoma. She was in the kitchen making breakfast for her boys when she overheard the news story on the television. There weren't many details because I refused to talk to the media, but it was enough to trigger Camille's curiosity. On a whim and with a premonition, after getting as much information as she could, she arranged a babysitter for her sons and then headed to Texas.

When Camille left hours after she arrived, I gave her my promise that I would find Wild Man. She gave me her phone number and the name of the hotel she's staying in for the next week. I have every intention to call her with good news soon.

I roll to my other side, my eyes drifting closed. Today was a long day and all of the new information has left me exhausted, but I can't get comfortable. The bed is too soft and the smell of my apple-scented candles is irritating me. The blankets are too restricting, so I kick them off, but then I don't like having nothing covering me so I pull just the sheet over me. I miss the warmth of Wild Man. I miss his heavy arm wrapped around my stomach as he pulls me back against his hard chest. I miss his steady breath fanning across my ear as he sleeps. The kiss to the back of my neck he always gives me before he drifts off. There are so many things I miss about him.

I kick the sheet off me and get up from the bed. At my window, I pull the curtains aside and push the pane of glass open halfway. I want to feel the fresh breeze on my skin when I sleep. It won't be the same as sleeping in Wild Man's tree hut, but who knows, maybe it'll help just a little.

I crawl back in bed, bringing the sheet up to my waist. I'm naked because I can't stand sleeping in clothes now. The slight breeze that comes through my window feels good, and I release a long breath.

My eyes drift closed and I will my brain to let go of all its erratic thoughts.

Within seconds I'm drifting off to sleep.

*thirty*

WILD MAN

The window that I approach is half open, but there's
something that's covering the square hole. It's not solid,
more like a meshy type of thing, so it won't be hard to cut through.
I pull the big knife from the pants that I'm wearing.

Jeans. That's what Ben called them.

I hate the way the rough material feels against my skin. I don't
know why people choose to wear the things. And the shirt isn't
much better. The cloth isn't as restricting and coarse as the jeans,
but it's still irritating and uncomfortable.

It's the shoes that I refused to put on though. Those things felt
too tight on my feet, even though Ben said they were the right size.

I remembered *momor* saying that people can't go without
clothes in her world unless they're in their home. If they do, they
go to the place she called jail. I'd rather be constricted by clothes
than be put in a place where I can't leave if I want. So clothes it is.
Not the shoes though. I don't think I'd go to jail if I don't wear
those.

My knife slips easily into the mesh stuff, and I quickly slice

253

downward and over until it falls away. I quietly hoist myself up and over through the square hole. It's dark in the room, but my eyes are adjusted to the darkness enough that I see a bed that's lifted off the ground. I don't know if this is where *momor* is, but it's the only room that had a window open. The door in the front and back were locked.

Before I get to the bed, I know the person on it is *momor*. I can smell her. She always smelled the same, even after she bathed. Something sweet, like some kind of flower or fruit.

My cock hardens and it makes the jeans I'm wearing even more uncomfortable. I'm in *momor's* house, so the clothes are coming off.

I stop at the end of the bed. *Momor* has the blankets thrown off her, showing me her beautiful skin. I want light so I can see her better. I want to look at her face, so I'll know that I'm actually here. That she's right in front of me and not just part of my dreams.

I put my knife on the end of the bed and reach over my shoulders, pulling the shirt over my head and dropping it on the floor. My cock is so hard that I have to pull the jeans away from my body to be able to get the metal closure down without pinching my skin.

The light from the moon coming in through the window shines on my female. She hasn't moved since I came in. She's on her stomach with her hands under the pillow. One of her legs is bent and angled upward, leaving them spread open. She's naked. In her position, the shadows of her body cover the area between her legs, so I can't see the spot I want to see.

I put a knee on the bed and crawl on top. The moment my hand touches the skin of her ankle, some of the worry, desperation, and anger drains out of me.

I have my *momor* back. I feel her against my hand, so I know it's true.

I start at her feet, my lips sliding across her soft and familiar skin. She doesn't wake up, and I don't want her to yet. I don't know if she'll fight me like she did in the beginning, and I need to have my hands and mouth on her. The crazed images of her being taken away from me, hearing her scream my name, has kept me on the edge of sanity. I need to feel her, taste her, take in her scent to know she's real.

She's been gone for too many days with her family, and I don't know if being back in her world has driven away the feelings she was starting to have for me. When her family was taking her away, she acted like she didn't want to go, but maybe being away changed her mind.

I lick up the back of her leg, a low growl rumbling from my chest as I taste her. I missed having her on my tongue.

When I reach her upper legs, I push the one that's bent further up, spreading her open more. She's still asleep, but her body weeps her juices. I can smell it and it nearly drives me mad. My cock that's pressed against the bed throbs and produces a bead of liquid. I want to rear up, mount her from behind, and ram myself inside her tight body. I will do that, but only after I've eaten her.

I drop my head and take the first taste of my female in way too many days. I groan when her juices explode on my tongue. *Momor* moans, her hips lifting off the bed, as if, even in sleep, she's seeking out my touch.

I push my tongue inside as far as it'll go but it's still not enough. I want all of me inside her, just as all of her is inside me. She consumes my body and my mind. She's a part of me, so much so that if she were to be ever permanently taken from me, I'd no longer live. It would be impossible, because I need her to breathe.

I play with her little back hole, the one I haven't fully taken yet, pressing the tip of my tongue inside. *Momor* pushes against me, and I groan against her. I thrust my hips on the bed, but the blankets don't feel right. I need something different. I need my female's wetness sliding against me. I need her snug body surrounding my cock, strangling me with her need.

I lift my head, getting to my knees. With gentle movements, I roll *momor* to her back. Her eyes are still closed, but her breathing has deepened. She's not awake yet, which shows just how tired she must have been when she went to sleep. But she'll wake soon.

I push her legs apart and lay my body between them. I hook one of her legs over my arm, angling her pussy in the right position. My cock nudges against her opening. I grit my teeth and hiss out a breath. She feels good. Like her body is the only place I'm supposed to be. She was specifically created to perfectly match me in every way.

I don't ram my hips forward like I want to. Instead, I slowly slide inside, watching her face as each inch goes in. I tense my stomach muscles, forcing my seed to stay in place. I'm not ready to release yet. I want her awake when I fill her with my seed.

Her eyes slide open, and at first it's like she doesn't see me.

"Wild Man," she whispers, her voice husky. She lifts her hand and lays it on my cheek. I close my eyes at her touch. "You're always in my dreams."

I open my eyes, turning my head and kissing her palm. "No dreams, *momor*."

Tears puddle in her eyes, one falling free to slide out the corner. I feel that tear like it's a lick of fire on my skin.

"I don't ever want to wake up. I want to live in my dreams with you."

Her voice is so sad and it makes my stomach feel like I ate something rotten.

"Not a dream, Ever." I push my hips forward, wedging my cock in as far as it'll go, and pressing against the part of her that she likes. "I'm here. With you. Real, not a dream."

When her beautiful brown gaze still doesn't look like she really sees me, I settle my weight on the arm I've got hooked around her leg and wrap my fingers around her throat. I tighten my grip, feeling the heavy thump of her heart against my palm, hoping that if I steal some of her breath, she'll snap out of whatever dream state she's in.

"Fey," she croaks. Her eyes widen and her tongue comes out to lick her lips. "Oh God, Fey." More tears come and she chokes out a sob. "You're real?"

"Yes."

I flex my hips and it's then that she comes fully awake and aware that I'm deep inside of her. Her hand flashes out, fisting my hair and drags my mouth down to hers. We kiss like we'll die if we don't. I feel like I will if I don't. I need her lips to live. I need her touch to breathe. I need her surrounding me in every way possible for my heart to beat. It's a kiss full of yearning and desperation.

"I told you I never let you go," I tell her. I pull my hips back, lift her leg higher and to the side, and drive back inside. "My *momor*. Your Wild Man. Always."

*Momor* still cries, even as she lifts her hips to meet my thrusts. Her walls tighten around my cock, tempting me to release my seed. I pump inside her again and again and again.

Never again will I be without this. Without my female. Never again will she be without me. Her male.

I bury my face in her neck and lick the mark that's faded. I growl when I latch my teeth on the spot and suck. She bucks her hips, her body demanding I give her more. I give her everything I have. I slam inside her and retreat, only to charge forward again. Her nails rake down my back, leaving her own marks behind. Ones I'll proudly wear.

When her lips fall open and her walls tighten around me, and I know she's finding her release, I drop my mouth back to her. I want to feel her cries of pleasure against my lips. I want to breathe in her pleasure as I fill her with my seed.

I kiss her until both of us are breathless and need to separate to fill our lungs with air. I let go of her leg and she wraps it around my waist like she has the other one. She tightens her hold, like she'll never let me go. Our faces are so close that I can see the thickness of her eyelashes.

"I love you, Wild Man."

Her words have the pounding muscle in my chest constricting.

I brush the damn hair from her cheeks. "I love you, my *momor*."

"I can't believe you're really here," she says, whispering her fingers over my forehead and cheeks.

When she grazes my lips, I press a kiss against them. "I always come for you."

She smiles, but her lips tremble. "I missed you so much."

I drop my head for another kiss. Since *momor* gave me her mouth the first time, I can't get enough. I'll never get enough.

Something loud bangs against the wall and a bright light fills the room. I'm on my knees in the next second with *momor* shoved behind me. My eyes meet a man who stands in the doorway.

In his hand is something metal, and he's pointing it straight at my chest.

# *thirty-one*

EVERLEE

The second I see Joe standing in the doorway pointing a gun at Wild Man, a deadly look in his eyes and his finger a mere centimeter away from the trigger, I know he intends to kill him. Joe, just like the rest of my brothers and our dad, is an excellent marksman. Even if his target wasn't directly in front of him only a few feet away, he wouldn't miss. Joe could hit the bullseye a hundred yards away. The only reason he hasn't fired yet is because I'm behind Wild Man and he wouldn't take the chance the bullet would slam through Wild Man and hit me.

A ball of fire erupts in my stomach at knowing Wild Man is so close to death.

We're both on our knees facing the door and we're both naked. It should feel weird—for me at least—with my brother in the room, but it oddly doesn't. Or rather, it does, but my concentration isn't on finding clothes. My only thought process is to get Joe to lower the gun.

I grab Wild Man's arm and inch my way closer to him. The

closer I am to Wild Man, the less of a chance Joe will pull the trigger.

"Put the gun down, Joe," I say, surprised at how calm and collected my voice is when my entire body is shaking like a leaf.

He doesn't acknowledge my request, just keeps his hate-filled glare on Wild Man. "Get away from my sister."

"No."

Rika walks up behind Joe, stopping just inside the doorway. Her hand flies to her mouth and her eyes go as big as saucers. "Oh, Jesus," she mutters.

"Get the fuck away from her," Joe growls. "Or one of my bullets is going through your skull."

"Do it," Wild Man snarls. "*Momor* is mine. Kill me. Dead is only way I'll leave her."

I watch the muscle in Joe's jaw clench as he gnashes his teeth together.

"Please, Joe." My voice cracks on his name.

Nothing in his body changes except for his eyes as they meet mine behind Wild Man. "Off the bed, Ever, and come to me."

"No." My nails dig into Wild Man's arm. "If I leave this bed, you'll shoot him."

"Damn right I will. The bastard deserves to die for what he's done to you."

At his rancorous tone, anger mixes with the fear swirling in my stomach. I shuffle my knees forward with every intention of getting in front of Wild Man. Of course, Wild Man doesn't allow it. He blocks my way by throwing out his arm.

He keeps his eyes locked on Joe as he says, "No, *momor*. Stay behind. I protect."

I press my body against his. "You don't need to protect me from him. He won't hurt me."

"Behind me."

Lord fucking help me from over-protective men.

Moving fast before he can stop me, I duck under his arm and

force my way in front of him. I push my back against him, which knocks him slightly off balance. His arm goes around my waist, and I know he's getting ready to toss me behind him again.

"Stop!" I scream so loudly that I wouldn't be surprised if the windows rattled. I feel the heat of Wild Man's glower on the back of my head, but shockingly, he doesn't try to shield me again. He just wraps his arm around my waist and pulls me back against him so tightly, a whoosh of air leaves my lungs.

Joe's moved his arm to the side so the gun isn't pointed at me. With his closed mouth and the slightly uncomfortable expression on his face it reminds me that I'm butt naked. I grab the robe at the end of my bed and hold it up in front of me.

"You can't kill him, Joe," I tell him.

"The hell I can't. He needs to pay for what he put you through. If I don't do it, one of the others will and you know that."

"And do you know what happens if you or they do?" I ask.

"What?" he grates out.

I put my hand on my lower stomach, just under Wild Man's arm. "You kill the father of my unborn child."

---

I'M DRESSED IN A PAIR OF BLACK LEGGINGS AND AN OVERSIZED T-SHIRT. MY long mass of hair is tossed up haphazardly on top of my head. Wild Man wears a pair of jeans and a dark-blue t-shirt. It's weird seeing him in clothes, but not in a bad way. I'm obsessed with his naked body, but he looks just as sexy in ratty jeans that hug his lean hips and sculpted ass.

I didn't want him to find out about the baby the way he did, but I knew, if anything would get through to Joe, it would be the knowledge that I'm carrying Wild Man's child. And I was right. As soon as the words left my mouth, Joe's jaw went slack and the hand holding the gun fell to his side, like the deadly metal became too heavy for him to carry.

Moments after that, Spencer came rushing into the house, who must have been the one stationed outside to keep watch and heard the ruckus. Joe shoved him away when he tried to come into my room and gently pushed Rika out behind him. Before the door was slammed shut, he shot me a glare over his shoulder. "Get dressed."

When Wild Man and I were once again alone, I wanted to talk to him, but I couldn't find the words I wanted to say. My head was all over the place, but mainly focused on the fact that he was actually here. I still couldn't wrap my head around it. I watched him as we dressed, while his gaze stayed pinned on my stomach. The look in his eyes was possessive. I wanted to go to him and fall into his arms, then never let him go. Now that he's here, the ramifications of what could have been his fate hit me hard. I almost lost him for good.

The proof of that is on his face. One of his eyes is still bruised, the color a nasty yellow mixed with spots of black. There's a cut on his eyebrow and another on his forehead that looks almost healed. The bruises on his chest and ribs had the muscles around my heart tightening. I wanted to sucker punch Dad and my brothers for leaving a single mark on him. It hurts too much to imagine the condition he was in eleven days ago.

I was leading him into the living room where my house was once again filled with testosterone when Wild Man saw all the men. His arm snapped around my middle, stopping me just inside the room, and I was dragged against his side with his big protective hand on my stomach. He shot each one a glare. I could only imagine the ways he was killing them inside his head. The look Dad and my brothers gave him was no less hostile.

I peeled his arm from around me and took him to the couch. He sat on one end and when I tried sitting beside him, he took my hips and pulled me down on his lap sideways. His legs fall apart, and I lay mine between them. I don't think the intimate position was a good idea in front of so many pissed off faces, but I stayed in place anyway. I wanted to be in Wild Man's arms, and from the way held me with his hand back over my stomach, as if protecting the small life growing inside me, he needed me there as well.

"Jesus, Ever," Dad mutters, pacing a hole in my carpet as he drags his hand through his hair. "You're fucking pregnant?" He stops and his eyes swing to mine, then flicker to Wild Man, before he resumes his walk to the window only to turn around again.

He's no more surprised than I was when I took the pregnancy test I had Rika get for me a week ago. I thought for sure having my period meant I wasn't pregnant, but I guess I'm one of those people who spots during a pregnancy. Or maybe it was the stress of the situation that brought on the spotting. Rika got a multi-pack, and I took all three. Each one came back positive, the double pink lines showing almost immediately. I decided to take the tests on a whim. It was just a feeling I had.

Until thirty minutes ago, Rika didn't know I took the tests. Of course, since she's the one who bought them for me, she asked me every day if I took them, but I always told her no. I wasn't ready for anyone to know yet. I wanted to find Wild Man first. He was the first person who should know he was going to be a father.

So much for that plan.

I look at Dad, watching the agitation in his body. "Yes."

"How long have you known?" he asks without looking at me.

"Does it really matter?"

His narrowed gaze meets mine. "How long, Ever."

"Since the third day I was back."

A twinge of guilt hits me. Not for keeping this from Dad, but from the hurt look on Rika's face. I'll explain later why I hadn't told her. I know she'll understand.

"Fuck," Dad mutters. "I assume you'll want to keep the baby?"

My fingers dig into Wild Man's arm at Dad's hurtful question. "Don't make me hate you," I tell him. "Because I'm really damn close."

Remorse flickers in his gaze before he moves them to Wild Man. "What about you? How do you feel about being a father?"

"I'll be good Peepa," he answers in his deep voice. "Always protect *momor* and our baby."

"Peepa? What the fuck is that?" Ethan asks.

"It means papa," I answer.

"And *momor*?"

I look at Spencer. "I don't know what it means, but it's what he calls me."

Dad ignores all that and asks. "And how will you provide for them?"

I talk before Wild Man has a chance to. "That's not something we need to worry about right now. We'll figure it out later. I have plenty of money saved, and I'll still be working at the paper. I can provide for us for the time being."

"I'll be damned if I'll allow some man to leech off you, Everlee. I'll sooner toss his ass back out into the woods, this time making sure he doesn't leave, before I let that happen."

My blood pressure raises, making my cheeks heat with anger. I've had enough of people thinking they can push me around and make decisions for me. That shit stops now.

I push against Wild Man, intending to get up, right in Dad's face, and make it very clear that he needs to back the fuck off, or I won't be held accountable for my actions. Wild Man holds me in place.

"*Momor* is mine. Our baby is mine. I protect them both. I feed and shelter them. I make them happy. I make them laugh. I give them everything they need." He pauses a moment, in which Dad looks at him blankly. "*Momor* is strong female. She'll be strong Noeny. Because you good Peepa to her."

I'm surprised to hear the reluctant gratitude in Wild Man's tone, like he respects Dad for a job well done in raising me.

His eyes move to each of my brothers. "Wanted to kill you for taking my *momor* away." Four sets of eyes narrow and their bodies go rigid. "No more. You take to protect. Good brothers."

Tears prick my eyes.

Wild Man looks back at Dad, his fingers splaying wide over my stomach. "I protect *momor* now. I die to protect her and baby, like you would. *Always*." That last word is emphasized with a growl.

"Shit," Dad mutters. "Fucking shit."

I just manage to keep the smile from my face. If there's one thing Dad understands, it's the incessant need to protect family at all costs. He must have seen something on Wild Man's face that made him finally believe the severity of Wild Man's feelings for me. I know without a doubt in my soul that what he spoke is the truth. He would do anything to ensure my and our child's safety.

In a way, that thought is scary. The intensity of a love like that could be dangerous. I would never want Wild Man to step in front of me and take whatever damage is headed my way. But then again, I'm sure he feels the same way.

Dad walks up to us, his expression giving nothing away. He stands there, his eyes drilling into Wild Man, completely ignoring my presence. He stays that way for several long seconds, seconds that feel like minutes.

Then he slowly lifts his hand, palm sideways. I have no idea if Wild Man knows what a handshake is, but I guess he deduces what Dad is after. The hand not splayed on my stomach lifts and meets Dad's. I internally wince at their white knuckles, knowing they are both gripping the hell out of the other hand.

"You hurt her in any way, and I'll make what me and my boys did to you feel like a pat on the back. You got me."

"Got you."

Dad drops his arm and takes a step back. He looks around the room to my brothers. "We're leaving."

All of them, except for Mad, seem to accept Dad's decision and start moving toward the door. Mad still has his hard gaze pinned on Wild Man. He looks two seconds away from springing forward and tackling him. He's the one who's the most like Dad, so his protective instinct is strong.

"Maddox, let's go," Dad barks.

It takes a moment, but he eventually spins around and stalks out the door, taking his still pissed off vibes with him.

When Rika gets up from the chair she's been occupying, I slide off Wild Man's lap. She still looks hurt from me not telling her about the pregnancy tests. I walk to her and take her straight into my arms.

"I'm sorry," I say in her ear. "I hated not telling you. I'll explain later, okay?"

She nods and pulls back. Some of her hurt fades as she looks at Wild Man over my shoulder. When she brings her gaze back, there's a hint of mischievousness.

"He's yummy."

I can't help but laugh. She's definitely not wrong.

"I'll call you later."

"You better." Her chin drops and she looks down at my stomach. "I can't believe you're pregnant. I'm going to be an aunt."

I smile and pat my belly. "I can't believe it either. You'll be a kickass aunt."

"Damn right I will."

I close the door after Rika leaves and turn to face Wild Man. He's standing only a few feet away from me, and boy does he look intense. His gaze rakes down my body, then back up. By the time he reaches my eyes, I'm pretty sure I've soaked through my panties, and from the thick bulge behind the zipper of his jeans, he's not faring much better.

"We need to talk," I tell him, trying my best to ignore the way my body wants to melt for him. There are things he needs to know.

"Fuck first. Talk later."

Eh, those things can wait.

# *thirty-two*

WILD MAN

I place a kiss against *momor's* stomach before I lay my arm over her legs and put my head in my hand so I can stare up at her. She's leaning against the piece of wood against the wall that's part of her bed. I brush my fingers over her legs until I reach the dip between the v of her legs. I can feel the combination of our wetness that leaks out of her.

"I like this," I say, swirling my fingers around.

It's not our releases I'm talking about—although I like that too — but the bareness of her pussy. I noticed it when I ate from her when I first came into her room, but I was too overcome with my need for her to have really paid attention. The hair that she had is now gone and the smoothless that's left behind makes my mouth water.

"This is how I normally keep it."

"Good. I do the same."

Heat pools in her eyes and my cock moves against my thigh. I already want to take her again, but I was rough with our last fucking, so I want to give her body a little time to recover. Especially since she's carrying our baby.

I'm going to be a Peepa. I want to throw my head back and roar to the sky in triumph.

"I like this bed. Soft."

She smiles. "I liked it too before I found you. When I was brought back here, it was too soft. I missed the bed in our tree hut."

"Missed just the bed?"

Her smile gets bigger. "I may have missed the man who always kept me warm in it and always fucked me so good."

I growl, lifting my hand to fist her hair. I drag her head down and lean up so our lips meet. I'll always crave her kiss. I'll always need it like my body needs my heart to beat.

"I missed you, Wild Man," she says against my lips. "So much. I was so worried about you. I wanted to come back, but they wouldn't let me. I was going to make them today, but you got to me before I could."

"I wanted to come soon, but I couldn't." I don't want to worry her by telling her how injured I was but, I need her to know I would have been here quicker if I could have. "I was hurt."

A line forms between her eyes. She lightly runs her finger over the marks still on my stomach. "They told me they weren't sure if you were alive or dead. How bad was it?"

I don't answer that. Instead, I say, "Teeja found me. Brought me food. Kept animals away."

"Teeja is a good friend."

I nod.

"How did you find me here? You've never been out of the forest, right? And where did you get the clothes?"

I pick up a piece of her hair that's lying on her chest and slide my fingers through it. "Ben gave me paper long ago. It tells how to get to his home. It took me a day to find home. He was surprised to see me, but knew why I there. He heard of you from people when brothers took you from me." I bring her hair to my nose and breathe in deep. "He knew your Peepa name and found where you live. He gave me clothes and gave me paper to tell where you live."

"I can't believe you came for me."

"Always, *momor*."

Wherever my *momor* is, is where I will be.

"Phenix."

I tilt my head to the side. That word sounds familiar, but I don't know how.

"That's your name," she says softly, her deep brown eyes watching me. "Fey is the name your older sister called you."

"Sister? I don't—" My mouth slams shut when a fuzzy memory fills my head. A female, a young one, with dark brown hair that's twisted on both sides and hangs over her shoulders. Bright pink pieces of cloth hang from her hair. She's smiling in my head.

*"Come play with me, Fey."*

I snap my eyes shut, trying to hold on to that memory. Wanting more of it to form.

"You have an older sister, Wild Man."

My lids open and find *momor* looking at me. She has the same smile on her face as the girl in my head.

"Her name is—"

"Cammie," I finish for her.

"Cammie. Yes. Camille." *Momor* slides her fingers through the hair on my face so she's cupping my cheek. "She's been looking for you for years. She wants to see you again."

For the first time in my life, I have no words. Not because I have nothing to say, but because I don't know *what* to say.

I have a sister.

Cammie.

Now that her name is in my head, more faint visions appear.

Sitting at a small table while Cammie gives me a little cup. There's nothing in the cup, but we pretend there is and drink from it.

*"Would you like more tea, Fey?"*

Me sitting on something as Cammie pushes me. I go forward and backward. I felt like I was flying.

*"Higher, Cammie!"*

Cammie lying in a bed in a white room. She has something stuck in her arm and there are beeping sounds.

"Why are you sick, Cammie? You won't die, will you? You can't leave me."

*"I'll never leave you, Fey."*

The last time I saw my big sister was the day me and Peepa and Noeny went to the forest. We were both sad she couldn't go with us. Peepa helped me crawl on the bed so I could give her a big hug.

*"Tell all the little baby animals I said hi. And bring me a pretty rock home."*

Cammie had a bunch of rocks in her room that she kept in a box. She said they were her favorites because they were neat shapes and colors.

I don't know why I forgot about her. I've held onto some faded memories of Peepa and Noeny, but it was like Cammie disappeared. Maybe my young mind knew, when I was left on my own, that it would be too hard if I kept Cammie with me.

I focus back on *momor*. Her eyes are wet, but she has a small smile on her face.

"How do you know Cammie?" I ask, my tone deeper than normal.

I listen intently as she tells me how Cammie showed up here and everything my sister told her. She talks about my sister with excitement, and I can tell she's happy for me. I'm happy too. I thought I was left alone in the world, but then *momor* showed up and I wasn't anymore. Having her made me realize how lonely I felt. Without her, I was nothing.

But now I have a sister. Not only a sister, but her two sons. *Momor* said I was an uncle.

"Do you want to meet her?"

"Yes."

*Momor* laughs at how fast I answer. Now that I remember my sister, I don't want to wait.

"Now. Want to see now."

She laughs again and her dark eyes glitter like there are stars in them. She tugs lightly on my beard.

"Let's wait an hour or two. It's still pretty early. We'll wait until the sun comes up and then I'll call her." She shifts her legs, and I remove my arm from over them. She gets up from the bed. Her naked body tempts me to pull her back down. I don't like it when she puts something on that covers her body. "For now, I'm going to blow your mind by making you my famous omelet."

---

I can't stop looking at my sister. She can't stop looking at me either, so I guess it's okay.

She's beautiful. Long brown hair, almost as black as mine. Her eyes aren't as dark, but the lines of hair above her eyes are the same shape as mine. I only know that because after *momor* and I were under the falling water, I looked in what she called a mirror for a long time. I stared at every part of my face, studying it closely. It was weird looking at myself.

"You look just like Dad," Cammie says. Her face is still red from when she cried earlier. "He had the same black hair and was thick like yours. You have his eyes too, and we both got his height, although you're much taller than me. But it's mom who gave us her high cheekbones and full lips."

We're on the long thing with padding called a couch. I'm sitting in the middle with Cammie on one side and *momor* on my other side. *Momor* has my hand in hers, squeezing my fingers. She's had a hold of it since we first sat down.

"Mom and Dad adored you. They adored us both." She rubs her lips together. "I have some pictures of them if you want to see."

I clear my throat when it feels like something is stuck inside it. "Yes."

She grabs a bag she has on the floor by her feet and pulls out a small box. The top is flipped open and she pulls out several small shiny papers. She holds them out to me, and I take them with hands that shake.

I look down at the top one. It's of a man and a woman who look familiar. They both have wide smiles on their faces. They look like they are looking out of the picture and straight at me. Peepa has his arm around Noeny's waist and she's turned toward him a little with her hand resting on his stomach. Peepa has hair as black as mine, just as Cammie said. He's taller than Noeny, his chin higher than her head. Noeny's hair is deep red, like the color of leaves when it starts getting cold. Her skin is lighter than Peepa's and she has little dots of color on her nose and cheeks. She's more beautiful than I remember. They look happy as they smile at me.

I look at the next picture. This one Peepa is holding Noeny with one arm under her legs and the other around her back. She has one arm around his neck and her other hand is on his cheek. They aren't looking at me this time. They look at each other, their smile not as big, but still filled with love and happiness.

I move to the next picture and this one holds my attention more. Peepa and Noeny are standing in front of a big tree. One of his arms is draped over Noeny's shoulders. In his other is... me. The little boy version of me. My legs are hugging his hips and Peepa's arm is under my butt with his hand on my leg. A little girl— Cammie—is hugging the other side of Noeny. We all look forward with big grins on our faces.

The last picture tightens my chest so much that it's hard to breathe. Peepa and Noeny are on a couch. Cammie sits across both of their laps, her butt on Peepa's thighs with her legs lying on Noeny's. In her arms is a bundle of light blue blankets, my tiny scrunched up face peeking out of them. All three are looking down at me.

"That was the day Mom and Dad brought you home from the hospital," Cammie says. "I was at home with a babysitter. I was too young to really remember, but Mom said I couldn't wait to meet you. She said as soon as they walked in the door, I demanded to hold you right away." She laughs, the sound coming out choked. "I was so proud to be your big sister and promised to be the best one you ever had."

"You were," I say in a hoarse voice.

"You remember me?"

I glance up. Tears slide from her cheeks and drip off her chin. *Momor* reaches around me and offers Cammie another tissue. She has a small pile of used ones on the table beside us.

"Little. I remember tea parties." Cammie laughs. "And playing outside in rain. I remember you holding my hand and talking under sheets."

"We used to build forts made out of sheets in your room." She wipes her nose with a tissue. "I'd sneak into your room at night after we were supposed to be in bed and we'd huddle under one. We'd try so hard to be quiet so Mom and Dad wouldn't hear us, but we always ended up giggling and they'd catch us."

I grin. It's not really the memories that make me smile, but the sound of childish laughter I can hear in my head.

"Can I," she stops and her throat moves. "Can I hug you?"

I don't answer with words. I reach out and pull my big sister into my arms. She falls against me, her arms going around my middle and pressing her face in my shoulder.

"Never ask," I rumble in her ear. "Always hug me."

She cries against my shoulder, her tears soaking my shirt. "I've missed you so much, Fey."

"Missed you."

The warmth of *momor's* hand touches my back, and I hear her soft sobs behind us. I don't want her to cry, but I can't stop it. Not when my own eyes have tears in them.

"I'm going to get us more coffee," *momor* says when Cammie and I pull apart.

I grab her hand before she can walk away and bring it to my lips. "Thank you, *momor*."

"*Momor*? Is that what you call Ever?"

We both look at Cammie.

"Dad used to call Mom *mon amour*. It's French for 'my love'. Dad's father was French, and he lived there for the first fifteen years of his life, until he and our grandmother, who was American, moved to the states." She looks from me to *momor* and then back. "Even if the endearment is altered, he would really like that you use the same for the woman you love."

*Mon amour*. Now that Cammie has said the word, it does sound right. I can almost hear Peepa's voice saying it.

But Ever will always be my *momor* to me.

And she agrees when she looks down at me with a smile and says, "I like *momor* better."

# thirty-three

EVERLEE

I fight back my laughter as I watch Wild Man fiddle with the remote for the television. He gives the thing a look so dark I'm surprised it doesn't melt in his hand. Mr. Bones lays across both of his bare feet. My cat doesn't do new people. He's skittish and hides any time someone unfamiliar is in the house. But he took to Wild Man right away.

It's been a few days since Wild Man broke into my window and took back what was his. It's strange to have him here, seeing him wear clothes, attempting to do modern things. His life up to this point has been so simple. He lived off what nature gave him. I know his adjustment will be a struggle, but I'll help him every step of the way.

Once things settled that first day, I was concerned he would want to go back to the wilderness. While a part of me misses the simplicity of that life, and I probably always will, I can't imagine staying there forever. And I want Wild Man to experience the way life should have been for him. For everything he's been through, he deserves that. The thing with love is, sometimes you make sacrifices. I was willing to go back with Wild Man if that was what he truly wanted. I didn't want to force this life on him if it would make him unhappy.

When I brought up the subject to him, he firmly and quite literally growled the word 'no'.

"We stay. Better for *momor*. You miss family."

My heart melted. Is it really no wonder why I fell in love with the man? While I was willing to sacrifice my entire life to be with him, he was willing to do the same.

But just because we won't be living in his tree hut anymore, doesn't mean we're leaving that part of his life forever. Next week, we plan to go back. There are things there he wants to get.

Cammie left yesterday to go home to Oklahoma. She's coming back in a few weeks and she's going to bring her boys. We learned through her that the boy's father was some guy she met while she was on vacation in Key West. They had one wild night and the next morning he was gone, never seen or heard from again. She had no way of contacting him to tell him about the pregnancy because they never exchanged numbers and they only shared first names.

I bring the two bowls of cinnamon applesauce with me to the couch and sit beside him. I'm tempted to take the remote from him and find something to watch myself, but he'd just scowl at me and wouldn't give it over. This isn't the first time he's become agitated at something new and complicated, and each time he does, he refuses help, stating he wants to figure it out on his own.

It takes him another minute of him pressing buttons before a movie starts to play. I have no idea what it is because I'm too busy watching him. That's what I do when he's in the room. My eyes are always riveted to him. I'm fairly certain I could look at him until the end of time, and I would still want to gaze at him in the afterlife.

Ethan came by a couple days ago with a suitcase full of old clothes. He's the one closest in size to Wild Man. Tonight, he's wearing a pair of ratty, faded jeans. The material is so worn that there's a couple of spots so thin holes are beginning to form. The jeans may be old and should probably be thrown away, but damned if Wild Man doesn't look good in them. He's barefoot and has no shirt on. His long black hair is mostly down his back, but with his body bent as he rests his elbows on his knees, some fall over his broad shoulders. I don't know if Wild Man has plans to ever cut his hair, but if he does, I think I might tie his ass to the bed so he can't. I love his hair. The same thing with his beard.

Typically, when we're in the house alone, we both go naked. I grew used to not wearing clothes, and I find wearing them now is irritating and uncomfortable. Of course, Wild Man doesn't complain. He says he loves looking at my body and me not wearing clothes makes it easier for when he wants to fuck me. Or make love to me. The only reason we're wearing them now is because we just got off a video call with his sister.

I sit with my back against the arm of the couch and my bowl of applesauce in my hands. When he settles back, I tuck my toes under his thigh and give him his bowl. I watch his face as he takes the first bite. This is his first foray with applesauce. Well, he probably had some as a small child, but he doesn't remember it.

"Well?" I ask, licking the bottom of my spoon as I wait for his reaction. With each new food he tries, I sit on pins and needles. I want to learn all his favorites and dislikes.

He's half turned toward me. He looks down at his bowl as he scoops up more and brings the spoon to his mouth. His jaw moves back and both as if he's assessing the flavor.

"Good."

His answer is lame, and I let him know this.

"Good?" I ask, my tone incredulous. "This is divine. It's perfection in the form of squished apples and cinnamon. Good is what you would say about ice cream or an everything bagel."

He gives me a look that suggests I've lost my mind. He's the one who's gone insane.

I lift my spoon to bring another bite of perfection to my mouth, but a drop falls on my chest. I drop the utensil back in my bowl so I can use a finger to swipe off the mess, but before I can, I'm stopped when the bowl is suddenly no longer in my hand. Wild Man has snatched it away and he puts both of our dishes on the coffee table. He turns more toward me, his hand going up my legs to my knees. He lifts one and puts it between him and the couch. His hands go up further to my waist, and then I'm being dragged down the couch.

"What are you doing?" I ask, my breath stuttering in my throat.

"You made mess." His eyes lock on the drop of applesauce, which conveniently landed at the top of my cleavage. "I clean it."

One of his hands goes under me, arching my back. He leans over me, dropping his mouth to my cleavage. I let out a husky moan when his tongue darts out and swipes away the mess.

"Mmm...," he groans. "You right. It is divine. My new favorite."

I laugh lightly, but the sound ends on another moan when he swirls his tongue deeper between my breasts. I arch my back more and lace my fingers through his hair, pulling his face closer.

"More, Wild Man."

I'm wearing a thin tank top, so when he grabs the front of it and yanks, the material rips easily. I've already taken my shower for the night, so I'm braless. My boobs bounce free, the tips already turning into hard little points. Wild Man growls, the deep sound making goosebumps pebble on my skin.

He takes one of my nipples between his lips and sucks hard, scraping his teeth over the tip. He pops that one free and goes to the other one.

"Oh, god, yes. That feels so good," I moan.

Wild Man lifts his head, and I look down. His lips are wet from his kisses.

"My *momor*," he rumbles.

"Yes. Always."

His eyes flare and he sits up. The shorts I'm wearing are ripped down my legs, along with my panties. Once I'm naked, he takes one of my legs and hooks it over the back of the couch. He places my other foot down on the floor. I'm spread wide open, and I feel my juices leaking out of me onto the couch.

"My pussy," he grates.

"Yes," I reply, my voice broken from the onslaught of desire wreaking havoc on my body. This man drives me insane with lust.

He slides a finger between my folds, and I lift my hips to meet the touch. He barely grazes my clit before he's sliding back down and pushing the tip of his finger in my hole. I whimper, the sound needy and desperate.

"Please, Phenix."

As I knew it would, his eyes darken at hearing me use his full name. He thrusts his finger inside as far as it will go, giving me just what I wanted.

"Two fingers, *momor*?"

"Yes," I moan.

He pulls out and rams two fingers inside. I cry out at the intrusion, lifting my hips off the couch. He thrusts and retreats, driving me crazy with my need for even more.

"Three? You want three fingers fuck you?"

I open my eyes, dazed at how easily this man controls my body.

"Or you want my mouth, eating pussy?"

I lean up on one elbow and fist a handful of his hair. I yank his head down toward my pussy. "Both. Give me both, Phenix."

With a muted growl, he falls on me. His mouth attacks my pussy like it's the last thing he'll ever consume. With a cry, my arm gives out and I fall backward. The foot that's on the floor is lifted when Wild Man aggressively shoves my leg back, lifting my ass off the couch. I'm as spread open as I can be with a crazed man feasting on my pussy.

He licks and slurps and sucks and nibbles on my clit, all the while ramming three fingers inside me. My head thrashes as I lift my hips and smash his face against my pussy. The vibration of his growls and the roughness of his beard scraping all over me adds fuel to the flames consuming me.

When my orgasm hits, it takes total control. Wild Man keeps thrusting, the juices seeping out of me making each one slicker. I grab his hair and shove him closer, lifting my hips, grinding myself on his face.

I'm boneless and sapped completely of energy by the time he lifts his head. His beard is soaked with my release, and coupled with the satisfied look in his eyes, it renews my need for more.

I watch with languid eyes as Wild Man gets up from the couch and yanks off his jeans. Once he's naked, his long, hard cock bouncing around, he grabs me under my knees and pulls me further down the couch. With one foot planted on the floor, he throws his other leg over my torso so his cock bobs right in front of my face. Gripping his shaft, he angles the tip down toward my lips, a small dot of pre-cum glistening on the tip.

"Open, *momor*," he growls. "Suck."

Suddenly ravenous to have his cock in my mouth, I spread my lips open. He feeds me just the head, and I clamp my lips around it, sucking away that delicious little drop. I love the way he tastes.

He hisses out a breath, his head tilted down with his hair falling all around his face. He looks savage at this moment. Like an animal ready to take his mate.

I suck the head, wanting more of him, needing him to fill my mouth all the way. He presses his hips forward and another inch slides inside. I lift my head, intent on taking more and he takes advantage. Gripping a handful of my hair, he snarls down at me as he guides my head up at the same time he pushes his hips down. He goes to the back of my throat and my eyes water.

"Yes, *momor*," he grates, his teeth bared. "So good."

I hum in the back of my throat. He lets out a groan and sinks deeper, wedging his cock through the tight muscles. I swallow, constricting those muscles, knowing it'll drive him crazy. I want him to lose his mind with lust. I want his control obliterated.

He grunts, his already tight grip in my hair growing stronger. He jerks my head back and rams his hips forward again. I sink my nails into the globes of his ass and my hips lift off the couch. I don't know what I'm reaching for. I just know my pussy is weeping so much juices the couch will be soaked.

Wild Man falls forward, catching himself on the arm of the couch. I tip my head back for a better angle, my eyes sliding open to meet his intense black pair.

"More, *momor*," he grunts through his clenched teeth. "Deeper. I fuck your mouth."

He thrusts, and I didn't think it was possible for him to go deeper inside my throat, but he manages to. I let one of my hands wander down my body to my pussy. I strum my clit and the shock of that first touch has my back arching off the bed and a low moan vibrating through my chest.

"Fuck your pussy while I fuck mouth."

And I do. I shove one of my fingers inside my slick pussy at the same time he shoves his cock down my throat. I match my thrusts to his. Tears leak from my eyes and slide down my cheeks as he takes my mouth hard and fast, choking me on his cock. I fuck my pussy as deep as I can.

A tingle builds in my lower stomach, preparing me for what I know will be an electrifying orgasm.

Wild Man's moves become wild and frenzied, his thrusts deep and savage. He uses my hair to pull my head back, only to use it to slam forward again. Over and over. My throat feels raw and abused, but in the most delicious way. I pull my finger from my pussy and press it to my clit, swirling the tip around the tight bundle of nerves.

With my other hand, I wet my fingers with my juices and bring them to Wild Man's ass. I slide my fingers between his cheeks until I feel the pucker of his asshole. His grunt is deep and gravelly when I press against the spot, pushing the tip of my finger inside his tight hole.

"*Momor*," he growls. His thrusts become wild and uncontrolled. A man possessed by his lust.

I push my finger deeper inside him and feel for the spot I know men have. When I find it, I press against it. Wild Man lets out a loud bellow and jams his cock in my throat as deep as it'll go, effectively cutting off all of my airflow.

His shout of pleasure and the strumming of my clit sets off my release. I arch my back, the muscles in my stomach tighten as I'm thrown over the edge. I can't vocalize my release with his dick in my throat, but that's what makes it more intense.

He grunts and groans as I feel the warm jets of his cum slide down my throat. I greedily swallow every drop.

He releases my hair as I slide my finger out of him and he pops out of my mouth. My chest pumps up and down as I take in large gulps of air.

Wild Man's stamina has always amazed me. Maybe it's because he's making up for lost time or he's just been graced with a magical cock. Either way, he's still very hard.

He lifts me from the couch and falls on his ass on the cushions with me straddling his lap. From the look in his eyes, he's not done with me. Which suits me just fine, because I'm not done with him yet.

With his hands on my hips, he poises me over the head of his cock, then slowly slides me down until I'm fully seated on him.

"Give me mouth, momor."

I drop my head and give him what he wants.

*thirty-four*

EVERLEE

I never imagined I would miss the treehut. The whole time I was stuck there, all I thought about was a way to get free, and that I never wanted to see it again. Standing here now, looking at the dead firepit, the log Wild Man would sit on with me on his lap as we fed each other, and the area we slept in, it makes me sad that we won't be living here any longer. I'll miss this place more than I probably should. This is where we started. It's where we fought, laughed, and got to know each other. It's the place where I fell in love with Wild Man. Part of me never wants to leave again.

Wild Man piddles around the area, gathering the things he wants to take with him. My brows go up when he lifts a section of the ground. It's a door made out of logs that's covered in leaves and in an area that a person wouldn't walk. He reaches in and pulls out the pack he stole from me all those weeks ago, along with my gun and taser. My stuff was literally right below us the whole time.

I laugh, because the thought is funny. I had the means to escape within feet of me and I never knew. When I think back to that time, I realize that I didn't truly try to escape. I mean, I did, but I could have tried harder, fought more. Someone else would have. Maybe my heart was telling me something. I tried following the reasoning in my head telling me I had to leave this place and Wild Man, but my heart wouldn't allow me to.

None of that matters now though. I'm where I'm supposed to be and with the man who makes me happy.

It doesn't seem right for Wild Man to be in the treehut with his clothes on. My own clothes feel itchy against my skin. Today he's wearing a pair of black cargo pants, a hunter green t-shirt, and a pair of black boots. His hair is braided down his back, but some of the strands have come loose. When I first taught him how to braid, he really liked it because it kept his hair out of his face. He prefers a braid than a ponytail. Now, more often than not, he has his hair twisted and pulled back instead of loose. I have to admit, the look is damn hot.

"I'm going to miss this place," I tell him. I sit on the log and start going through my pack he handed me, refamiliarizing myself with its contents.

"We come back," he replies, stuffing some stuff into the black duffle bag we brought with us.

"I hope no one finds it and destroys it."

"Teeja will keep people away."

That's another thing I'm going to miss. Teeja and his beautiful family.

A strangled laugh escapes my throat when I come across the handy dandy little silver bullet in my pack. I forgot I brought it with me, which is stupid because I always take it with me when I go on trips. Jamie—aptly named after Jamie Dornan because that man is fire—and I have had a lot of sweaty nights together.

Wild Man walks over and stares down at the bullet. "What is that?"

I tip my head back slowly and regard his expression when I press the button on the bottom. It comes to life in my hand, the vibration strong and the hum low. My lips curl into a little smile as his eyes narrow. It takes him a moment to understand, and when he does, the black in his eyes flare. For a moment, I think he might toss me to the ground like he has so many times before and mount me from behind. And honestly, I would be more than okay with it.

His gaze moves to me. "You show me at home how you use it."

Anticipation ripples through me, making the area between my legs tingle.

"Okay." I can't keep the huskiness out of my voice.

With another heated look, he goes back to packing the duffle. I drop the bullet in my bag, looking forward to getting home and introducing Wild Man to something new, especially something so pleasurable.

I love teaching him new things. I love watching the awe on his face. He's adapted really well to life in civilization so far. I'm actually really impressed with how well he's doing.

Something rustles near the doorway and we both look over just in time to see Teeja trot into the treehut. Right behind him is Vena and their litter of pups.

"Teeja! Vena!" I call, scrambling up from the log. I drop to my knees in front of them. "I'm so glad you came."

I hold out my hand to Vena and she butts her head against it. I laugh as I slowly stroke the top of her head. Teeja nudges my other hand for some scratches. I rub between his ears.

Drefan bounds up, his tails wagging, and props his front paws on my thigh, just like he did that first day. His tongue hangs out the side of his mouth.

I laugh. "Hey, Drefan." He yips and starts running in circles.

Nemu and Khelan come up to me next, more sedate than their brother, but still appearing happy to see me. Khelan licks my hand and plops down, rolling to his back for some belly rubs. I oblige him and pet Nemu with my other hand. After I've lavished the pair with my attention, I look at Devika, who's standing beside her mother.

"Devika," I call softly and hold out my hand. She's always been the shyest of the bunch.

She walks over, slower than her brothers, and sits on her haunches once she's in front of me.

"Hey, girl. I missed you." I rub my hand along her head and down until I reach her tail. She stares up at me, her head tilted back, her eyes curious. She lets out a little sigh of contentment.

I love every member of this wolf family, but Devika has always held a special place in my heart. I hate knowing we're leaving them behind and we very well could never see them again.

Teeja and his family stay while we finish packing up Wild Man's things. Tears prick my eyes as I take a long look at the treehut before we walk out. Wild Man says we'll come back, but who knows if the place will be the same when we do.

As if sensing my sad thoughts, a solid warmth hits my back and an arm comes around my waist. Wild Man presses his lips against the side of my neck, over the same spot he always marks, even still.

"We'll be back," he tells me again, his voice a deep rumble.

I nod, too choked up to form a verbal response. I force my lips into a smile before I turn to face him. He kisses my lips before reaching for my hand. Together, we leave the treehut, knowing that I'm leaving a small part of me behind.

---

AFTER WE SAY GOODBYE TO TEEJA AND HIS FAMILY—A TEARFUL GOODBYE on my part—Wild Man leads me in a direction away from where we need to go to leave the forest.

"Where are we going?" I ask.

"Something I need to do," is his only reply. He's tense and his lips are a flat line.

I don't ask him to elaborate. I just stay silent beside him, something telling me he needs this quiet time. Walking with him now is a lot easier than it was when we were out here before. Having shoes and not worrying about shredding my feet makes a big difference.

I start to recognize the way we're going and my heart lurches in my chest. I've only been this way once. When he showed me where he buried his parents. The field of wildflowers is just as vibrant as it was the first time, despite the temperatures dropping lower.

My throat closes as we step under the low hanging branches of the tree and stop at the two piles of rocks. By leaving these woods, Wild Man is not only giving up the only home he's ever known, but also the resting place of his parents. We *will* come back to this forest, if for no other reason than to visit his parents.

Wild man sets the duffle down and pulls out a small retractable shovel. He gouges the dirt and begins digging a hole at the bottom of the graves, directly center between the two. When the hole is about a foot deep and a foot in width, he drops the shovel to the ground. He reaches inside the duffle and pulls out one of the skulls. I blink back tears as he looks at it a moment before he carefully sets it in the hole. He does the same to the second skull.

I can't hold back the tears when I look inside the hole and notice he's placed the two skulls so they face each other. He carefully begins shoveling the dirty back in the hole. As he does this, I look around, swiping at the tears sliding down my face. Once I find what I'm looking for, I pick up two rocks about the same size as the ones on his parents' graves and place them down beside where Wild Man is. I go back for more.

By the time I've gathered enough rocks, Wild Man is already placing them on the grave. Once he's done, he gets to his feet. I immediately move into his arms. He wraps me up tight, as if needing me in his arms as much as I need to be there.

I tip my head back. "Are you okay?"

He clears his throat before he speaks. "Yes."

"We can come back anytime you want."

He nods.

"I love you."

Some of the torment leaves his eyes. "I love you, *momor*."

I pull back from him and grab his hand. "Come on. There's something I want to do." When he reaches for the duffle, I tell him, "Leave it. We aren't going far."

I lead him back to the wild flowers and bend to pick a bright blue one. I hold it up between us. "Help me pick some flowers."

We pick several of each color until we have two bundles of beautiful flowers. I grab his hand again and take him back to the graves. I set my bundle on top of his father's grave. Wild Man sets his on top of his mother's.

I let Wild Man decide when we leave. After we stand there for several moments, his arms around my waist as we stare down at his parent's resting place, he lets me go and grabs the duffle bag. Together, we leave the beautiful but sad place.

We come across the waterfall and pool of water, and I tug on his hand to stop.

"How about one more bath before we leave?"

His gaze immediately fills with desire, just the reaction I was hoping for. Sex is the perfect distraction. Anything to replace the somber look in his eyes.

I shiver when my hair is suddenly grabbed and I'm pulled against his chest with his eyes boring down at me. "No bath. Fucking."

I lick my lips and give him a lavenous smile. "Fuck your pussy, Wild Man."

I squeal with laughter and delight when he growls and tosses me over his shoulder.

*epilogue*

WILD MAN

I glare at the doctor as *momor* lets out another wailing cry of pain. The grip she has on my hand should be painful, but it only reminds me of how much she's hurting and there's not a damn thing I can do to help her. The stupid fucking doctor said it's too late to give her the numbing shot. I'm half a second away from ripping the doctor to shreds and forcing her to give my wife whatever the hell she needs to make the pain go away. It's tearing me apart seeing her like this.

"Wild Man," she pants, her grip around my hand tightening even more. "Stop it. I'm fine."

When asked if she wanted an epidural during labor a few months ago, *momor* told the doctor no. She was insistent that she deliver without the aid of medication. I didn't argue, because I didn't fucking know it would be this bad. I knew it would be painful—pushing something the size of a watermelon out a hole the size of a pea had to be—but I didn't realize the magnitude. Each time *momor* screams in pain, I swear my heart dies a little.

After one last glare, in which the female doctor ignores, I turn to *momor*. "I don't like seeing you in pain."

Her face is flush with red and sweat coats her forehead. She takes short little breaths as she waits for another spasm of pain to hit her.

She smiles, but it's not the real one I love so much. "We knew this was coming, right? Once we hold our babies in our arms, it'll all be worth it."

Twins. Not one, but two little babies.

We were happy when we heard the news. Now, a part of me is scared shitless, because this won't end when she delivers our child. She'll have to endure it even more until our second baby is born.

"Alright, Everlee. I want you to give it all you got with this next contraction," the doctor says in a tone so calm it grates on my nerves. How in the hell can she appear so relaxed? My entire fucking life is laying right here, sounding like she's dying from so much pain.

*Momor* nods. Her teeth clench and she blows out a readying breath. When the next contraction hits, she crushes my fingers so much it feels like the bones are breaking. But I don't care. If this helps her in any way, she can break every bone in my body.

She lets out a jarring scream and her face turns a deeper shade of red. Seconds later, a loud wailing sound fills the room. I jerk my head down the bed where the doctor is. She holds up a tiny baby that's covered in red and white gooey stuff. The little arms flail around and his mouth is wide open as he screams. All I can do is stare in awe.

"Congrats momma and daddy." The doctor smiles. "Here is your healthy baby boy."

Almost immediately, the grayish cord connecting baby to momma is cut and he's handed over to a nurse holding a blue cloth. I want to demand they bring him back, but the grip on my hand reminds me that this isn't over.

I look back at *momor*. She's smiling, even as more tears leak from her eyes as she watches the nurse walk away with our son. I bring her hand to my lips and kiss the back of it.

"He's beautiful," she whispers, her voice hoarse from screaming.

"He is."

The doctor sits back down on her stool. "Baby number two is coming fast, Everlee, so as much as you want to take a break, I'm going to need you to push again, okay?"

"Yeah," *momor* replies weakly.

Our daughter comes a few minutes later. If I thought our son's crying was loud, his sister nearly pierces my ears.

"You did so good, *momor*," I whisper, my face close to hers. "So brave. So strong."

She gives me a smile that wobbles. "Thank you."

"Thank *you*, for giving me this precious gift." I bend and kiss her lips. "I love you."

She sniffs and wipes her hand across her tear-stained cheek, giving me another one of her beautiful smiles. "I love you."

What seems like hours later, after *momor* has been cleaned up, two nurses walk over with our babies. One of them gently sets our son in his noeny's arms and I get our daughter. I am utterly transfixed as I stare down at the tiny person cradled against my chest. Her little face is scrunched up as she sleeps. She has the smallest nose and a mouth shaped like a bow and she has a head full of nearly black hair.

My heart instantly fills with love.

I look down at *momor* and our son and that love grows. Tears slide now *momor's* cheeks and she gazes at him with adoration. His hair isn't as dark as his sister's. More the color of *momor's*. And his face is a little slimmer.

"What are their names?" one of the nurses asks.

*Momor* doesn't look away from our son as she says, "His name is Alexander."

Alexander was mine and my father's middle name. I'm man

enough to admit, my eyes became watery when *momor* told me she wanted to name our son after me and peepa.

My throat is tight when I give the nurse our daughter's name. "Josephine Athena."

"Beautiful names," the nurse says.

Our daughter's name is after both of our noeny's. We couldn't have thought of a better way to honor the parents we no longer have.

*Momor* looks at Josephine, and I know what she wants. I carefully settle our daughter in her other arm. Her gaze goes from one to the other, her eyes shining happily.

"I love you, Josephine." She presses a kiss on her forehead. "I love you, Alexander." Our son's forehead is next.

When she looks at me, I lean down and kiss her lips.

I was content out in the wild all alone, maybe even happy. It wasn't until I had *momor* that I knew what true happiness was.

This woman and our two children will forever and always be my life.

---

"Look what I found, Daddy!"

Josie comes running up to me and holds out her little hand. In her palm is a rock nearly the size of her hand. It's black and smooth and closely resembles the shape of a heart.

"Do you think Auntie Cammie will like it?" she asks, her gaze hopeful.

"I think she'll love it."

With a squeal of delight, she runs off, immediately going to her brother to show him her treasure.

My sister still collects rocks. Any time we visit her, she always tells the kids one story about where one came from. Even after hearing many of the stories, their favorite rock is the one I gave her the first time *momor* and I visited her.

When Peepa, Noeny, and I came to the wild for our last visit, I did find a rock to bring back to Cammie. Although I had forgotten Cammie and the reason why I needed to, I kept the rock all of those years. When I gave it to Cammie and explained what it was, she burst into tears. She now calls that her favorite rock.

A loud yip echoes in the forest and a moment later, a pair of pups comes bounding across the ground in front of me. Alex and Josie laugh as Loki playfully jumps on Ares' back. The pups roll around until Ares pins Loki to the ground. Loki and Ares, along with Nala, are Devika's pups. Devika and Nemu are the only two wolves we see now when we come to the forest. Teeja and Vena have been gone for a few years now, and we believe Drefan and Khelan have moved on to other parts of the forest.

With a smile on her face as she watches the rambunctious pups, *momor* walks over and tries to sit beside me on the log. I grab her waist before she can and drag her down on my lap.

We're in my old treehut. It's nearly the same as when we left it all those years ago, except it's been cleaned up a bit. We don't come as often as we used to, but we still like to bring the kids out here a couple times a year for a weekend. *Momor* thinks it's important for our children to know where I spent most of my life and where she and I met. I love that she wants to share my past with them.

"Do you ever miss being here?" she asks.

I pinch a piece of fruit between my fingers and bring it to her mouth. Her eyes smile as she opens her lips to take it. Any time we're out here, this is what we do. We feed each other like we used to.

"Yes and no. I miss the freedom and the quietness. The simplicity of living in the wild and not having to worry about what I do, say, or how to act." The arm I have wrapped around her pulls her closer, and I lower my voice. "I miss having you naked all the time and being able to fuck you whenever or however I want."

Her eyes flicker with heat and she shifts on my lap. "Maybe we can have Dad or one of my brothers watch the kids one weekend and we make a special trip out here."

My cock twitches in my jeans, and I barely hold back my growl. To have my *momor* naked and readily available for an entire weekend?

Fuck yes.

"Did you ever imagine your life would turn out this way?" *momor* asks as she watches our children play with Loki, Ares, and Nala. Devika and her wolf mate, Treyvan, lie on their bellies close by.

Honestly? No, I always thought I would die like my parents. By some wild animal, stronger and smarter than me. Maybe a bear or cougar.

I kiss the side of *momor's* neck. "No. I never expected to find you, but the moment I did, I knew my life was about to change."

She lays her head on my shoulder and kisses the underside of my jaw. I still have the beard and long hair. The one time I mentioned cutting it, I thought *momor* was going to attack me. She got a cute crazed look in her eye and demanded to never mention it again.

"When I first came to this forest to find you, you were just a myth. I didn't even know if you were real or not. But even so, you already had a piece of my heart. When I saw you in that pool of water, you stole a little more of it. I never expected for you to be what you were, and boy did I tear off more than I could chew those first few days." she laughs.

I still don't regret the things I did to her. Had our story changed in the slightest, we might not be where we are today.

She sits up straight and turns so she's facing, laying her hand against my cheek.

"I can't imagine my life without you, Wild Man." She kisses my lips, and still, even after seven years, I can't get enough of her taste. "When I came here, I never thought it possible to tame the Wild

Man rumored to live in the forest, but I did." She grins cheekily. "And as I did that, you made me wild for you."

She did tame me. She taught me how to love. How to cherish the things I hold close to my heart. She gave me back to my sister and gave me a new family. She showed me what true happiness is. Before her, I was just a nameless man and only existed.

Now I'm Phenix Alexander Salone. Gabriel and Josephine's son. Cammie's brother. Father to two beautiful children, Alexander and Josephine. And husband and lover to Everlee, my *momor*.

I more than exist. This brave and gorgeous woman found me and gave me life.

*other books by alex*

JADED HOLLOW SERIES
Beautifully Broken
Wickedly Betrayed
Wildly Captivated
Perfectly Tragic
Jaded Hollow: The Complete Collection


THE CONSUMED SERIES
Mine
Sex Junkie
Shamelessly Bare
Hungry Eyes
The Consumed Series: The Complete Collection


HELL NIGHT SERIES
Retribution
Vindication
Vengeance
Wrath
The Hell Night Series: Complete Collection


WESTBRIDGE SERIES
Pitch Dark
Broad Daylight

Salvaged Pieces

## BULLY ME SERIES
Treacherous
Malicious


## ITTY BITTY DELIGHTS
Heels Together, Knees Apart
Teach Me Something Dirty
Filthy Little Tease
For I Have Sinned
Doing Taboo Things
Lady Boner
Lady Boss
Lady Balls
Lady Bits
Itty Bitty Delights: 1-5
Itty Bitty Delights: 6-9


## STANDALONES
Whispered Prayers
Haunted
Dear Linc
Just the Tip
Uncocky Hero
Until Never
Beautiful Chaos
The Wild Man

*about the author*

Alex Grayson is a USA Today bestselling author of heart pounding, emotionally gripping contemporary romances including the Jaded Hollow Series, The Consumed Series, The Hell Night Series, and multiple standalone novels. Her passion for books was reignited by a gift from her sister-in-law. After spending several years as a devoted reader and blogger, Alex decided to write and independently publish her first novel in 2014 (an endeavor that took a little longer than expected). The rest, as they say, is history.

Originally a southern girl, Alex now lives in Ohio with her husband, three cats, and one dog. She loves the color blue, homemade lasagna, casually browsing real estate, and interacting with her readers. Visit her website, www.alexgraysonbooks.com, or find her on social media!

Made in the USA
Monee, IL
28 December 2024